MYSTICAL PATH TO MYSTIQUE

A Novel by Gene Stirm

Way West Productions, Publisher
California, U.S.A.

ISBN-13: 978-0-9826828-0-7

First Edition
First printing, May 2010

To Patricia

Acknowledgments

My profound thanks to my wife Patricia, without whose love and support this work would not be possible.

To fellow writer Chelley Kitzmiller, thank you for your contribution and editing expertise. John Acosta, the inspiration for the Old Man and all my friends and associates that through the years inspired the bits and pieces that make up a work of fiction. And to my friends at Ft. Independence, thanks.

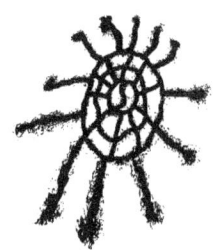

CHAPTER 1

In the dark.

Deep in the bowels of an old Los Angeles apartment building, Dave Hoffsted searched the antiquated electrical board. A spark punctuated by the ring of his cell phone sent him skyward. "Ah shit!" He juggled the phone to his ear. "Hello," he said, annoyed at the interruption.

"That's no way to answer a business phone." The squeaky voice of Shirley, the apartment manager chastised. "How much longer are you going to keep us in the dark down there?" Us didn't include her; she was comfortable at her home in Long Beach.

"What time is sunrise?" Dave's aggravation built.

"Don't take that tone with me mister. The power's been off for five hours and irritated residents are calling me at home every few minutes."

"I'm doing my best in this fire trap. If the owners would get off their butts and upgrade the damn electrical, we wouldn't have these problems," Dave bitched as he continued to probe, desperate to find the source of the outage. "I've got to find the short. Every time I throw the power main on, it kicks back off."

"That's not good enough, we've got to have the lights on now."

"What am I supposed to do, stick a wire up my ass and fart the lights on?"

"I've had enough of your attitude. Keep it up and I'm going to write you up."

"You can take your damn write up and shove it you know where."

"We'll see about that. Be in my office at nine a.m. sharp. Now quit screwin' around down there and get the power on." The phone went dead.

"Bitch!" Dave continued to probe. With the penlight's batteries near spent, it shed only a faint glow on the eighty years of make-do, frayed, twisted wires and old fuses rewired a dozen times. He probed down the long strips of fuses in an attempt to find the problem before being left in total darkness. Sparks flew when the probe shorted across a live wire. "Damn!"

Dave was vaguely aware that just inches from his hand a thin black coil of wire hung like a viper ready to strike, its mouth full of copper fangs. In the shadows among the decaying electrical wires, it waited silently for its' prey to move closer. Complacent of the hidden killer's potential, Dave slowly moved his hand within striking distance. Without warning it attacked, sinking its copper fangs into the fleshy heel of his right hand, it released a jolt of its full power.

Dave flew backward to the basement floor hard, the electrical current broken. The wayward wire recoiled back into the dark. Evidently the wire had come loose from its connector earlier that day and attached itself to a near by bus-strip, creating a dead short.

Flat on his back, entopic stars blazed before Dave's eyes then disappeared. Disoriented, he felt around the cold bare concrete floor for his penlight. Above him, a man's face appeared in the dim green glow of the battery powered emergency exit sign. Fear gripped Dave and he froze in terror. The right side of the face was painted solid black, the left with vertical lines, alternated

2

black and white stripes. The paint glistened. Deep amber eyes glowed, penetrating Dave's soul. "Holy shit," he yelled, as he located the penlight. It's still worked, but when he flashed it around him, he saw that he was alone.

"You're hallucinating asshole," he assured himself as he lifted his six-foot frame from the floor, woozy, wondering, what the hell hit him?

He stood a moment then returned to his task. The wire that had come loose and bit him, once again created a dead short. "There you are you little . . . ." He reconnected the wayward wire to its proper terminal. The penlight sputtered its last, just as he threw the power main. Overhead fluorescents flicked to life. He closed the makeshift door that tried to pass as an electrical closet, took a last look around the basement, an old converted boiler room that was now used as a laundry room. "One of these days this whole friggin' place is gonna go up in a blaze of glory."

The wooden stairs creaked as he climbed to the first floor hall of the 1920's, four-story brick apartment building, one of hundreds built in the mid Wilshire district of Los Angeles. These once luxury dwellings had fallen into disrepair. The buildings not destroyed by the 1994 Northridge earthquake were retrofitted to new standards. Now, the Miracle Mile had become a Mecca for the Hollywood want-to-bes and studio workers willing to pay sky-high rent for small rooms in old buildings. They called them retro, where vintage was chic, and wore-out was hip, as long as it didn't pertain to people.

Dave had been the building's maintenance man for two years, a stretch longer than usual in his long career of menial jobs. Tonight he felt neither chic nor hip, simply old and tired. He stepped into the small cantankerous elevator and pushed the forth floor button.

The elevator paused, then jolted on its journey upward. The innards of the building slid by the open-grate car. After each of the elevator's frequent breakdowns, he hoped it would be un-repairable and replaced, but each time Romel, the elevator re-pairman, resurrected the thing with the assurance, *'Señor Dave, es mucho bueno, like I fix back en Mexico City'.*

He tripped out of the elevator on the forth floor, the car had landed three inches short, again. A stark hall led to his studio apartment in the back of the building, provided as part of his pay package. It was twenty past eleven when he entered his room, a hot Monday night in July.

The apartment looked out over the parking lot of an all night diner, a 24-hour pharmacy with drive-through and a few blocks beyond, Beverly Hills. The noises from the busy streets filled the air. On the weekends, the traffic, emergency vehicles, fighting drunks and other assorted street people created an ongoing melodrama. The late night entertainment always came at the expense of a good night's sleep. Tonight however, only the constant din of traffic accompanied the cool breeze starting to blow in from the ocean.

Dave was the only on-site apartment personnel, so his company cell phone served as the building's emergency hot line. Of course, he got called for everything, whether it was an emergency or not. The usual night call, if not a meth-head tweaker who wanted to rent an apartment at two a.m., was about a neighbor's bedroom workout. When conditions were right, and they usually were, a sexual romp on any floor was heard loud and clear. The copulating co-habitants kicked off rounds of performance evaluations in the form of catcalls, jeers and the occasional cheer. Sometimes even applause, often after the thud of a collapsing bed.

He showered the tedium of another long day down the drain. The one consolation of a late night shower was plenty of both hot water and water pressure. Sometimes in the morning rush, when everyone was getting ready for work, he'd be lucky to get enough water to make a pot of coffee.

Out of the shower, he put ointment on the small red burn on his hand. The throb in his arm from the electrical shock had quit sometime during his shower. *You are one lucky son-of-a-bitch, a stunt like that could of killed you.*

He turned out the lights and stood naked in the dark at the open floor to ceiling French window, where he saw his reflection in the glass. *Not bad for fifty-two, at least no beer gut.* The gentle breeze cooled him, a welcome refreshing touch.

It was in moments like this that the pain of being alone became apparent. He thought of a spoiled marriages, his childrens' rejection and the messy divorce that started him on his path of self-destruction.

After a brief moment of indulgence in self-pity, he was ready for bed and maybe, a full night's sleep. As he turned from the window, he saw the face from the basement reflected in the glass, standing behind him. He froze and stared, behind the paint were the distinct features of a Native American. Not a Hollywood Indian, but a sepia-toned face from a late 1800's Edward Curtis photograph, strong and proud. Their eyes locked for an instance before the strange figure disappeared like Alice's cat.

Dave turned, a sharp jolt shot through his right arm as he stared into the empty pane of glass. *What the hell's going on here? Maybe your flop on the floor knocked a screw loose. You're seeing things.* Then as quick as it came the pain was gone.

At last in his bed he hoped for an undisturbed nights sleep. Sleep came slowly. The haunting face kept churning in his head. At last his needed sleep came.

*   *   *

Dave was in the middle of a vast valley that stretched as far as he could see north and south. Soaring mountain ranges flanked the valley on either side and at his feet were grass and sagebrush spread across the gravely desert soil.

In the far distance, a lone figure walked toward him. It was a man, naked in the blazing sun, except for a flesh-colored strip of leather wrapped around his waist. Dave could make out sandals on his feet and a claw and feather necklace around his neck. His shoulder length hair was tied back with a band.

But it was his face, the painted face from the basement, which caused a cold chill to run up Dave's spine.

The Indian stopped twenty feet in front of Dave. "Come home Dave, you must come home."

"Home? I have no home."

The Indian pointed to the north: "Yes you do. Your home is Mystique. North, beyond the waters they call Tahoe."

"Mystique? I've never lived in Mystique."

"You must come home before it's to late."

"Too late! What do your mean, too late?"

"Come!"

"What if I don't?" Dave asked angrily.

"You will cease too exist."

"But I live in L.A.." Dave turned toward the south. "My job, I have commitments." When he turned back, the Indian was gone.

The obnoxious ring of his cell phone brought Dave out of his disturbing dream. At least he thought it was a dream.

The electronic ring-tone came from his jeans pocket, somewhere in the heap of clothes on the bathroom floor. Its muffled chirp refused to quit. The haze of sleep cleared as he stumbled to the bathroom in search of the modern instrument of torture. "Hello!" his voice cracked, "Maintenance".

"My toilet is overflowing!" the panicked voice on the other end explained. "It's running all over the floor!"

That's the one call Dave knew he had to act on, no matter what time of day or night. Fire, flood or blood, were the only real emergencies in this business. He was wide-awake now. Overflowing toilets meant water through the ceilings, contaminated water, flooded floors, major cleanups and a general pain in the ass. "Is that you, Gladys?" he asked the familiar voice as he slid into his jeans and pulled on the first tee shirt he found.

"Yes, apartment 307, hurry!"

"Oh geeze, not again."

"Come, hurry."

He stepped into his boots and was off, grabbing a pipe pliers and toilet plunger from the stash of tools he kept in his apartment. He noted the time: five twenty-two a.m.

In seconds he knocked on the door of apartment 307. "Maintenance!" he yelled loud enough to wake the entire building. No response. He pounded and yelled even louder. He knew she was hard of hearing and scatterbrained as well. He reached for a master key on the ring hanging from his belt, started to insert it and heard a stir from within.

"Who is it?" the elderly woman asked.

"Dave, the maintenance man."

"Who?"

"It's Dave, Gladys. You called about your darn toilet running over."

"Oh yes." The dead bolt snapped open, the safety chain pull back against the doorframe. "Who is it?" The woman peered at him through the crack.

"It's Dave, the maintenance man. You called me about your toilet." She looked him up and down then closed the door.

"I'm not dressed."

"Dammit!" His teeth clenched, he was about to pound his fist through the door when it swung open.

The elderly woman stood blinking at him, her pink terry bathrobe gaped open to her panties and bra, her hair uncombed and her feet were stuck into huge pink fuzzie slippers.

"Don't get so up-tight, it's not good for your blood pressure. The toilet's stopped running over, It's just plugged up now, you can come back later." She started to close the door, but Dave stepped forward.

"If you don't mind I'd like to fix it while I'm here."

"Well, if you insist."

"I insist."

"Come in then young man, come in."

"Thank you." Once inside he realized by the increasing mess, that Gladys' forgetfulness had turned to senility. She had lived in the same apartment for twenty-seven years. Because of rent control, she paid less than half the going rate and couldn't afford to move. The signs were clear that she needed a place with supervision. He hated to be the one to report her, but by the looks of the disarray, uneaten food and piles of trash on the floor, he had little choice.

He made his way through the clutter to the bathroom, the old lady in pink shuffling along at his heels. *Wonder what I'll find this time. Last month it was a ceramic skunk, the time before a slipper.*

The stench greeted him first. "Oh Christ!" He blurted out repulsed. The toilet bowl was packed with toilet paper, piss and shit. There were clothes hung from every conceivable spot and heaped on the floor, wet from the toilet's putrid overflow.

"Did you drop anything in there again?" *Dumb question, she wouldn't remember.* "You forgetting to flush?"

"Sometimes," the old lady admitted, giving him a toothless grin.

"Jesus Christ," he said, his disgust evident in his voice.

His empty stomach wrenched as he worked the plunger into the commode. Confident the clog was nothing more than paper and crap, he plunged vigorously. The smell worsened, but the clog didn't budge. Determined to unclog the mess without a trip to the basement for the auger, he gave the plunger one more push. The contents spewed up out of the bowl and high in the air, drenching him and the old lady. Dave gagged, the toilet flushed.

"Praise the Lord, it works," the old lady undaunted by the unexpected baptism, rejoiced.

Dave made a hasty retreat to keep from vomiting on the spot.

"Who's going to clean up this mess?" the old lady asked, as she followed him out the door.

"I don't know, but it isn't gonna be me." Without a backward glance, he ran from the apartment, dry-heaving all the way up the stairs to his own apartment.

*   *   *

After a long shower, Dave still felt contaminated. He sat at the kitchen table, nursed a cup of black coffee and read the want ads. He'd been following the same routine for twelve years, since just after his divorce.

He was distracted by a glint of reflected light. It came from a ring that was too large and too flashy to be practical and had long been reallocated to the status of paperweight. He picked it up and remembered the night he received it.

The Clio Awards, he had swept the awards, Gold, winning for three different advertising campaigns he had created, including the one with a dancing frog that aired during the Super Bowl.

One big night, one little indiscretion and bang!

After the divorce, his downward spiral began. His ex-wife took everything but wanted more. She wanted his balls nailed to the wall of her fancy office but settled for money. She didn't need it with her rich new husband and she, an attorney.

Dave realized the less money he earned the more it angered her, so he hatched his plan. For years he took low-paying jobs and stayed ahead of wage garnishments by switching from one dull job to another.

Seven years ago, he surrendered to her demands and gave up all rights to the children. The boys, in their teens, wouldn't have anything to do with him anyway. Only after their stepfather adopted the boys did his ex let him off the financial hook. Now, at his age and with a resume full of low-end jobs, he was stuck at the bottom with no apparent way up. His deliberate dumbing down had him firmly in its grip.

When he went to return the ring to the stack of papers, he noticed the return address on an unopened letter that he put on the table and forgotten. Mystique.

He opened the letter and a check fell out.

> *From, William Baker, Esq. Mystique, CA.*
> *Dear Mister Hoffsted:*
>
> *I am pleased to inform you that after a long probate your mother's estate has been settled.*
>
> *Your inheritance includes the sum of $1727.31; check enclosed, along with a full accounting, and the deed to the property, 100 acres near Mystique, California, which waits transfer into your name. The property is free and clear and taxes are paid through December of this year.*
>
> *I would advise you to come to Mystique as soon as possible to complete the transfer and sign the necessary documents.*

Dave had forgotten about the property at Mystique, an area on 395, several miles north of Susanville near the Oregon border. He thought it had been sold years ago.

> *Your prompt reply will be appreciated.*

"I'll be damn." Dave picked up the check and returned the letter to its envelope. "Thanks mom."

The cell phone in his shirt pocket chirped. He looked at the clock, ten after eight, officially on the clock, as if that mattered. He was on twenty-four-hour call. There was no overtime, just comp-time. Of coarse, there was never a convenient time to take your comp-time, so it just accumulated.

With the day's shitty start, he wondered if it could get any worse.

"Hello, maintenance,"

"Hello Davie, my sink is all plugged up and I'm having dinner guests tonight. Can you be a dear and help me out?"

"Yeah, Aaron, I'll be right down".

"Oh thank you, you're such a dear. How did you know it was me?"

"Psychic."

Dave grabbed the five-gallon plastic paint bucket he had made into a tool caddy and started out the door. Two tenants, Cathy, a script reader at Universal, and Sam, a production assistant at Fox, were ahead of him in the hall. Both were young and beautiful, which is required to work in Hollywood these days. He passed them at the elevator on his way to the stairs and made a quick descent of the two flights to Aaron's apartment. Before he could knock, the door swung open.

"Come in, come in." Aaron, decked out like a parrot, in a brilliant Hawaiian outfit, motioned him in. Aaron was a makeup artist at Warner's, very flamboyant, if not downright flaming, and pushing fifty.

"You handsome man you," he gushed, as he gave Dave a thorough once over. "New shirt, black, looks good on you, but blue is better, brings out those blue eyes. Oh, and canary yellow MAINTENANCE printed all over the backside, how delicious."

Without a word, Dave went straight to the tiny galley kitchen and checked the sink.

"Looks like another grease clog." Under his breath he added, "My lucky day, at least it isn't shit."

"What?"

"Nothing, just talking to myself." Dave emptied his tools from his bucket onto the floor with a clatter and grabbed the large pipe pliers. "You've been dumping grease down the drain again." He knelt to remove the clutter from under the sink. On hands and knees, he placed the bucket under the sink and removed the trap. In seconds, the water drained into the bucket.

10

Dave could feel Aaron's eyes fixed on his butt. "Shirley said not to use drain cleaner." He was on the defensive. "It just happens, I can't help it."

"Right, eats holes in these old metal drain pipes. This whole building needs to be re-plumbed with PVC. Things have changed since they built this place." Dave backed out from under the sink and bumped into Aaron's feet.

"Do you mind giving me some space? Stand over by the door." Aaron hovering over him like a vulture gave him the creeps.

With a piece of coat-hanger wire from amongst his collection of tools, Dave pushed the clog out of the trap and into the bucket with a splash.

"Ugh, nasty," Aaron shrieked.

"If you think this is nasty, you should have seen the mess in the toilet of apartment 307 this morning."

"Spare me the details, I can just imagine."

Nobody's imagination is that good, Dave thought.

Back on all fours, he ducked his head under the sink to re-place the trap. Dave sensed that Aaron had moved closer. He was about to tell him to, back off, when the old queen goosed him.

"Oops, I slipped!" Aaron declared his innocence.

Dave jumped. His head slammed hard into the cast-iron sink with a loud thud. He scrambled to his feet in a rage, face red and blue eyes ablaze. His head still hurt from the hit the night before and the jolt compounded the pain.

Aaron shrieked and backed away. "I'm sorry, I'm sorry, I couldn't help it."

"Don't you ever touch me again, ya hear?" He held the huge pipe pliers up to Aaron's face.

"I promise, but I swear, it was an accident."

"Accident hell, one big mistake." Dave glared at Aaron, irritated, dazed and confused. His head throbbed. He ran his fingers through his hair and found a large knot. "I ought to bust you one on the head. Now get in the other room."

"Yes, sir," Aaron disappeared into the living room. "Do you want some ice? I can get some ice for your head," he offered from the other room.

"No, just stay where you are and leave me alone." Moments later Dave finished his work, gathered his tools in a temporary pouch made out of the front of his shirt and left the apartment. Once outside, he tried to regain his composure. He'd never hit anyone in anger is his whole life and hoped never would have too. But Aaron pushed him to the limit.

"I'm sorry," Aaron squealed through the closed door. "I didn't mean any harm, please forgive me."

"Piss-off!" He headed to his apartment with his bucket of water sloshing.

Back in his apartment, he dropped the tools on the table. His hands trembled uncontrollably. He was overreacting and knew that Aaron meant no harm, but the incident opened a door to memories he wanted to keep closed.

He stepped to the open window to calm himself. Last night's sweet cool breeze was gone. In its place, the stink of gasoline and diesel fumes rose from the hot asphalt.

I wonder if it stinks like this in Mystique.

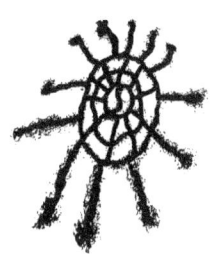

CHAPTER 2

"Sit down."

Shirley didn't look up from her Daily Vacancy Report.

Dave leaned against the doorjamb of the office. "I'd rather stand." It was fifteen minutes after nine.

"I said, SIT DOWN."

Dave threw himself into a chair. "Happy?"

"No." She continued to read the report.

He sat perfectly still. She wouldn't get him to squirm no matter how long she took. His eyes burned into her head.

"You're making this easier." Still focused on her paper she added, "You're fired."

The words hit him in the gut like a fist, but he didn't flinch. He had told her to stick-it before and it didn't get him fired.

She waited for Dave's response. When it didn't come, she lifted her head, their eyes met. Dave was aware that at that moment a simple, I'm sorry, would have diffused the situation and saved his job. But he would rather go to hell than utter a conciliatory word. He was being an asshole but didn't give a damn.

She took a deep breath. "You've been here two years. I've tried everything to make you happy, but nothing I did pleased you. Why?" She paused. He knew what she was after. She wouldn't get any sign of repentance out of him.

Dave sat stiff-backed unblinking. He tried to hide his tension, but could feel ripples in his cheek muscles, and wondered if it would betray him. He would rather die than give an inch to any woman.

"In that time . . . ." Her voice cracked. She cleared her throat. "In that time, I've had nothing but complaints from both residents and fellow workers. You're a looser and with your," she cleared her throat again, "poor work record I wonder why the company ever hired you. At first, I felt sorry for you and gave you the benefit of the doubt."

Dave looked out the window. He had heard it all before.

"I . . . we can't have your attitude any longer." She again waited for a rebuttal. "Don't you have anything to say for yourself?"

His lack of response angered her more and he knew it. His silence put him in the power position. Without spoken words, he told her 'to go to hell'. The charged energy in the room was like an aphrodisiac for him. He loved it.

"You have seventy-two hours to vacate your apartment and be off the property. Is that clear?"

"Yes." Dave answered with no emotion.

She held up an envelope. "Here's your pay, plus two weeks severance, accrued comp-time and vacation." Dave reached for the envelope. She held out her other hand, "Keys and cell phone first . . . please."

"I'll keep my keys, I have my tools in the maintenance room and my things in my apartment."

"You can keep your apartment key. When you are ready to get your junk out of the maintenance room, I will accompany you. Now turn over the rest."

"You don't trust me." Seeing her anger exhilarated him.

"You're damn right I don't trust you." She was not amused. "I'll tell you what."

"What?"

"If you are out of here by six o'clock tonight, I'll throw in another two hundred bucks as a bonus."

"Cash?"

"Cash."

"You're on! All I want are my tools, clothes and TV. My bed is yours." A sinister grin crept across his face. "I know you've been wantin' in it ever since I've been here."

She looked away. He knew she was attracted to him. She tried to conceal how she felt, but he saw it in her eyes. She wasn't his type, he went for the cheap-with-no-commitment-kind. He waited until she turned back.

"The rest of the crap the company calls furnishin's, you can . . . never mind."

Dave stood and took his bundle of keys from his belt. He removed his apartment key from the ring and held it out so she could see it. Then he dropped the rest on her desk with a loud thud. His cell phone followed. With that, Shirley handed him his paychecks.

"Thank you, ma'am." He snatched the envelope and started out. At the door, he stopped and turned back to her as if he was about to speak. She looked up, her anger boiled. With a large gesture, he pulled off his company shirt.

"You can keep the shirt," she quickly replied.

He threw it at her. It fell short and landed on the desk. "Keep your fuckin' shirt." He left and without turning back, waved goodbye. "Two hundred bucks cash if I'm out by six o'clock." His voice rang down the hall. "I'll look you up when I'm ready to get in the maintenance room."

*   *   *

At eleven a.m., Dave looked up from the alley at the open window of his vacant apartment. He locked the back of the camper shell on his twelve-year-old Ford Ranger. Everything he owned except for the few tools he would get later was in that pickup. The dark blue king cab, like him, was in good shape for its age.

Leaving the pickup, he walked to the corner, turned west, and started up Wilshire Boulevard the four blocks to the bank to cash his checks.

He had hung around this part of the Wilshire corridor long after he left its high-rise executive suite at the advertising agency that he made rich and powerful. He realized all he really was, was a glorified salesman. *Account Executive, what a joke, but what more could you expect from a four year degree from a state college?* They wouldn't even let him in the lobby now. He would leave the area for a while. Try other parts of the state, hoping to get it out of his blood, but something always drew him back to its shadows.

As he walked, he thought about Mystique. *A hundred acres, it must be worth something.* He remembered visiting the property with his parents when he was twelve. The family had camped there for a couple of weeks. Since then, he heard that a small community grew up near by. *I'll drive up and see if there is any hope for the place, maybe a fresh start, or else sell it and move-on. Get away from this place for good.*

Tonight however, he would drive out to his sometimes girlfriend Lois's place in Upland. He figured he'd stay with her a week or two. Maybe they'd drive over to Vegas for a couple of days before he headed north.

*   *   *

He left the bank with a wad of money in his pocket, his pay, the cash from his mom and savings, a little less than five grand. As he walked back to the corner deli for lunch, he said his goodbyes to the boulevard, this time for good. He could see himself reflected in windows and shiny facades. *Stand straight,* he told himself. *Can't let anybody think you're defeated.*

He had seen a lot of strange sights on the sidewalks of L.A.. And the character he glimpsed in the windows walking behind him was a dilly. The guy was damn near naked. He looked in the faces of the people that approached but surprisingly nobody reacted. He would have turned around for a better look but he didn't want to appear to be an obvious gawker. In the next bank of windows, he tried to inconspicuously study the reflection of the nut walking behind him, now less than ten feet back.

Suddenly the cold chill of panic gripped him. "Shit! It's the face, the Indian," he yelled, turning and crouching at the same time. There was no one there. He looked at the reflection in the window and saw the faint image of the Indian disappear into the air like a puff of cigarette smoke. Several people on the street stopped and looked at him, the hot flush of embarrassment rushed over him. They politely smiled and went on their way. He stood and walked away, fighting the impulse to run.

"Dammit Dave, you've gotta get a grip on yourself," he muttered as he reached his pickup, anxious to put distance between himself and Shirley, the apartment building, Wilshire Boulevard and the Indian.

*   *   *

The Pomona Freeway was jammed, Dave knew it would be at this time, but he'd refused to leave the apartment complex until the last minute. At ten to six he picked up his tools, turned in his key and collected his two-hundred bucks.

He pulled off the freeway at Mountain Avenue and drove north. He should have called Lois and let her know he was coming.

The two of them had been dating off and on for about three years, nothing serious so far. She was convenience without commitment when the need arose. He would drive over when he could get away, spend a night or two, and then back to the grind.

There was no romance in the relationship, just convenient sex, lacking any semblance of passion. There hadn't been passion in Dave's life for years. He had given up on the idea of real romance, convinced that true love was only in books and movies.

Lois had been a little distant the last two months, his lack of visits no doubt. She had let it be known that she liked their romps as much as he did and seemed to have twice his stamina. Now, he would make it up to her. *Clear the rust out of my old pipes.* She would be happy to have him around for a while he assured himself.

After today's kick in the ass, he felt he might even try getting a little more serious about their relationship. He would ask her to come with him to Mystique. If the property looked good, he'd ask her to stay, he thought. She had no real attachment to

Southern California either. It seemed like a good idea. They could both make a fresh start.

*   *   *

It was after eight o'clock when he pulled up in her driveway.

"Surprise!" he announced as she opened the door. "Guess what, honey, I got canned today, so I'm movin' in for a couple of weeks."

The look on Lois's face wasn't one of surprise, but shock. She just stood there with a blank stare as he gave her a quick kiss. She didn't kiss back, she didn't even pucker. With an ear-to-ear grin, he waited on the porch for her reaction.

There was a long awkward silence. Then someone moved inside the house. A big red-haired orangutan of a man stepped up behind her. He looked to be in his early thirties. A tank top revealed his hairy chest and heavily tattooed arms and shoulders. Dave thought for a second that this might be a son that she'd neglected to mention.

"Who is it, honey?" the ape asked, as his thick lips kissed her ear. He tickled the back of her neck with his short fat index finger and glared at Dave.

"An old friend," Lois replied without blinking, "I'll take care of it. You go finish dinner." She turned back to Dave. "You should have called."

The word 'it' rang in Dave's ears. The sound of her voice and the look on her face said it all.

Dave felt like the orangutan had just run out on the porch and kicked his nuts clear up into his throat. He was left speechless.

"You should have called!", she repeated, as if a phone call would have lessened the blow. Their relationship wasn't much, but he thought it worth more than, 'you should have called'.

It. The word kept repeating. He had been shit-on, hit-on, canned and evicted, and now was reduced to an *It,* all in one day.

He returned to his pickup like a whipped dog, his tail between his legs. He could see Lois still standing at the door as he drove away. The orangutan stood behind her.

Anger, hurt, pain, humiliation, emasculation and frustration all buzzed in his head until there was no reasonable thought left.

*   *   *

After hours of aimless driving, Dave got a grip on himself near Hesperia, at the I-15 and the 395-highway turnoff. It was past two a.m., when he started north on 395. When the last of the city lights disappeared in the distance, he pulled to the side of the road, turned off the engine and hoped to find some sleep. The silence of the empty desert road rang in his head.

He looked in the rearview mirrors, nothing there. Tonight he would even welcome the mysterious visitor from the basement. "Well, I guess you got your way after all. I'm on my way to Mystique. I hope you're happy."

He reclined his seat as much as possible and tried to make himself comfortable. A Ranger king-cab wasn't made for sleeping, but it would have to do.

Dave looked up at the high desert night sky with its millions of stars. "Unbelievable." He had forgotten how many stars there were in the sky once you got away from the city.

A shooting star flashed across the heavens.

CHAPTER 3

"Save yourself. Gary! Dammit Gary, don't do it!"

Dave jolted awake. Another one of those terrible dreams, this time about Gary, a buddy that was disabled in Viet Nam. A sense of dread hung in the air like a cold fog. For years, Dave has been plagued with nightmares of Gary, along with two other deceased high school pals, Joe and Donny, his three best friends who's lives had been tragically cut short. It took him a moment to safely tuck the memories back into their closet in his mind.

A flame red desert sky reminded him where he was and how he got there. His body ached and needed to move. He slid out of the pickup and stood. Twisting his upper body, he tried to work out the knots. The pickup seat made a lousy bed.

Stiff-legged he made his way to the opposite side of the pickup to relieve himself.

The sun peeked above the distant mountains. Its rays, like hot lava, flowed over the cinder cones, Joshua trees and creosote bushes of the Mojave Desert. The clear orange sky turned to yellow and then blue, a sure sign of the heat to come. Dave admired the beauty of the desert landscape long after his necessity was relieved. He had thought of the California desert as an inconvenient hellhole on the way to somewhere, anywhere. This morning he saw it through different eyes.

In the side mirror, a dark shadowy figure moved. "What the . . . ?" he whipped around, startled by the movement he saw. "Who's there?" His nerves knotted in his back. *Someone is watching me.* After zipping his pants, he walked around the pickup and even looked underneath it. Whoever, whatever he'd seen wasn't there now. He sat on a boulder a few yards from the pickup and rubbed his eyes. *Your losin' it man. Really losing it. There's nothin' there.*

"Leave me alone," he yelled, jumping to his feet. Then in a whisper he repeated, "Leave me alone." *Now that's stupid. It's all in your head. A good night's sleep and a couple of days away from L.A., will set you straight.*

A growl from his empty stomach reminded him that he hadn't eaten since noon yesterday. He remembered Kramer Junction was about an hour's drive up the road.

Back in the saddle, he grabbed his sunglasses off the dash and flipped on the air-conditioner. The sun's heat was already penetrating the cab. Before the radio signal faded, a blabbermouth weatherman predicted a temperature of one hundred-eight for the high desert, with wind. *It must be ninety already.*

*   *   *

The gas gage nudged empty as he reached the junction. Four corners with a half a dozen gas stations, a couple of eateries and a souvenir shop huddled together, each vying for a chance at the traveler's wallet. The price of gas was expensive no matter which station you chose. An independent station with a mini-mart looked like it could use his business.

The only other customer pulled out as he pulled up to the pumps. The heat slapped him in the face when he opened the cab door. "Christ, it's hot."

A sign on the pump read 'Please pay cashier first.' "Great." He headed for the mini-mart door.

Near the door was propped a cardboard cutout of a figure from an Old Western movie. *South of the border, down Mexico Way*, the old song played in Dave's head as he approached. When he was almost to the door the figure moved. "For cryin-out-loud!" Dave said as he took a step sideways. A slight grin crept over the weathered face of the shriveled little man.

Dave took off his sunglasses and greeted the old man with a, "Howdy." Struck by the man's western belt buckle, Dave commented, "Like that buckle." A gold 'S' on the large engraved silver buckle, blazed in the desert sun. "Win that riddin' bulls?"

The old man just smiled and nodded his head up and down like a wobble-head-doll.

"It's sure gettin' hot," Dave said as he passed. The only response from the old man was a broader grin. "Nice buckle."

Dave stepped inside the mini-mart and handed the clerk cash. "Fill-up on three."

"Number three, thank you." The clerk's answer revealed his East Indian lineage.

Back at the pump, Dave watched the old man as he gassed up. On his way to get change, he again commented on the weather to the old man.

Getting the restroom key from the clerk he moved his pickup to the side of the building. Making a pit stop to freshen-up, he grabbed his shaving kit from the back of the pickup and headed for the men's room. Finished shaving, he had splashed his face with water when he saw the painted face from the basement in the mirror. Dave spun around so fast he fell. "Dammit! This is getting ridicules." Dazed, he pulled himself up by the washbasin and rushed outside.

The spring hinges slammed the door behind him, and he leaned against the door as if to trap the mysterious visitor inside. The strange dream of two nights ago replayed in his head. He broke out in a cold sweat. A sense of dread came over him. It wasn't a fear of the Indian but a strange foreboding, as if some strange dark secret was about to be revealed. It took him a minute to shake it free. *You must have taken more of a jolt than you thought.* He ran his fingers through his hair. The back of his head was still sore to the touch from the fall in the basement and Aaron's sink.

Once composed, he tossed his kit in the back of his pickup. A growl from his stomach demanded breakfast.

Back in the mini-mart Dave provisioned himself with junk food, sodas, beer, ice, a large cup of fresh coffee and a half dozen hot bean burritos.

"Anything else?" the clerk asked.

"Yeah, a fifth of that Old Turkey whiskey you've got behind the counter should do it." *That'll chase away that demon.* "Who's the old guy by the door?"

"I don't know. He showed up here a few days ago." The clerk rang up the items. "He's waiting for someone. The night clerk got that much out of him. I think he only speaks Spanish." He grabbed a plastic bag. "That will be ninety-seven sixty."

"Good God," Dave grumbled as he paid the clerk with a hundred-dollar bill. "Hope he's not lost. You know, one of those old guys who wandered off from the funny farm."

"Funny farm, what is meaning, funny farm?"

"Rest home, you know, nursing home, mental hospital."

"Oh funny farm, yes, I get it. No, I don't think so." The clerk made change after double-checking the bill. "Two dollars and forty cents."

"Keep it."

"Thank you." The clerk stuffed the change in his pocket. "He's okay, just waiting for someone he's suppose to meet here.

Dave stowed everything in the back of his pickup except the coffee, two sodas and burritos. He was about to climb in when he decided to offer the old man a soda. With soda in hand, he turned and saw that the old man was gone.

Through the mini-mart window Dave could see that the old man wasn't inside, and he knew the bathrooms were locked. *Strange, I didn't see anyone pick him up.* The road was deserted as well. Shaking his head he returned to his pickup.

The engine cranked to life. As he pulled onto the highway and started to accelerate, Dave could see the mini-mart in his rearview mirror. His attention was back at the station, curious as to what had happen to the old man.

He felt the pickup begin to drift off the pavement. Instinctively he jerked the wheel and his attention back to the road. A hitchhiker stood directly in his path.

"Oh shit!" He slammed on the breaks. The pickup went into a skid on the loose gravel of the shoulder. It stopped in a cloud. Dave peered through the windshield and swirling dust. A young man stood just inches from his bumper.

Adrenalin pumped, Dave's heart pounded like a jackhammer. He had a death grip on the wheel.

Once his fear subsided anger took over. "Dumb kid!" Dave slammed the pickup into reverse. The tires spun as he backed-up twenty-feet. "Fuckin' asshole, tryin' to get yourself killed?" he yelled out the window. The gears ground as he forced them into first. The pickup lunged forward and veered around the stranger. Dave stomped on the brakes again. With a screech, the wheels locked, sliding on the small rocks. He flung the pickup door open and flew out.

"What in the hell's the matter with you?" Through the dust, Dave could only see the dark shape of the hitchhiker as he turned toward him. Suddenly he realized the confrontational position he had put himself in and froze. A gust of hot wind pushed the dust off into the desert. There came a strange recognition. "Joe?" His mouth hung open as he stared at the hitchhiker.

The hitchhiker stood motionless. The young stranger appeared completely undaunted by the near mishap.

Dave calmed enough to speak. "You scared the hell out of me. I could have killed you."

"I thought for a moment you would." The hitchhiker said, as he lifted the brim of his black Stetson and lowered his aviator sunglasses. "I'm glad you've got good brakes."

Though still shaken, Dave's anger started to diminish as his mind filled with questions. There was no one on the road when he pulled out of the gas station and in this barren landscape there was no place to hide. He looked at the mini-mart and then back at the hitchhiker. Looking the young traveler over carefully, he realized there wasn't really a resemblance to Joe. Without thinking he asked, "Need a ride?"

"Yes."

The young man accepted the offer before Dave could re-nege. The situation seemed out of Dave's control, like someone was speaking through him. "I'm headed north, up the backside of the Sierras, to Mystique, if yeah want a ride that far." *You just invited a complete stranger to share a ride all the way to Mystique.*

"That would be great, I'm heading that way, too." The stranger told Dave, with an appreciative smile.

What do I do now? Dave's mouth gapped open. *Introduce yourself stupid.* "Ah—I'm Dave, Dave Hoffsted." He bolted forward as if somebody just kicked him in the butt, and stuck out his hand.

"My name is Trent, pleased to meet you." A fraction before their hands touched a bright blue-white spark jumped between their palms.

"Whoa!" Dave flinched at the shock. "I must have picked up some static electricity back there," ending the handshake.

"Thanks for the ride," Trent said, not reacting to the electrical discharge.

"Didn't you feel that?" Dave questioned, looking at his hand.

"The static? Yeah, it happens a lot out here in the desert, the dry air."

Dave glanced from his hand to Trent. *You're stuck with him. Sure hope it's not a mistake.*

"I'll put your pack in the back." Dave grabbed a strap of Trent's backpack, it was heavier than he expected. "Whattya got in here, rocks?" He attempted a joke.

"Yeah, of coarse, and the kitchen sink, too."

Dave opened the back of the camper shell and lifted in the backpack, then turned to Trent expecting him to hand over the well worn handmade buckskin bag hanging over his shoulder.

"I'll keep this with me, if you don't mind." Trent's hand gripped the colorful woven strap, guarding the well-worn bag.

"No problem, there's plenty of room." Dave said as he climbed in the cab. "Get in before you roast." He slid the cans of soda and the burritos to the center of the bench seat as Trent climbed in. Trent placed the buckskin bag on the floor behind his feet and fastened his seatbelt.

Dave buckled up and started out once again, this time with a young stranger-riding shotgun. Dave cast a discreet glance out of the corner of his eye at Trent. Other then a stranded motorist, this was Dave's first hitchhiker. He was apprehensive, but much to his chagrin, he welcomed the company.

Trent had on black cowboy boots. *That is a good sign. And jeans, appropriate for out here. But a black tee shirt.* "Wasn't that shirt a little hot out there in the sun?"

"Not too bad, I wasn't out there long before you stopped."

Dave stole another sideways glimpse at Trent. The knit of his tee shirt clung to his muscular upper body. When Dave spotted his belt buckle, his thoughts spun, *the old man's belt buckle.* "Where did you get that belt?"

Trent looked down at his buckle. "My grandfather gave it to me." He continued to look at the buckle, running his right index finger over it slowly.

"What does the 'S' stand for?"

"Salvador!" He rolled his 'r'. "My great-grandfather was from El Salvador, and he took the name Salvador as his sir name when he immigrated to America. I'm a Salvador too."

"You're Hispanic?" Dave questioned. "Trent is an unusual name, it isn't Spanish."

"I'm French, English, Latino and Native American." There was a sense of pride in his voice. "Trent means, flowing waters, to the People of the Northeast." He turned his head and looked at Dave. "So what's your fascination with my belt buckle?"

"Oh, ah, ah . . . ." Dave stuttered. "There was an old man hangin' around the gas station back there. He was wearin' the identical belt buckle. I just thought it strange—it's not very common."

"No it's not. Interesting coincidence."

An empty rumble from Dave's stomach reminded him that he still hadn't eaten. He shifted his thoughts to food and reached for a burrito, jockeyed it with the steering wheel and peeled back the foil wrapping. Once exposed, he took a hearty bite. It was dry and only a little tastier than cardboard, but it was food. He washed it down with coffee.

Out of the corner of his eye he caught Trent watching him eat. His large sunglasses didn't hide everything. "Want one?" Dave asked, making a gesture with the burrito. "There's plenty. No coffee, but there's a soda."

"Thanks," Trent said eagerly helping himself to a burrito.

Dave wondered as he drove, where the kid had come from. He seemed to have just appeared out of nowhere. Did he spend the night on the road and where did he sleep, but the questions would wait, at least for now.

Trent made quick work of the burrito.

"Help yourself to another," Dave insisted.

Trent seemed almost surprised that he had finished the first one so quickly. "Oh, okay, thanks, I didn't eat breakfast this morning."

By the way the kid wolfed down the burrito, Dave figured the he hadn't eaten for a day or two.

For someone on the road, Trent looked clean and well groomed. Little dark curls stuck out from under the back of his hat. Dave tried to guess his age. *Early-twenties, maybe younger, hope he's not a runaway-teen.*

"How old are you?" The words rolled out of Dave's mouth before he could stop them.

"Twenty-three." Trent answered as he finished his second burrito. "The burritos really hit the spot. Thanks. I owe you."

"My pleasure."

The road north was clear and with very little traffic headed south. The heat of the desert penetrated the cab and fought with the air-conditioner. Dry hills dotted with sage and creosote brush, stretched in all directions. Ahead and to their left, the southern end of the Sierra Nevada's created a hazy blue wall leading north.

"I've never picked up a hitchhiker before," Dave said. "I've heard stories about hitchhikers." Dave tried to explain his reservations. "Ya, you know," Dave struggled to clarify, "about robbers, killers, runaways . . . ."

"Perverts," Trent added. "Do I make you nervous?"

"Oh no, no. You look pretty safe." *Perverts,* the very word Dave was thinking. He tried to cover his misgivings. "It's just new to me."

"Well, there is a first time for everything,"

"Yeah, I guess you're right." Dave smiled, but his apprehension built.

"Well . . . ." Trent slowly leaned forward, pulled off his dark glasses and gave Dave a serious look. "If it will make you feel any better, you look pretty safe yourself, you don't look like a rapist, pervert or serial killer. You aren't one, are you? No, I got it, you're just a runaway, a runaway from the big city." After a pause, Trent began to laugh.

The truth in the runaway comment surprised Dave, then he realized Trent was joking and joined the laughter. The seed of friendship germinated and with it came an exchange of trust. Dave's shoulders loosened and his grip on the wheel relaxed.

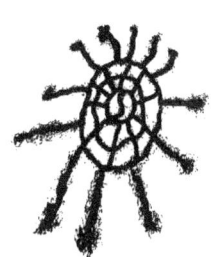

CHAPTER 4

"Run you damn fool. RUN!"

Dave yelled at another ground squirrel as it darted in front of his pickup. "Damn fools, they wait until you're right on top of them before they run."

"I think it's their private game of chicken," Trent laughed. "Trying to see how close they can get to the tires and not get run over."

"By the number of flattened remains on the road, their timin' isn't all that good."

"At least they provide easy meals for the ravens."

Curious to know more about his passenger, Dave switched the subject. "Gonna meet up with someone up north?"

"Nah. Just traveling."

"That's kinda what I'm doing, tryin' to clear my head and see the country. Thought I'd drive up the 395 to Mystique, stay off the freeways and away from big cities. Kick back a couple of weeks and take a break from the old grind." Dave drove on for a minute.

He wasn't sure why but he felt the need to tell the truth. "Ah shit! No use lyin', the truth is I got canned yesterday, then found out my girlfriend's got some young buck livin' with her. It's like you said, I'm a runaway from the big city. I got a piece of land up at Mystique and I'm hopin' I might make a go of it there."

Trent didn't respond. After a while, Dave glanced over at him. Trent faced forward, his eyes hidden behind his dark glasses. He felt the kid was more than a mere hitchhiker. Maybe it was just his imagination. He couldn't put his finger on it. Was it his quiet gentle manner or the way he appeared out of nowhere? And how did he happened to have the exact same belt buckle as the old man?

"I was at a pretty low point this mornin'." Dave said, breaking the silence. "Don't know why I offered you a ride, but I'm glad t' have your company."

"Guess I was in the right spot."

*   *   *

Try as he might, Dave couldn't get any more information out of Trent other than he had no close family or any particular place he called home. So after some time asking questions and getting short answers, he gave up asking and just talked.

"I use to live up near Susanville, when I was a kid. Mystique's about fifty miles north, it wasn't a town then, just a gas station with a bait shop. Back then they called it Mystique Corners, named for an old abandon farmhouse across from the bait shop that was supposed to have been haunted. That's when my folks bought some property there. Property was dirt cheap then."

Dave enjoyed Trent's willing ear. He slowed the pickup, turned into a pullout and stopped.

Trent looked at him. "Something wrong?"

"Gonna grab some more cold drinks out of the back."

A moment later he jumped back in the cab with four cans of soda and a bag of cookies. "Damn, it's hotter than hell out there," Dave said as he handed Trent a soda. "Would you want to live out there?"

"No thank you." Trent opened the can. "Would you?"

"Not on your life."

Back on the road, the AC struggled to catch up. Each hill looked like the one before. Fatigue was setting in.

Trent broke the silence. "So, how old were you when you left Susanville?"

"You really interested, kid? You don't mind me callin' you kid?"

"No, I don't mind and, of course, I'm interested."

"I was eighteen. Left home right after high school graduation." Dave watched a large black SUV approach from behind through his rearview mirror. The vehicle didn't slow. It passed them as if they were standing still. Dave laid on the horn as it passed.

"That idiot's got to be pushing a hundred," Trent said shaking his head in disapproval. The SUV was soon out of sight.

"My dad was killed in a car crash when I was a freshman in high school," Dave said. "Fell asleep at the wheel and hit a tree. Can't say I shed many tears over it. We weren't very close." Dave held up the bag of cookies. "Help yourself."

"Thanks."

"I thought we should stop and stretch our legs, maybe the next town."

"Sounds good." Trent picked up the miss-folded map from the dash. "Inyokern is the next town on the highway, it looks like it's about twenty miles."

"That'll do."

Trent leaned against the door and folded his arms across his chest. Dave munched on the cookies. The large black SUV that had passed them was stopped along side the road. Two men stood on the passenger side and by their posture, it looked as if they were relieving themselves.

"No wonder they were in such a hurry." Dave remarked as he gave the men a toot of the horn.

"You sure it's the same SUV?"

"I think so. Nobody else has passed us."

Just then another suicidal squirrel made a break. Its course took it under the pickup. In a second, Dave could see the bewildered critter through his rearview mirror, sitting in the middle of the road. "He made it."

"I'll be, I thought for sure he was a goner."

Dave carried on his one-sided conversation about leaving Susanville, college, his career, marriages and divorces. Trent seemed a willing listener.

"Back in the sixties," Dave continued, "it was some crazy times. Free love, Hippies and Viet Nam." Dave looked over at Trent. "You ever been in the service?"

"Military? No!" Trent answered, seemingly surprised by the question.

"You young guys today, you got it made. No draft. Back then it wasn't that way. Viet Nam, and everyone was afraid of the Russian Commies and the Red Chinese. Shoot, that's why we moved to Susanville, to be safe from an A-bomb attack. You know, before we moved some of our neighbors in San Jose, built bomb shelters in their front yards. What the hell good would that had done them?"

"False security I guess," Trent paused, "like stocking food for Armageddon."

"So you never did time in the military." Dave lingered a moment. "Neither did I. Back then, when Viet Nam was goin', everyone was gettin' drafted. Shit, did Nam ever turn into a mess, just like Iraq, only back then the American people woke up to the truth, but it took years. I had a bad knee and ear, so I was 4-F, the only lucky break I ever got. My buddies, they weren't so lucky. They're all dead now because of the military, one way or another. We started in the sixth grade together. The four of us went all the way through high school together." Dave's memories were so vivid he could see their faces. "They're all gone." Dave glanced at Trent, assuring himself he was still listing.

"There was Gary, big guy, six-foot-four, strong as a horse, loved sports. And Donny, wanted to be a movie star, good-lookin', athletic. All the girls were gaga over him. He starred in all the school plays. Then there was Joe, my best friend. He looked a lot like you. Same colorin' and build. You could be his son, if he'd had one."

"Joe?" The desert passed outside Trent's window.

"That's who I thought you were for a moment back there. Crazy?" Dave asked, looking over at Trent. "I'm not borin' you?"

"No, not at all. Please, go on."

"I remember our high school graduation." Dave chuckled to himself. "Well actually the night after the graduation. It was the last time we were altogether. Joe and I went campin' for two weeks after graduation, at our favorite place in the mountains, near Lassen. Supposed to be just the two of us at a place called Castle Rock. Donny and Gary surprised us; they came up together and brought a couple of cases of beer. All of us at The Castle, a big rock that looked like a castle on top. We made camp at the base. It wasn't a regular campground, just a spot a couple of miles up an old dirt-logging road. There was a creek for water and the bushes to do our business."

The black SUV came up behind them and started to ride their bumper. "I wonder what's wrong with this jackass behind us."

Just then the SUV jerked into the other lane, swerved around them and cut back in inches from their front bumper. Dave slammed on his brakes and laid on the horn. "Jackass."

"It sounds like you had the fixings for a celebration."

"Well we had one hell of a party that night. That was the name of the game, get wasted. We were all feelin' no pain."

"Must have been fun."

"It was, 'til the next day. Oh God, the next day." Dave's face twisted with a grimace as the memory of that morning thrust itself into his consciousness.

"Paid the piper?" Trent flashed a knowing smile.

"Yes sir. I thought I had died and gone straight to hell." Dave took a drink of soda. "I woke about mid-day to a loud growl. At first, I thought it was a bear. It was Joe puking his guts out. The moment I moved, I joined him. It was my first hangover, and it was a humdinger.

We had a tent, but Joe and I had passed out under a tree. God knows where Donny slept. We found Gary, sprawled out, bare assed naked and dead to the world, layin' out in a clearin'. He must've lain in the sun all mornin'. He was cooked, his butt looked like a tomato. We finally got him into the tent. He lay there two days, couldn't stand anything to touch his backside. Donny nursed him, poor Gary was sicker than we realized. Sun poisoning, I think they call it. We never did find his clothes, we had to loan him some of ours to go home in. Our clothes were too small and he looked like a clown in them. He was one sick puppy. You ever do anything that stupid?"

"I think you've got me beat."

"God, I think of those guys all the time, especially Joe, like it was yesterday. I always expect to see them. I can't believe they are dead all these years now." Dave looked over at Trent. You any relation to a Joe Colombo from Susanville?"

"No. Not that I know."

"Damn! Somehow you remind me of him and yet you don't even look like him." The memories of the camping trip returned to Dave.

"Joe and I stayed our two weeks. It sure went fast after the rocky start. We didn't drink any more beer that trip." Dave looked over at Trent for a moment.

"The day after we got back from the Castle, Joe left for the army. That was the last time I saw him." Dave drank more soda. "I got a letter from him every week. Then they stopped. I started gettin' nervous. I hoped he was just out on field maneuvers, but I had this feelin' somethin' was wrong."

"One day I got this letter from Joe's dad. I knew it was somethin' bad. Joe's dad had never written me."

Trent sat up, straightened his hat and looked at Dave.

"Well, is seems that Joe and his buddy were out practicin' on the gunnery range. His buddy's gun jammed and miss-fired, blew the poor guy's brains all over Joe. It really messed with Joe's head. He cracked up. Six weeks later he took a rope and hung himself in his barrack's store room." Dave paused, visibly shaken. "Maybe if I had driven down, we could have talked, things would be different."

Dave hit the steering wheel with the heel of his hand. "GUNS! Damn things, never had any use for guns." He took another drink of soda.

"I had a cap gun when I was a kid. Played cowboy and Indian with the rest of the boys, had that toy gun for years. Then one day my dad took me out squirrel huntin' with a real gun, a twenty-two rifle. I was nine or ten. I shot at a lot of squirrels, 'til I finally

36

hit one. I never knew a squirrel could cry. Blew me away, I cried for hours. My dad was pissed, he called me a sissy. When I got home, I took that toy gun out and threw it in the Susan River. I haven't had a thing to do with guns since.

"I don't have much use for guns either."

The black SUV was stopped beside the road again and as they passed it pulled back on the road behind them and started flashing their lights.

"I wonder what the hell they want."

"Pull over and find out," Trent said.

"I don't like this, it's a pretty lonely stretch of highway."

"They seem determined to talk, why not find out what's up?"

Dave reluctantly slowed and came to a stop at a turnout. He left the engine running and stepped out of the pickup and stood beside the open door. The men jumped out of their vehicle and approached Dave.

"What the fuck's the matter with you, man?" the driver yelled. "You ran us off the road coming out of Bakersfield this morning."

"I wasn't in Bakersfield. I came from L.A., up the 15 to the 395."

"It sure as hell looked like your pickup. So what's your problem, man, honkin at us when we stopped to take a piss?"

"I honked because of the way you were driving. I didn't run anyone off the road." Dave backed toward the pickup. "I'm sorry but it wasn't me, you are mistaken."

"I want to know what the fuck your problem is." The men stepped closer.

"Didn't you hear? The guy said you have the wrong man." Trent stepped up beside Dave. "I have been with him since this morning at Kramer Junction. You have the wrong man so get back in your vehicle and go on." Dave sensed Trent step closer.

"Yes, sir. We don't want trouble." The driver of the SUV said, suddenly apologetic. "I guess we made a mistake."

"You sure have." Trent agreed.

Dave watched the men as they got back in their SUV, turned around in the middle of the highway and laid rubber as they sped off. Dave's knees nearly buckled as he turned to Trent. Trent smiled as he quickly put something back into the buckskin bag hung over his shoulder.

"I was scared shitless," Dave confessed, as he looked at Trent's bag.

"Why?" Trent asked, as he slid his hand out of the buckskin bag and took hold of the door for Dave.

"I don't deal well with confrontation." Dave climbed in the pickup.

Trent closed Dave's door and quickly got in on his side. Dave sat trembling.

"You gonna be okay?"

"Yeah, just need a second to calm down."

"You've got to confront your fears, most are nothing but paper tigers. I'm sure that's the last we will see of those two."

"How did you know they would back down?"

"I didn't, but we couldn't let them run us off the road."

"I don't know what I would have done if you hadn't been here."

*   *   *

The two men drove along in silence. Dave relaxed and soon started to snack on some cookies. He reached for his soda but his can was empty.

A bump in the road dislodged a small packet of papers from the sun visor. It landed at Dave's feet.

"What's that?" Trent asked.

"Not sure, registration papers I think."

Dave picked up the packet, it was held together with a paperclip. He glanced at it as he drove. "It's an old vehicle registration, an expired proof of insurance card, a sandwich shop card . . . ." He tried to keep his eyes on the road. "And an old photo." Dave turned the photo over and looked at the image.

"Holy shit!" He gasped.

"What's a matter?"

"It's a picture of Joe and me, haven't seen this in years. I wonder how in the hell it got stuck up there." Dave showed the photo to Trent. "Look, can you see a resemblance?"

"No."

Dave grew misty-eyed. "That picture was taken the day he left for boot camp."

"How about a pit stop," Trent suggested. "The sign said there's a rest stop two miles up the road."

"Yeah, I've sucked up enough soda to piss a river. I thought we would be comin' to a town, Inyokern?

"We passed the turn off a good forty miles back."

"I need a break, thinkin' about the guys kinda made me blue."

"I'm sorry I brought it up."

"No, thanks for listenin'. Most guys would have jumped out of the pickup and run off into the desert just to get away from my long-winded-story."

"Maybe I'm not like most guys."

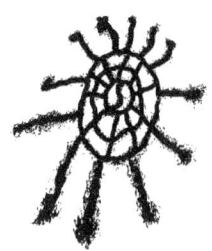

CHAPTER 5

"If there is a hell, this is it."

Dave stood beside the pickup and looked over the Coso Junction rest stop. It beckoned the weary traveler with a promise of cool shade, but with a hundred-ten degree temperature and twenty-five mile an hour winds, its looks proved deceptive.

"Death Valley is about fifty miles that way," Trent said pointing east. Just then, his hat blew off sending him on a chase across the parking lot. It took a good run for him to catch up with it. Hat in hand he started back.

A large black SUV with the hood up was parked across the parking lot. Dave's heart skipped a beat when he first spotted it, but when he saw that two forlorn women stood looking at the engine, he was relieved.

"You ladies have a problem?" Dave asked as he approached.

"Do we ever!" The woman in a tan western-style slack suit, answered. She was near tears, her brown hair blown around her face. "Hi, my name's Betty." She managed a smile as she held out her hand to Dave.

"I'm Dave." He gave her soft hand a gentle shake.

"This is my daughter Susan." The young woman she introduced was more comfortably dressed for the weather. "We stopped to use the restroom and when we got back, it wouldn't start. The damn thing's completely dead."

"Mom!" Susan rolled her eyes with embarrassment.

"Well, let's take a look." Dave poked his head under the hood and stared for a moment at the jumble of wires and hoses. Staring at the battery, he checked for loose wires or any other visible indication of the problem.

"It's dead, just dead. It won't even turn over," Betty explained. "I tried to call for help but my cell phone is dead, too."

"And the pay phone is out of order," Susan added.

"Sorry, but I don't have a cell phone either."

Trent joined the group, with their heads under the hood. Dave made the introductions. He could not help but notice the quick once over Susan gave Trent.

Trent returned the look with a smile before he turned his concern to the SUV. "What are you looking for?"

"It's dead. I've checked everything I can think of," Dave answered.

Dave double-checked the battery cables before moving to the fuse panel under the dash. With a yank, he pulled the cover off the fuses. "I need some light." As the three stood and watched, he retrieved a flashlight from his pickup and was back under the dash. His legs hung out the door as he tried to find a comfortable position to work.

"Out here, two stranded ladies with their hood up is like a red flag for the bulls, if ya know what I mean." Dave explained as he inspected each fuse for the possible culprit.

"We have little choice but hope for help from a kind soul like yourself."

"Can I offer you gentleman a soda or cold water?' Susan asked.

"No thanks, ma'am," Trent answered for both of them.

Dave's legs thrashed about trying to find a better position as he continued his hunt under the dashboard. He fought back the expletives he'd like to have added. Finally, he relaxed and slithered out from under the dash. With a grunt, he stood, dusted off his pants and sat in the driver's seat.

"Watch yourself," he called out. "I'm gonna give it a try."

The women stepped back from the exposed engine. Betty held up her crossed fingers. Dave smiled and held up his left hand with is fingers crossed before trying to start the engine.

There was a breathless moment of anticipation, but hope faded when nothing happened.

"Damn!" Dave let out his frustration on the steering wheel. "Sorry!"

The two women stared at Dave. Now it was Susan who looked like she was about to cry as Betty's optimism turned into disappointment. Dave sat in the SUV disheartened.

"Stay there," Trent told Dave. "I want to try something."

Trent leaned under the hood and hovered over the engine, blocking Betty's view. He took something out of the buckskin bag that hung from his shoulder. Dave tried to see what he was up to through the space between the frame and hood, but wasn't able to make out what Trent was doing. Susan was too busy watching Trent to notice his mechanical skills.

After a few seconds, Trent stepped back from the vehicle. "Now, try it again."

Dave turned the key and the SUV sprang to life. Betty and Susan let out a cheer as Dave bounded out of the SUV.

"What the hell was it? What did you do?" Dave yelled over the hum of the engine.

"The negative clamp on the battery was loose. I stuck my penknife blade in the terminal and it started. Turn off the engine and I'll tighten it."

Trent pulled an all-in-one tool from his bag and cleaned and tightened the clamp on the terminal. Dave stood confused, his ego tweaked. He shook his head in disbelief.

"I know I checked that," he said to himself. "Twice."

"Oh thank God, I didn't know what I was going to do," Betty trilled.

"We'll have you on your way in a minute," Trent told Betty. "You shouldn't have any more trouble."

"How far are you going?" Dave asked.

"Near Susanville. Do you think we can make it there, will it be okay?"

"Oh sure. Trent will fix it as good as new. Susanville? We're headin' up that way ourselves."

"You won't have any more problems ma'am," Trent interrupted. "However, you might want your mister to check it when you get home."

"There's no mister."

Trent looked up as he finished tightening the terminal.

Betty opened her purse. "Now, can I thank you gentlemen?"

"Close your purse ma'am, it's our pleasure to be able to help," Dave said as he held the door for Betty.

With a thud, Trent closed the hood and stepped to Susan's side of the vehicle.

"Look, Mom, the cell phone works, too."

Betty laughed, looked at Trent and winked. "Thanks again boys and have fun."

Her remark puzzled Dave, but before he could question her, their eyes met. There was a strange moment of recognition. Dave froze, his jaw dropped. But before Dave could form a word, Betty put the vehicle in reverse and backed out of the parking space. All he could do was watch her drive off.

"I swear I know her from somewhere, but I can't imagine where."

"Maybe in another life."

"Yeah sure." Dave laughed.

When they were out of sight, Trent turned and started toward the toilets. Dave hesitated a few seconds and just looked at the empty road. When a blast of hot wind nearly took off his sunglasses, he turned and followed Trent.

The only light in the concrete walled bathroom filtered through a single small skylight. The acrid smell of urine filled Dave's nostrils as he stepped up to the urinal next to Trent.

"It stinks in here." Dave stared at the wall in front of him. "Damn! The battery terminals appeared fine to me."

"Well sometimes things aren't always as the appear." Trent looked at Dave. "Looks can be deceiving."

Trent left Dave at the urinal, washed and stopped at the doorway to wait.

From the washbasin, Trent was a blur in the stainless steel panel that served as a mirror. "Couple of good lookin' gals, those two. That Susan was really givin' you the eye. How would you like to get her in the sack?"

"Hmmm?"

Looking at Trent's blurred image in the mirror Dave repeated, "I said, how would you like to get that Susan in the sack?"

Dave turned when there was no answer. Trent was gone. Dave stepped out the door. Trent was sitting on a picnic table clear across the grass, near the pickup. *How did he get over there? Good God, it must not have been Trent in the mirror.* Dave rushed back inside the bathroom, it was empty and there was no one else around.

Idiot! You're loosing it. Dave shook his head. *Got to stop this shit, I need some rest.*

*   *   *

Trent sat on top of a table near the pickup. His legs folded under him lotus style as he stared trance-like off into the desert. Dave had opened the hood of the pickup and checked the oil and belts. When he was finished, he joined Trent.

"Over that hill," Trent pointed, "about five miles is the Coso Hot Springs, a sacred place to the native people. The U.S. Navy fenced it off in the forties and leased it out for a geothermal electric plant. A couple of times a year they let the local natives come in and have ritual healing baths and worship in their traditional ways."

Dave sat quietly for a while and looked out at the desert. "It sure is a damn shame how they treated the Indians."

Trent continued to stare off into the distance.

The hot wind weakened to a breeze and cooled a little.

Dave lay down on the bench and folded his hands behind his head.

"So Dave, you ever think about getting married again?"

"Shit no."

"Not even if you find the right gal?"

"I've given up on marriage and, if it weren't the occasional need for some pussy, women altogether. They're nothin' but a nuisance."

"The gal with the car trouble, Betty, sure put a smile on your face."

"I'm a man. I didn't say I gave up sex, just marriage. I noticed you were all grins, too. Don't tell me you weren't thinkin' about gettin' that Susan in the sack," he said again, this time making sure Trent heard him.

"So, you were telling me about your buddies."

"That's right, change the subject." Dave laughed. "I need somethin' to drink." Dave went to the pickup and returned with two cans of beer. "It's time for a brew. You drink beer?"

"Sure, thanks."

"Well, with Donny, that was sort of weird. As I said, he was real good looking and hot with the ladies. He bragged about how good he was in bed, too. Made all the guys jealous with his locker room stories. But don't get me wrong, he was real likeable, always lots of fun."

Dave stopped and looked away. "Well, after high school Donny moved to L.A., to try his luck in Hollywood. He and his roommate came back to Susanville for Joe's funereal. He really had gone Hollywood by then, flashy and phony. It wasn't long after that he was drafted. He got sent somewhere in the south, Mississippi I think, or Alabama. He wrote a couple of times, then nothing. Well, about three years went by and I get this long letter. He's livin' in San Francisco with some *guy* he met in the army." Dave took off his sunglasses and looked Trent in the face. "He was gay for Christ sake."

Dave watched for a reaction. Trent showed none.

"It seems," Dave continued, "he got caught screwin' around with some soldiers on base. And when I say screwin', I mean it literally. They court-marshaled him, locked him up for six months, then threw him out of the army. A year later he wrote again. He was alone and havin' a hard time gettin' a decent job, with his

46

dishonorable discharge and all. He asked me to help him get a job with the newspaper I work for in San Jose. I didn't. I didn't want anyone to think I was friends with a queer.

"I saw him one time after that. It was about ten years later. He was real sick and stayin' with his Mom. She called me sayin' he was askin' for me. When I got there he was in bad shape. It seems he turned to prostitution and got into drugs. I just stayed with him for a couple days; that was all I could do. Three weeks later, he died . . . of AIDS."

"How did the military cause his death?" Trent asked.

Dave finished his beer. "In high school, he wasn't gay. Somethin' happened to him in the goddamn Army that made him change." He turned to Trent. "I don't know why I'm telling you all this shit."

Dave bolted toward the pickup. "Drink up, let's get goin'."

*　　*　　*

Back on the road, Dave watched a car pass and move on down the road in front of them. He looked at Trent who was staring out the passenger side window. He studied the young man as he drove. *Eerie. It's as if I've known him for years. I'm telling him things I've never told anyone and I know nothing about him, not a damn thing.*

Trent made himself comfortable by leaning against the door. Dave started to whistle the old folk tune 'Good-night Irene'. Trent tried to conceal his amusement, but chuckled out loud.

"What?" Dave asked.

"That song."

"What about it?"

"I haven't heard it since I was a little kid. My grandfather used to whistle it all the time."

"Does it bother you?"

"No, just memories. Good memories. 'I'll kiss you in my dreams'."

Dave continued to whistle and Trent closed his eyes.

*　　*　　*

Trent was asleep with his head against the window. Dave glanced over at him. The kid's face was as strong and flawless as a Michelangelo marble. *Glad I picked him up. Maybe he'll bring me some good luck.* A bump in the road woke Trent. Dave stopped whistling.

"Did my whistlin' wake you?"

"No, no. I shouldn't be sleeping. I'm supposed to be keeping you company."

"That's okay. You looked tired."

"I didn't get much sleep the past few nights, I was waiting up for someone."

"I planned on stoppin' for the night." Dave paused as he weighed his thoughts. "I was gonna get a room, somethin' cheap. Heck, we can share. If you'd like. Twin beds."

"Sure, that sounds fine. We can split the cost."

"I'll take care of the room kid, you can spring for dinner."

"It's a deal."

Dave started to whistle again, then stopped. His thought shifted to Betty and her daughter at the rest stop. "They were a couple of good-looking gals and they live in Susanville. I should have gotten their address."

"You never know, we might see them again."

"Dream on." Dave glanced at Trent. "You must do pretty well with the ladies."

"Fair!"

"Yeah, fair! My ass. I bet they flock all over you."

Trent smiled. "So, what happened to Gary?"

"Always changin' the subject." Dave, pleased with Trent's interest, sat up straighter.

"It's hard dealin' with what happened to Gary. He was a big guy, strong, but a heart of gold. Would do anything for you. He enlisted in the Marines and got sent to Nam for a year." Dave paused for a moment. "Gary was patriotic, but not gung-ho like Joe. He didn't like it in Nam, was just doing his duty. He never complained, but I could tell from his letters, he was just puttin' in his time. I got a letter from him, about a month before he was to come home. He was countin' the days, could hardly wait."

"Then I got a call from his dad. He said, 'hello' then started to cry. Gary's mom had to get on the phone. She told me he had been injured. Two weeks before he was to come home, he stepped on a damn mine. One of those they call, Eunuch Makers. Got him bad. Took his legs off at the hips. He was half a man."

He drove on in silence for a minute. "When he got out of the hospital he tried to find a job. He accepted his condition real well, but I couldn't. I couldn't bear to even look at him. My wife thought I should get him a job at the newspaper, I told her that the paper wasn't equipped to hire anyone in a wheelchair. I did, however, raise the money to buy him an especially equipped handicap van so he could stay in Susanville and get around on his own."

Dave started to whistle again, this time a slow and mournful 'Good-night Irene'.

"A year after he got the van, he was in an accident. A truck ran a stop sign and hit him broadside. It killed him instantly . . . damn war."

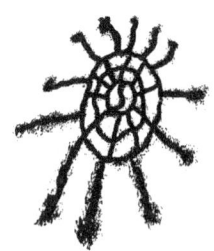

CHAPTER 6

"As the Duke would say. This town isn't big enough for the two of us." Dave said, as they approached the small town of Independence.

Dave's poor imitation of John Wayne brought a tolerant smile to Trent. "You missed your opportunity, they made all the Old Western movie's forty miles back at Lone Pine."

Dave was tired of driving and glad to be coming into the little town. The community was pressed hard against the Sierra's at the edge of the Owens Valley. A thin stand of trees followed a stream down the mountain and spread out into Independence.

The speed limit dropped to twenty-five miles an hour as they entered city limits and something told Dave, he had better obey. "Looks like the Courthouse is the biggest thing in town," he remarked as they passed the old three-story building.

Ahead and across the street from the Courthouse, he spotted a motel. "The Courthouse Motel," Dave read the name. "Damn, sounds like the county jail. I'll pass on the Courthouse Motel."

"I think I see another motel a couple of blocks up on the left." Trent leaned forward to get a better look.

Dave turned on the left turn signal. "It looks clean, but a little long in the tooth."

"Long in the tooth, what's that mean?"

"Old, kid, old, like me." Dave pulled into the motel's parking area. "I'll see if they've got a room." He left the motor running.

"I'll sleep on a cot if that's all they got," Trent said, as Dave closed the cab door.

Dave counted nine rooms on his way to the office. The office door was locked, but a handwritten sign read. 'RING BELL'. Dave pushed the button and waited. Impatient, he pushed the button again, and then walked around the side of the building to see if anyone was out back. No one was around. He came back to the door and rung the bell once more. With a glance at Trent in the pickup, he shrugged his shoulders. Frustration mounted as he peered through the window for any sign of life. Angered, he turned on his heals and headed back to the pickup, just then he heard the click of the office door's lock and the door creak.

"Hello," a voice called. "Sorry, I was in the kitchen."

It took Dave a couple of steps to come to a stop and turn. A white haired woman stood in the doorway. "I was washing dishes. Can I help you?" Her toothless grin immediately defused his irritation.

Dave reminded himself this wasn't L.A.. "Do you have any vacancies?"

Wiping her hands in a towel, her small eyes peered from a round, incredibly wrinkled face, "Sure do young fella. Come on in." Her blue and white checked bib apron and faded blue dress completed the image of a character out of an Old Western.

With a gentler walk, he followed the old lady into the office. A small counter near the door separated the so-called lobby from her living room.

"I'd like a double."

"I have a room with two queen beds. Would you like to see it?"

52

"Nah, as long as it has two beds it'll do fine."

"One night, you and your son?"

"Yes, but he's not my son." Dave was surprised by how observant the old lady was.

"It'll be forty-eight for the night plus tax. You'll need to fill out the card," She pushed a registration card and pen at Dave. "There is a payphone by number four and if you want ice, take the ice bucket in your room next door to the Burger Spot, they'll give you free ice, but you have to take the bucket from your room. Checkout time is eleven a.m. and no loud noise after ten p.m.. My son is the deputy sheriff and the jail is right down the street."

"We noticed the courthouse on our way in." Dave signed the card. "There's a bar and grill back a block, across the street. Is it any good?" He slid the completed card back to the old lady.

"It'll fill your belly and wet your whistle, That's about all yea can expect round here." She looked over the card. "That will be fifty-three dollars."

After Dave paid for the room, she handed him a key. "Only got one key. Have a good stay."

"Thanks. Good afternoon." Dave walked quickly back to the pickup. "Got us a double. Room one."

Dave moved the pickup to in front of the room. "This is it." The sidewall of the room butted up to the sidewalk next to the highway.

"Close to the road." Trent stood beside the pickup. "Hope it's not too noisy."

"I don't think anyone would dare be noisy in this town."

Dave circled to the back of the pickup, took out his hat, a suitcase and the bottle of whisky. Trent, his buckskin bag over his shoulder, grabbed his pack and they headed for the room.

The door bumped against the bed as Dave opened it. A strong disinfectant smell greeted him. "Well, it smells clean!"

"Small."

The second bed was against the opposite wall with a under-sized nightstand between. "I'll take the one by the door." Dave tossed his hat on the bed and turned on the air-conditioner. A mirrored dresser with a TV perched on top filled the rest of the space. "It's not big enough to do much dancin' in here."

Trent left the door open, worked his way to the far bed and placed his bag and backpack on the foot. He dropped backward onto the bed. It squeaked. "Noisy, but not bad," he said testing the mattresses' firmness.

"Probably has had a lot of action through the years." Dave put his suitcase on the luggage stand near the bathroom and grabbed the ice bucket. "I'll run next door to the burger joint for some ice while the room airs out."

*   *   *

Trent jumped when Dave returned. In the short time Dave was gone, he had fallen asleep. Dave took the ice to the bathroom and returned with two water glasses full of ice and the bottle of Old Turkey Whiskey. Dave sat on his bed, placed the ice filled glasses on the nightstand and generously poured the golden liquid.

"Whoa!" Trent sat up when he realized that Dave was pouring the glasses full of whisky. "I don't drink that much."

"We are celebrating independence. Can't refuse that." Dave set the bottle on the nightstand and handed Trent a glass. "Here's to independence."

"Independence from what?"

"Oh shit, who cares?" Dave clicked his glass to Trent's then downed half its contents as Trent watched.

Dave grimaced. "Come on, drink up, this is a celebration." He leaned back and kicked off his boots as Trent took another polite drink and placed his glass on the nightstand. Dave refilled his glass then held the bottle out for Trent. "More?"

"No thanks, not yet."

"Well, it's here. Help yourself when you're ready." Dave sipped his drink as he grabbed the TV remote and started to flip channels. "I want to kick back a bit before dinner. Okay with you?"

"Fine. I think I'll hop in the shower."

Dave continued to channel surf as Trent took off his boots and pulled off his tee shirt.

"I think I'm going to have a steak, red rare," Dave continued to surf the channels as he talked. "Then we can find the closest bar and have some fun, get wasted. Can you go for that?"

"Not really." Trent took his shaving kit and clean under-wear out of his backpack. "The getting wasted part, I'm not much of a drinker."

"Me neither, but I feel like tiein' one on tonight. What do yea say, give it a go? Have some fun."

Trent turned his back, undid his pants and slid them off. "I'll come along to keep you out of trouble." Trent left his pants on the bed beside his buckskin bag and headed for the bathroom.

"What makes you think I need your help to stay out of trouble?" Dave said as Trent closed the bathroom door.

"I got one of those feelings."

Dave had no problem hearing Trent through the closed bathroom door. The sound of water came from the shower; as the door swung slowly open. Trent pushed it closed a second time, but moments later, it started to creep open again. "The door won't stay shut."

Dave, still running through the channels paid little attention. "Good thing I'm not modest."

"Yeah, well I might be." Trent pushed the door closed one more time, it held a short time, then slowly began to creep open again.

Dave noticed a reflection in the dresser mirror. From where he lay on the bed he could see Trent in the shower through the clear plastic shower-curtain. *God wasn't stingy when He passed out body parts to that kid.* "Maybe you're the one that will need help stayin' out of trouble."

"What?"

"I said," Dave raised his voice loud enough that Trent could hear over the running water, "maybe you're the one who needs help stayin' out of trouble."

"Oh, I'm capable of taking care of myself."

"I bet you are, kid. I bet you are," Dave answered softly. He wondered if Trent was aware that he could be seen in the mirror. Apparently not.

Dave shifted his focus to a news program and took another drink. He looked back at Trent lathering shampoo into his hair and quickly put down his glass. The influence of the alcohol was already fogging his judgment. With a watchful eye, he slid over the bed and started looking through Trent's pants. The right front pocket had the all-in-one tool that had saved the day at the rest stop, a penknife and some change. The other pocket contained a small-carved stone fetish in the shape of a bear, the kind the Zuni make. He examined it before he slipped it back into the pocket.

He pulled out Trent's wallet and hesitated, checked the mirror to make sure Trent was still occupied in the shower and then pulled out the cash and counted it, eighty-six dollars. The only other things he found in the wallet were a photograph of a dark haired young woman and a New Mexico library card. There were no other forms of identification or any other clues about his identity. He slid it back in the pocket.

Dave reached for Trent's buckskin bag and started to open it. Just then the water shut off, "shit," Dave jumped and tossed the bag back on the bed. It opened long enough for him to glimpse a small handgun inside before the bag folded closed.

Trent stepped out of the shower and Dave quickly returned to his place on the bed. He could see Trent take a towel and start drying off, but the image of the gun stayed in his head. *What the hell is he doing with a gun? Traveling alone, it may not be such a bad idea. Wonder if he pulled it on the guys in the SUV? That would account for their sudden change in attitude.*

Trent spotted Dave in the mirror and modestly turned his back. Dave was embarrassed at being found out and took another drink. *Shit, he'll think I'm a pervert.*

Trent came out of the bathroom with a towel around his waist and sat on his bed. Taking a sip of his drink, he looked at Dave over the rim of his glass. Dave fidgeted with his drink and flipped the TV channels. "Did you find anything?" Trent asked.

"What?" Dave panicked. How could he explain going through his pants and bag? *Think of something, stupid, fast.*

"Did you find anything?"

"Ah, ha," Dave stammered, words wouldn't come. He felt his face flush hot.

"Anything interesting . . . on the TV?"

"Oh! Shit no, nothing interesting." Dave fumbled to fill his glass and took a gulp.

"You'd had better slow down, you're face is as red as a beet." Trent sat back and looked at the TV.

Dave's nerves calmed, but then he remembered the gun. *Would he use it on me if he thought I was trying to rob him?*

"You gonna catch a shower before dinner?" Trent asked.

"Maybe before I go to bed."

"You'll need to block the door if you want any privacy."

Oh shit, he knows.

"The water sure felt good." Trent dried his hair.

"Yeah, the water looked good."

Trent razed his glass in a toast. "Here's mud in your eye!"

"Yeah! Salute!"

They downed their drinks.

Oh shit, did I open Pandora's box? Is he thinking I'm expecting something? Dave began to squirm. *No, he's not that kind, but if he did—what the hell should I do? And that gun!*

Trent stood, picked up his jeans and a fresh tee shirt. "I'll be ready for dinner in a minute." He returned to the bathroom closing the door and apparently blocked it shut.

Stupid, stupid, stupid, don't ever do anything that stupid again.

Moments later Trent returned from the bathroom dressed and started to put on his boots. "Let's go eat."

"Give me a minute." Dave got to his feet. "I want to wash up and change my shirt first." He started for the bathroom.

"Can I watch?"

Dave turned and stared at Trent.

"I'm kidding."

"Don't kid like that."

Dave stood a moment, and then with a grin, became animated. He gave Trent a fake pulled punch to the stomach, at which Trent tucked, howled and rolled onto his bed laughing. "Hurry up, I'm getting hungry."

*   *   *

Dave was finishing up in the bathroom when he saw movement at the door. He assumed it was Trent. When he turned, it was the Indian standing in the doorway. Dave jumped backward, almost falling into the tub. "Shit!" The Indian was gone. Dave bolted through the door.

Trent sat up. "What's wrong?"

"I thought I saw someone." Dave stood near the dresser and looked in the mirror. "Maybe it was just a reflection."

"What did you see?"

"Nothing I guess, just a shadow."

"By the look on your face it was more than just a shadow. Tell me what you saw?"

"You'll probably think I'm crazy."

"Try me."

"Well, it started last Monday night. We had an electrical problem at the apartments, where I worked. I got knocked on my ass by a loose live wire. In the dark, I thought I saw a man's face." He sat on the foot of his bed. "Strange face, it was painted with black paint. The right side was solid black from the center of the face to the ear. The other half was striped, half inch black and white lines running vertical. It looked Indian—Native American. I've seen it several times since then, just glimpses, in windows and mirrors, it's been scarin' the hell out of me. And just now it was standin' at the bathroom door."

"What do you think it is?" Trent asked.

"I sure as hell don't think it's real. Maybe it was the electrical jolt, stress, lack of sleep, maybe I need glasses." Finding the remains of the Old Turkey in his glass on the nightstand, he finished it. "Nothing to say?"

"Interesting . . . you're probably right. Grab your hat cowboy, let's go eat."

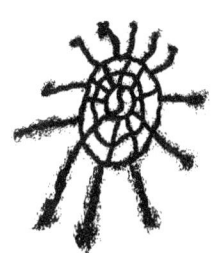

CHAPTER 7

"I missed my step."

Dave stumbled, the whiskeys effects being felt. The two made their way across the street. When they reached the Pine Tree Bar and Grill, Trent stopped at the restaurant entrance, but Dave headed straight for the bar's door. "Let's have a drink first. My treat."

Trent followed Dave into the small beer bar. "This place isn't much bigger than our room," Dave said, parking his butt on the first of the dozen chrome and tattered red vinyl stools.

"Probably the same decorator." Trent sat next to Dave and put his buckskin bag on a stool beside him.

A couple sat at the far end of the bar, the only other patrons. Dave looked around for the bartender. The guy at the end of the bar turned his face away as the gal pointed to the open doorway that led to the dining room. "She'll be right back," she mouthed.

Trent looked over the collection of old beer signs with their cords draped precariously over the dark aged mirror behind the bar. "This place needs a good cleaning."

Three bare light bulbs in the remains of an old fixture hung from the high ceiling and filled the room with a dull light that didn't quite conceal the cobwebs that flopped in the breeze of the squeaky swamp cooler. The smell of stale beer hung in the air. "In L.A., the health department would close this place in a minute." Dave ran a finger on the bar to see if it was clean.

A cheery waitress entered from the dining room and slipped behind the bar. "What are you gentlemen drinking this evening?"

"Give us a couple of tap beers. Please."

She paused a second and looked at Trent. "You old enough sugar?"

"Yes," Trent said as he reached for his wallet.

"That's okay, I'll take your word on it. Now, do you want two mugs or a pitcher?"

"Make it a pitcher." Dave wondered what Trent was going to show her for identification. *That was a damn good bluff. The kid's got balls.*

The waitress placed the overflowing pitcher and two frozen mugs in front of them. "Want to start a tab?"

"Please," Dave answered.

"You gentleman need anything just whistle." She poured the mugs full then wiped up the spill. "I'm waitin' tables in the dining room. If you want dinner I'll bring you menus." She placed a bowl of party mix on the bar before she headed back to the dining room. The pair at the end of the bar were too busy with each other to pay attention to the waitress as she past.

Dave raised his mug, "Here's mud in your eye."

"Salute." Trent sipped his beer and munched on the party mix.

They drank in silence and discreetly kept an eye on the free show at the other end of the bar. The guys glanced at each other in the mirror and expressed their mutual amusement.

"He's gonna fuck her right there on the stool." Dave whispered.

"Maybe you should lend them our motel room key."

The couple throttled back their passion when the waitress hurried in to pour a mug of beer. Their hands-on activities heated up again when the waitress left.

"Aren't they a little old to be acting like that?" Trent asked.

"When it comes to nooky, you're never too old to make a fool of yourself." Dave elbowed Trent in the ribs. "I'll guarantee they're not married, at least to each other."

"What makes you think that?"

"What rock did you just crawl out from under?" Dave poured another mug of beer for himself and topped off Trent's. "You're never gonna get wasted drinkin' like that."

Trent took another drink and settled into munching on the party mix. "Stale."

That's why I don't touch 'em." Dave made quick work of the second mug of beer and refilled it.

"You know, talkin' about Donny this afternoon got me thinkin'." Dave hesitated for a moment. "After I found out that Donny was gay, I wondered if it was the army that did it or if he was that way before. That night at the Castle Donny and Gary were buddy-buddy. I wonder if Gary knew."

"Maybe, possibly Gary was gay, otherwise he was probably as naïve as you."

"When we were in high school, bein' queer was kept secret. Now the big thing is, coming out. God, that gives me the creeps. They use to think it was how you were raised that made you gay, now they're thinkin' different, thinkin' maybe they're born that way."

"It seems to make sense, being born gay."

"You think so? You think Donny was tryin' somethin' with Gary? You'll never convince me that Gary was anything but straight." Dave's voice rose with anger.

"I'm not trying to convince you of anything. I think you're getting loaded."

"Need a refill?" the waitress asked, checking in on the guys.

"Yeah, sure, another pitcher and some more nuts for my buddy." Dave took a quick look at the couple at the end of the bar.

They had cooled and seemed to be behaving themselves. "And a couple of what-ever they're drinkin' for our friends at the end."

The waitress brought a fresh pitcher of beer and refilled the snack bowl, then served the couple. The gal gave a friendly wave to Dave when the waitress pointed to Dave, but the dude only gave a slight nod, appearing suddenly shy. Dave nodded back.

"Your aren't gonna make me drink this pitcher all by myself too?"

"Hey, I've been drinking my share." Trent picked up his mug and drank about a third in a show of accommodation.

"You know, Joe and me, we were closer than brothers. We did everything together, went camping, slept in the same tent, swam naked in the creek, discovered the opposite sex, traded nudie magazines and stories." Dave put his elbow on the bar and leaned toward Trent. "Even talked about masturbating and the first time we got pussy. But we never did anythin', you know, with each other. Never even thought of it."

Dave stiffened up and poured more beer, missing the mug and pouring some on the bar. "Oops, the damn thing moved." He placed both elbows on the bar and steadied his head. "Shit, if I thought Donny took advantage of Gary, I'd of kill the bastard."

"Keep it down or I'm going to have to take you back to the room."

"Yeah, yeah, I'll keep it down. I was just thinkin' how Gary would do just about anything for anybody."

I'm sure if Donny tried to do anything Gary didn't want, he could have taken care of himself."

"Yeah, your right, Gary could take care of himself."

Dave straightened up and looked at Trent, "I gotta piss." He slid off the stool, his legs started to buckle when his feet hit the floor. Grabbing Trent's arm, he steadied himself.

"You need some help?"

"Shit no, the stool was just higher than I thought."

Dave followed the restroom sign to the men's room, a smelly little room also badly in need of cleaning. He stood over the toilet, but distracted by the graffiti, pissed down his leg and over his boot before hitting the commode.

The hair on the back of his neck stood up, as he suddenly felt a presence behind him. Then a voice behind him said, "I never did it."

Dave whorled around, lost his balance and landed on the commode. Gary stood in front of him with his metals gleaming on his dress Marine Core uniform.

"We never did it," Gary repeated. "At The Castle, when you and Joe got drunk, Donny and I went for a swim. After that we talked and got stinking too. The next thing I remember was waking up naked, sunburned and as sick as a dog. I knew Donny was gay, and I promised I would never give away his secret. Now you know."

Dave closed his eyes, when he opened them Gary was gone. He grabbed the sink with both hands, pulled himself up and looked at his face in the mirror. For a second he appeared eighteen.

He splashed cold water in his face in an attempt to get himself together. *First, the Indian, now this. Shit man get a grip.* When he made his way back to the bar, he was much more sober than when he left.

The couple was still at it, so hot and heavy they didn't appear to notice Dave as he passed. Trent turned at his approach, "Where have you been? I was about to send a posse after you."

Dave grabbed his mug and took a big swig. "You'd never believe me."

"It looks like you missed and you'd better zip up."

"Oh shit." Dave pulled up his zipper. He climbed on his stool and stared into the dark mirror.

Trent sat quietly. After a long silence, Dave spoke without turning his gaze from the mirror. "I know nothing happen between Gary and Donny that night at The Castle." No further explanation was offered.

Slowly his jovial mood returned. Dave poured some more beer. The gal at the end of the bar let out a squeal. Dave snuck a peek and then leaned toward Trent and whispered. "Don't look, but I think she's givin' him a hand job."

"Told you, you should have lent them your key." They both burst into laughter, which didn't seem to disturb the lovers.

Dave was nearly finished with his beer when the dude let out a loud moan. Dave yelled, "Bingo." Trent choked on a mouth full of beer. Dave slapped him on the back and they got the giggles.

The dude slithered off his stool and headed toward the bathroom. The gal looked at the guys and smiled. Trent leaned over to Dave, "You're next."

"Oh shit, you got to be kidding. I'm not that hard up."

The waitress checked in from the other room. "Can you handle another?"

"No!" Trent answered.

"Sure!" Dave insisted.

"No, thanks." Trent turned to Dave. "I'm gonna have to carry you back to the motel."

"No, I'm doin' fine."

"If you want any dinner you better order now," the waitress said as she brought another pitcher of beer. "The cook goes home soon."

The guys ordered their dinner and Dave poured more beer when the waitress headed to the kitchen. The dude returned from the bathroom a little less starchy, with his shirttail hanging out and hair as wild as his eyes. He grabbed his oversize Stetson and dropped it on his head, flipped a couple of bills on the bar and the pair started toward the door, arm in arm.

"Thanks for the beer." The dude grunted as they passed. The door closed behind them.

Moments later the waitress returned with place settings.

"The happy couple left," Dave couldn't help but comment.

"Those two—Becky's a single mother of three and he's married, a pastor from Big Pine. They come in every Wednesday night, fool around a couple of hours, drink a couple of beers and ... sorry if they disturbed you. Some preacher, if you ask me," she grumbled on her way back to the kitchen.

"That was more than I wanted to know." Trent muttered.

Dave's mood swung toward the reflective. "Kid when I went to the john, the weirdest thing happened."

"You pissed your pants?"

Dave took a drink of beer. "You're not going to believe me."

"Try me."

"I saw Gary, he was there in the john, as real as you are sitting here." Dave turned to Trent. "He said he and Donny never did anything."

Trent didn't respond.

"I know, you think I'm crazy or drunk."

"I believe you."

They both sat silent, nursing their beer until the waitress brought their meals. "Is there anything else you gentleman need?"

"I'm fine," Dave insisted.

She set out the condiments and headed back to the kitchen.

Dave filled his mug and looked at his dinner. "You know kid, there's lots I don't understand about queers. I lived in West Hollywood, the place was full of them." Dave poked at his dinner. "I had a couple of them make passes at me, but most seem to know if you're straight. Funny that way, I can't tell if they're queer unless they are really obvious." He put some steak sauce on his plate and cut off a piece of meat. "I just can't imagine suckin' another guy's"—

"Do you mind? I'm trying to eat my dinner."

"Oh sorry." Dave pushed at his potato with his fork then filled his mug again.

"Yes they know if you're straight. And besides, I think it's so dangerous out there for those unfortunate men and women, that most are real careful about approaching anyone."

"That's real profound kid, that's what I like about you. Real quiet, but when you do say something, it's real profound." Dave slurred his words.

"You've only known me for a day."

"No! One day?" Dave tried to focus on Trent. "One day, you sure?"

"Yes, you picked me up at Kramer Junction this morning."

"No shittin'! One day?" Dave poured the last of the beer in his mug and made a toast. "Here's to the first day of our last life. No, to the rest of our lives."

"I think you've more than succeeded at getting wasted."

"I love you kid. You're just like Joe and I loved Joe," Dave teetered on his stool. "Why did he have to go kill himself?" He

65

threw an arm around Trent's neck and tried to hug him. "I really love you."

"You're drunk as a skunk." Trent pushed Dave off him.

Dave laid his head on the bar.

The waitress returned. "He's fading fast," she kidded. "Are you finished?"

"Yes, thanks, and so is he I'm afraid."

"I don't think he touched his dinner. Want a doggie bag."

"No thanks."

Dave moaned, slowly raised his head and looked around. "Give me another beer."

"I think you had enough honey." She looked at Trent.

"Give me another beer, dammit."

"Do you have the bill?" Trent asked. The waitress pulled the check from her apron and laid it on the bar. She finished gathering up the last of the dishes and took the bus tub to the kitchen. Trent pulled out his wallet and laid four twenties on the bar.

"Don't give her all your money." Dave said as he laid his head back on the bar.

Trent sat Dave back up by lifting his shoulders. "Come on Dave ol' buddy, let's go back to the room."

Dave stood wobbly, "No! Dammit! I want another beer."

"Come on Dave let's go."

The waitress returned from the kitchen.

"No goddamn it! I want another beer."

"Sorry honey, but you had your limit." She scooped up the money from the bar and deposited it in her pocket.

Dave fought to sit back at the bar. "I'm not goin' anywhere 'til I get another beer."

"Please, can you give us a bottle of beer, to go?"

"Sorry sugar, but that ain't legal."

Trent held on to Dave with one hand and took out his wallet. "This is my last six bucks. Please, for me."

"Okay. Just take Prince Charming home."

Trent handed Dave the bottle of beer and put his buckskin bag over his shoulder. He grabbed the back of Dave's shirt to steady him. Grabbing the back of his pants he guided him to the door. "Okay, let's go." He turned back to the waitress. "Thanks." Puppet like, Dave staggered out of the bar dangling from Trent's steady hand. "Come on, easy now. One step at a time."

Once outside the warm fresh night air seemed to sober Dave a little. Trent was able to maneuver him easily down the block toward the motel. They stopped at the corner to let a lone car pass before crossing the street.

"Hey-hey! Where we going?"

"Back to the room."

"Fuck you! I want some more beer."

"You've got a beer in your hand."

"Well shit, why didn't you tell me? I like beer."

Dave hugged Trent around the neck. "You're a good kid, did I ever tell you that, you're a damn good kid."

"Yeah, you told me. Now come on and walk."

They started across the street, but Dave missed the step off the curb and fell in the gutter. Trent struggled to get him up. Dave offered little help. "Why did you let me drink so much?"

"I don't know. I'm just stupid I guess." Trent managed Dave to his feet. "This was your idea, remember?" When they reached the center of the road, Dave pulled to a stop, finished his bottle of beer and threw the empty in the street, it clattered and bounced but didn't break.

"Ah shit, I wanted ta see it smash."

"Your smashed enough. Now come on, walk." Trent grabbed the back of Dave's shirt and the waistband of his pants again and marched him toward the motel.

"Kid when we get to Carson City, I'm gonna take you to a whorehouse and buy you a hooker."

"No thanks, I'm not into that."

"What, you don't fuck?"

"I'm not into buying sex. Now walk."

A light was on in the manager's apartment, Trent looked at Dave's watch, eleven-thirty.

"Oh shit!" Dave stiffened up. "I don't feel so good kid."

"I wouldn't think so. You drank enough beer to make a mule sick."

"No, I mean it. I must of eaten somethin'. It's makin' me sick."

Dave started to vomit, just missing Trent. He vomited down the front of himself as he sunk to his hands and knees in the parking lot. When he finished emptying the contents of his stomach, Trent got him back up on his feet and pushed him to their motel door, keeping an eye on the manager's apartment window.

He propped Dave up against the wall with one hand and held out the other. "Can I have the key?"

"No, I don't have no fuckin' keys."

Trent felt Dave's pockets for the key. "They're in your pocket."

"Hey, hey! What the fuck you doin'? Watch that. No funny business. You hear me?"

"No funny business." Trent agreed as he retrieved the key. "Here we go."

The door swung open hitting the bed. "You're a good kid." Dave patted Trent on the cheek." Then he fell face first onto the bed, his knees hung to the floor. Trent struggled to move his feet enough to get the door closed.

Trent undressed Dave and tucked him into bed.

Dave looked up at Trent, "You're a good kid, you know that."

Trent touched the back of his hand to Dave's cheek. "Sleep well, me amigo. See you in the morning."

Dave drifted into unconsciousness.

CHAPTER 8

Trent closed the motel door silently letting Dave sleep, even though he doubted even the loudest noise could rouse him after last night.

In the velvet gray light of the predawn, he walked north on the once familiar streets, past the Command House, moved to its present site from the disbanded fort, and past the Winnedumah Hotel, now an ageing bed and breakfast. *Winnedumah*, the word hung in his thoughts as he walked toward the park at the edge of town.

"Winnedumah," he whispered as he walked to the park. Sitting, he leaned against a tree and looked up, across the narrow valley, over the Owens River to the Inyo Mountains and studied the ridge. There, standing tall was Winnedumah, the eighty-foot-tall granite monolith, the Winnedumah Paiute Monument.

As the cloudless sky lighted toward sunrise Trent thought back to an earlier time in his life, a time of family, happiness and community. He could almost hear the crackle of the open fire and laughter of the other children gathered in his grandfather's yard for the first story night of the season.

Papa Bear, the tribes Pohagunt, wouldn't tell any of the Great Stories before the first snows were on the Pahbatoyas, and the snakes-in-the-grass were gone. The Paiutes spoke no matter of importance or orally shared their myths before the beginning of November, for fear that Snake, the mystical messenger and tattle-tail, might overhear and thus steal the magic.

Papa Bear, Trent's maternal grandfather sat quietly in his old chair, the great Medicine Man's throne, sacred, the place of honor near the fire. Actually, it was an old wooden chair Papa Bear found by the road, apparently fallen from a passing truck, that he cushioned with odd bits of cloth, leather and padding. At the first whisper of "Winnedumah," by one of the more than twenty children sitting on the ground circled around the altar pyre, a hush fell. "Winnedumah," a second voice softly echoed. "Winnedumah, Winnedumah, Winnedumah," all the children began to chant melodiously. The legend of Winnedumah was always the first to be told. For the Nuume, Paiute People of Fort Independence, it was more than just a story of the brothers Tinnemaha and Winnedumah, and the intervention of The Great Spirit to save the People from their loathsome enemies the Diggers. It was their most sacred myth, the transformation of Winnedumah to the stone monolith, that now stood atop the mountain directly above the village like the spire of a great cathedral. A symbol for all to see and be continually reminded of the power of their God.

Trent vividly remembered the last hearing of the Great Legend. A few weeks after that night he would leave the reservation and travel with his parents to a new life in New Mexico. He saw his beloved Papa Bear only once again, when two years later, at the age of fifteen, he returned for a short visit and his Vision Quest ceremony.

The sound of a semi's Jake-brakes brought Trent out of his thoughts. He stood and breathed in once again the essence of his birth place, then crossed the street and headed toward the cemetery. As he walked, the shadows and flickering shafts of sunlight filtered through the groves of poplar. He was the only youth of the reservation that still practiced the old ways and was willing to face the riggers of a Vision Quest and Papa Bear was proud of him, though he was careful not to show it before the council.

On the morning his ordeal began, his Papa Bear drove him to the decayed remains of Bend City, up Mazourka Canyon. After a blessing from Papa Bear and without taking food or water with him, he hiked up the mountain wearing only a smoke tanned deerskin around his waist and yucca moccasins. He found a level spot, near the Winnedumah monolith, overlooking the fallen and broken Tennemaha, and far, far below the Fort Independence Reservation. There he drew a circle in the dirt with a stick, marked it as his sacred space and sat, and waited for his vision.

By the afternoon of the second day, the lack of food, water and sleep was already testing him. Then, as if on cue, a fierce thunderstorm blew in from the desert. Wind, rain and hail pounded him and lightning struck the top of Winnedumah. When the storm finally blustered off to the north, it left behind a cold wind to batter the mountaintop. Throughout the night Trent shivered against the freezing wind, rhythmically beating a slapstick, chanting and trying not to think of his misery.

As the sun rose on the third day the monolith was gone, in its place stood the handsome brave, Winnedumah. Trent fell to the ground before him. "Stand." Winnedumah commanded.

Trent stood, heart pounding. He dared not dishonor the great warrior by looking him in the eyes. "My son, you have brought great honor to me and to your People. Your path will not be easy. You have been chosen to take medicine to the Rainbow Tribes. You will have no home, no family and your possessions will be only what you can carry on your back." Winnedumah placed his hands on Trent's head. "The blessing of all people, all nations, all relations will be upon you for you are of the few."

A great eagle screeched above Trent and a feather fell at his feet. He bent down to pick it up, and when he rose, the sun glistened above the mighty stone Winnedumah, ending Trent's Vision Quest.

But before he descended the mountain, he took the deerskin from his waist, fashioned a bag, and placed the eagle feather inside. It was dark when he reached Papa Bear's house, cold hungry and naked, but a man that knew his destiny.

In the morning light, Trend stood before the simple stone marker that read, 'Papa Bear Whitaker, Fort Independence's Last Medicine Man.' He placed the stone fetish from his pocket in the soil in front of the marker, stood and slowly walked out of the cemetery.

*   *   *

Trent walked through the cafe entrance of the Pine Tree Bar and Grill a few minutes after seven and looked over the half dozen patrons. Richard, a local, raised his hand and Trent joined him. "Manahuu, sorry I'm late."

"Manahuu, eight years, not bad for a half-breed." The men shook hands and took their seats. When I got your call yesterday afternoon, I couldn't believe you've finally returned. All the arrangements have been made. Everything is set for eight this morning. We'll just have time for breakfast, that's if you haven't eaten."

Trent vaguely remembered Richard, one of the few remaining Fort Independence elders.

"You have turned into quite a man," Richard went on, "but I would know you anywhere. You look so much like Papa Bear and your mother, rest their spirits."

The waitress stepped up and refilled Richard's coffee cup. "Coffee?" She asked Trent.

"No thanks, water will do and some orange juice."

"Well, good morning," she said evidently just recognizing him. "Where's your friend?"

"He's still sleeping it off."

"I thought he would be in sad shape after last night. Richard is having the special, Huevos Rancheros, can I bring you an order."

"Sounds good. Flour tortillas, please." Trent watched her work her way back to the kitchen. Richard gave him a questioning look. "I told you on the phone, it is something I have to do."

"Why don't you stay and help your own people?"

"He is my people, all people are one. I can't stay."

The waitress brought Trent's water and orange juice.

Trent took a drink of the juice and asked, "Have you seen Willy?"

"Only once since he moved up north, he stopped by last April for a couple of hours. I asked him if he had heard from you, and he said no. We thought you would come back here to live. The People need your medicine, too."

"It looks like they prefer to gamble."

"Did you see the casino?"

"No, but I saw the signs on the highway."

"The elders weren't happy about it, but the younger members of the tribe wanted it and pushed the council into it."

"I had hoped for more from them."

"Since Papa Bear's death there hasn't been much guidance, but the casino is bringing in good money; it's helping the reservation."

"Good money? There are better ways."

"I wish you would have come back sooner. Nobody, not even your Uncle Willy, knew where you were.

"It was better that way." Trent sat silent for a long time before he spoke again. "I thought the elders would have taken care of Papa Bear's house."

"You are the only one who can perform the ceremony. The place is taboo to all others. Even the young ones that don't believe are afraid of Papa Bear's medicine. Nobody has been inside the house since his death."

"Why was Papa Bear buried in the white man's cemetery?"

"He's not, it's only a marker, the townspeople respected him and wanted to remember him. He was cremated and his ashes are with me, so you can do the ceremony and put him to rest."

"It will be taken care of today."

The waitress brought their breakfast.

*   *   *

In silence, Richard drove Trent the three miles to the reservation in his shiny new black Ford 150 pickup. Less than a dozen people stood along the road in front of Papa Bear's house. A fire truck from town was parked in the driveway. The two county firemen in the cab were the only ones that would dare enter the property.

Richard parked on the road in front of the house and Trent got out of the pickup with his buckskin bag and a small wooden box containing his grandfather's ashes. Beyond a few nods of recognition, between Trent and a few of the people in front of the house, there was no communication. The yard was over grown and the chair where Papa Bear use to sit when telling his stories had collapsed.

The old medicine man's pickup, tires now flat, was parked where he'd left it next to the house. Richard held out a set of keys to Trent. "It all belongs to you."

"No, it belongs to Papa Bear."

The screen door fell away the moment Trent touched it. He unlocked the door and pushed it open. Floods of childhood memories filled his thoughts as he looked around the small two-bedroom house. He didn't have time for nostalgia as he went directly to the fireplace. Above the mantle hung Papa Bear's two rifles and a shotgun. On the mantle was the old man's medicine bag and a photograph of a young Trent, his mother and father. Tears filled his eyes as he knelt and placed the box of ashes on the hearth. He carefully removed two loose floorboards to the left of the hearth and removed a similar box containing the ashes of his grandmother and placed it on the hearth beside Papa Bear's. There was a photograph of his grandparents on their wedding day. There was also a letter, which he opened. *I am proud of you. Papa,* was all it read.

Trent pressed both his hands into the remaining ashes of the final fire in the fireplace and rubbed them on his face. His face contorted as he allowed himself to mourn and weep openly. It would be the last time he could express his anguish over the loss of his Grandmother and Papa Bear. When he finally composed himself, he stood and slowly started toward the door without a backward glance.

Outside, he found a tree branch, wrapped the end with rags and dipped it into the kerosene Richard had brought. He then took the remaining kerosene and doused the house. When he had circled the house, he doused the pickup with kerosene. He kindled a small fire in the fire pit, then took a red flannel tobacco pouch from his buckskin bag, sprinkled some in the flames, then lit the torch. He circled the house once, then stepped on the porch and set it on fire. He repeated the circle, torching the house and pickup. The tinder dry house was quickly engulfed. Trent stood by the fire pit as the flames licked high into the air. The heat finally got so intense he had to step back. But before he could leave, he had one more task to perform, he gathered the remains of Papa Bear's chair and threw them on the fire.

He watched as the heat blew out the windows and flames pushed out from under the eaves. Suddenly, out of the corner of his eyes he spotted a familiar face, Catherine. He turned toward her and she smiled. She was the only face he remembered. She was a white girl who lived across the creek from the reservation. Her father worked at the Mt. Whitney Fish Hatchery. Three years older than Trent, but they went to school together. She was the only non-Indian to come and play on the reservation. The winter before his last visit to the reservation she married a tall, blonde, skinny, cowboy from Wyoming. They had set up home in a travel trailer on the reservation's campgrounds. That spring her cowboy went to the high country, tending cattle, not to return until fall. The day after Trent returned from his Vision Quest he met her walking alone by the creek near the campgrounds. Papa Bear said she took Trent's innocence. The truth was Trent gave it willingly. He spent his last week at Fort Independence learning the Divine Mysteries of making love, sharing the cowboy's wife and bed.

She and her cowboy had moved to a rental in town. The cowboy still spent his summers in the high country and made babies all winter. The four toe headed children that clung to her legs and her swollen belly attested to his diligence. As Trent stared into her eyes, his body remembered their time together and longed to stay and once again share her bed, but when she turned her eyes away he knew it was all in the past.

Within minutes the roof sagged, the walls began to bulge and pieces of the bat and board walls fell outward pulling Trent's attention back to the present. There were several pops as the fire consumed the contents, the memories, the joys and sorrows of a long life well spent. Then there was a loud bang followed moments later with the crash of the roof collapsing. "Winnedumah." Trent yelled, but the sound of his voice could not be heard above the roar of the fire. "It is done."

Trent's thoughts returned to Catharine, but when he turned back, she was gone. "It is better this way," he said to himself.

Within a few minutes the fire had completed its task and began to wane. His job was finished too.

He walked to Richard's shiny black pickup and the two men drove away. "I guess nothing can convince you to stay."

Trent never answered and never looked back as they drove away.

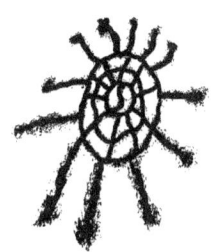

CHAPTER 9

"Why did you stay to help me, you should've saved your-self," Dave said.

Trent didn't answer; he just stared into space. Their Indian captors had stripped him and lashed him to the remains of a dead tree. Large pieces of his skin had been pealed from his chest, belly and legs. Thin trickles of blood striped his body and disappeared in the hot desert sand.

A forceful hand turned Dave's face back to the sun. He'd been stripped and his hands and feet staked to the ground. Small sharp rocks and desert debris dug into his back. Fingers forced his eyes open to a blazing sun. Like a hot poker the light burned into his head. A second captor tugged at a stick twisted in a rope that encircled Dave's head. He twisted it tighter. Dave arched his back in pain, which forced the sharp rocks to cut into the flesh of his shoulders. He slowly drifted into blessed unconsciousness.

The white-hot sunlight from the open door stabbed again into Dave's eyes and twisted his brain. Then he heard the door close as the light dimmed. His memory returned slowly, like thick syrup being poured into his head. *Independence.* Bad dreams and reality mixed.

"Are you awake?" Trent asked.

Dave couldn't answer. He tried to open his eyes, but even the dim light in the motel room burned in his head. He could sense Trent and heard the squeak as he sat on his own bed. Dave turned his head to speak when the headache hit. He thought his head would explode. Then his world began to spin wildly out of control. He grabbed the sheets to hang on for the ride of his life.

Before the bed crashed, he leaped from it and raced his stomach to the toilet, winning only by a fraction. Small consolation, the remains of last night's beer erupted with a roar. He convulsed long after his stomach was empty and with each wrench his shriveled brain slammed the inside of his skull.

Dave hugged the cool white porcelain bowl as round one subsided. Trent wet a washcloth and handed it to him. Knowing that any attempt of gratitude would surely bring on round two, Dave took the cloth and wiped his face.

Trent left Dave on the bathroom floor and sat on the foot of Dave's bed and waited. Dave cooled his face on the porcelain, knowing the fire in his gut would again explode. His expectations were not a disappointment.

Dave had lost count of which round he was in. His stomach was emptied, evident by the dry heaves at his repeated convulsions. "Oh God! I'm dying!" He wrenched once more. "I'm dead and gone straight to hell." His body helplessly contorted over the porcelain bowl again. "This has got to be hell."

After what seemed an eternity, the mercies of Bacchus finally descended enough that he could move. He crawled to his bed and collapsed. Trent had shifted to his own bed, still vigilant but silent. Dave's eyes painfully fluttered open and he looked at Trent.

"Kind of reminiscent of that night you and the guys spent partying at the Castle?" Trent joked.

Dave moaned.

"I've got something that will fix it."

"Oh God anything."

Without a word, Trent took a small paper packet out of his buckskin bag and went into the bathroom. He returned shortly with a glass of greenish liquid, placed it on the nightstand and sat on the bed with Dave.

He placed his hand on Dave's bare belly. Dave tensed, but relaxed when the warmth from Trent's hand began to penetrate and soothe his churning gut. When Trent placed his other hand on Dave's head, he could feel an energy move through his body from Trent's hands. It felt as if Trent somehow had taken control of the hangover.

After several minutes, Trent removed his hands and picked up the glass. "Here, drink this."

Dave struggled up on one elbow and looked at Trent's offering. "Is it poison that will put me out of my misery?"

"No, I'm afraid not, but it will help settle your stomach."

Just then another wave of nausea hit. "Oh God, give it to me quick." Dave looked at the glass of greenish liquid he was about to drink. "What's this, grass floating around in it? It looks terrible."

"Yeah, and it tastes worse." Then he added, "It's a Indian tea. Drink it."

Dave took a sip and made a face. "Oh God! What did you do, piss in the glass. It tastes like piss."

"Are you an expert on drinking piss? Shut-up and drink."

Dave took another sip of the bitter earthy-tasting liquid.

"Drink."

"He gagged as he force down the rest of the warm unpleasant fluid, and then fell back on the bed. The empty glass dropped from his hand.

Within minutes, the nausea was gone. Dave reached up and felt his head then moved it from side to side without pain. Gradually he sat up, avoiding any sudden movement.

"Shit! It's gone!" He shook his head more vigorously. "It worked! What the hell did ya do?"

"It's a Native American cure."

"Amazing." Dave stood and shook his head again with the expectation of the returned pain. He took a deep breath and stretched. "Absolutely amazing! Where did you learn that?"

"My people."

"Just how much Indian are you?"

"Half."

"You ought to setup a practice. You'd make a fortune."

"Yeah, right, if people are stupid enough to drink like you did they deserve the consequences."

"I know, but gees, that's amazing stuff. Thanks."

"Keep it to yourself."

Dave stood and looked at himself in the mirror for a moment then checked the time. "Shit! It's getting late, I'll grab a shower and then we can get goin'."

"I washed out your shirt and pants and hung them in the bathroom, I think they're probably dry by now." Trent started toward the door. "I'll go next door and see if I can scrounge up some coffee."

"Thanks," Dave said as the door closed. Trent had placed everything from Dave's pockets on the corner of the dresser, including the wad of money. He started to check it. *If he took your money he wouldn't still be hanging around, dummy.* Dave realized how fortunate he was, in the condition he was in last night, Trent could have cleaned him out and been long gone by now.

As he dug through his suitcase for clean underwear he spotted Trent's buckskin bag on the bed. For a moment he entertained the thought of looking inside for the gun, then realized trust far out weighed curiosity. He took a hundred-dollar bill and placed it on the bag then headed for the shower.

Dave was half dressed and shaving when Trent returned with the coffee. "What's the money for?"

"You, for dinner and the beer last night."

"Dinner was on me, remember."

"Yeah, but not the beer and I wasted dinner. You can get it next time." Dave finished shaving and put his stuff back in his shaving kit.

"But dinner wasn't this much."

"I didn't have change, and I owe ya a hell of a lot more then that."

"You owe me nothing." Trent held the hundred-dollar bill out to Dave in an attempt to return it. "Here."

"You keep it or you'll have to find another ride, capish?"

Trent stood with the bill still held out for a moment. "Thank you."

Dave took a drink of the coffee. "God that's good." He took another sip then finished dressing. He picked up his gray cowboy hat, dusted it and checked its shape. He had had it for years but never felt comfortable wearing it in L.A., last night was the first time it ever felt appropriate. He carefully placed it on his head and grinned at himself in the mirror. Out here it felt right.

"You ready to go?" Dave asked as he grabbed his suitcase. "We were supposed to be out of here a half-hour ago. The old lady will have the sheriff beatin' at the door any minute now to evict us."

*   *   *

Dave was at the wheel of his pickup still marveling at the speed of his recovery and how good he felt. "I should of asked before I started driving, that stuff you gave me to drink, does it have any side effects?"

"None that will impede your driving."

"Good."

"But I suggest you stay away from the booze for awhile."

"A long while," Dave agreed.

A short distance from town a line of trees intersected the highway and on the left was an Indian gas station and small casino and to the right the smoldering remains of a fire. "Looks like a house or somthin' burnt. Wonder why everyone is just standing around watching?"

"It's the Indian Reservation. Sometimes when someone dies they just burn the house. The older people believe it's taboo, bad luck to take the deceased's belongings. Before the White Man came they cremated the body with the house."

"That saves probate."

"Sometimes."

They drove on for a half-hour before any further exchange.

"By the way, where'd you go this morning?"

"Out for a walk. Wanted to see the town."

"Good, I'm glad you weren't sittin' there waitin' for me. Sorry I made such an asshole of myself. Hope I didn't embarrass you."

"You didn't. I had a good idea of what was going to happen."

"We should be in Bishop in less the twenty minutes, I'll spring for lunch."

"Thanks, but you don't have too."

"My pleasure, a little payback for your help last night and that magic elixir."

"Just some herbs."

"Whatever you say."

Trent opened his buckskin bag and looked inside.

"What all have you got in that bag-of-tricks?"

"Not much, just some personal things."

"What about that stuff you gave me?"

"I have a few remedies. Tricks as you call them. Enough to get by."

Dave remembered the gun. He wanted to question Trent about it but figured it wasn't the right time. *I wonder if there will ever be a right time. If I ask him about the gun he'll know I snooped in his bag.*

Trent closed the bag, latched it with the bone peg, and put it on the floor behind his feet.

"I was thinkin'." Dave paused. "Last night, in the bar, when I went to the can, and saw Gary. Do you think I really saw him or was I just drunk?"

"What do you think?"

"Damn it, don't play that game. You gave me the same answer when I asked you about seein' the Indian. I want—I need some straight talk. Am I going crazy?"

"I don't think you're going crazy. I believe you saw what you say you saw. My advice is that at this time just relax and see what happens. If it's stress or lack of sleep it will stop. If it's more, it will explain itself."

"Do you believe in an afterlife, spirits, God . . . ?"

"Yes."

"I don't, or didn't. I'm confused."

"Let it ride, things have a way of working out if we don't let our brain's get in the way."

"You are real profound. I know I was pretty drunk last night, but I remember what I said, and what you said. I owe you."

"No, you owe me nothing.

"You can be bullheaded, can't you?"

"I'm an Indian."

"What's that got to do with it?"

"Sitting Bull."

CHAPTER 10

"One greasy spoon is as good as the next."

Dave stopped at the first hamburger joint he saw. "Don't just sit there, let's eat. I'm hungry."

"You ought to be."

Dave moaned as he got out of the pickup and pressed his abdomen. "My stomach muscles are sore."

"They should be. You gave them enough of a workout."

"Keep rubbin' it in."

"Can't pass it up, got to keep reminding you," Trent joked as he opened the pickup door, his ever present buckskin bag over his shoulder. "When you choose—

"I know, I know." Dave poked Trent in the ribs with his finger as he past. "Sometime life doesn't give us much of a choice."

"Oh, I don't know," Trent answered, "sometimes we have more choices than we think."

"Quit the philosophy shit, okay?"

Inside the diner the men looked for a seat.

"Look, the gals from the rest stop." Dave poked his elbow in Trent's ribs.

"Will you quit that. You're making me sore."

"Are you girls following us?" Dave asked as he removed his hat.

"I think there might be a question on just who's following whom." Betty said.

"This is a surprise." Susan looked up at Trent. "We didn't expect to see you again."

"Mind if we join you?" Dave asked.

"Well, I guess." Betty hesitated a moment. "What the heck, Sure! We just ordered."

Dave slid in beside Betty then looked around for a place to hang his hat. Finding none he put it back on his head. He thought of how foolish he would have looked in his hat in L.A..

"I thought you would be long gone by now." Dave looked for a waitress.

"I had to take care of some business here in Bishop so we spent the night." Betty answered. "What about you guys?"

"We kinda got stuck in Independence last night." Trent quipped as he gave Dave a glance.

"More like bushwhacked." Dave added.

A perky middle-aged waitress brought coffee and took the men's orders.

"So Betty, you said you lived in Susanville?" Dave asked as he took a sip of coffee.

"Well actually north of there, but most people have never heard of the place, Mystique?"

Dave nearly choked. He looked at Trent, then back at Betty. "No shit! Oh, excuse me, but that's where we're goin'."

"No. Do you know someone up there?" Betty asked.

"No, but, I've got some property up there my parents left me, I'm thinkin' about buildin'."

"Well," Betty looked at her daughter, "isn't this a coincidence. I have a gift shop there, in Mystique."

"Maybe you know where I can find some work around there?" Dave asked.

"There's not a whole lot going on up there. What do you do?"

"Lots of things, I thought maybe I'd start a handyman business."

"And you?" Susan asked Trent. "Are you moving to Mystique too?"

"No, I'm just hitching a ride."

"He's kind of a nomad," Dave was quick to add.

"Yeah, just kicking around, seeing the country." Trent took a drink of his ice tea then turned back to Susan. "Do you live in Mystique with your mom?"

"Yes, when I'm not in school."

"Where's school?"

"U.C.L.A.."

"I drove down to Los Angeles," Betty explained, "and picked her up from school for the summer."

The waitress brought their order.

"So, you'll have to look us up when you get to Mystique." Betty suggested, breaking the silence of the meal.

"We sure will." Trent piped up.

"Oh, but I thought you weren't coming to Mystique." Susan said to Trent.

"I'm riding with Dave that far, then going on up into Oregon. I thought I might spend a few days in Mystique however. Maybe you can show me around?"

Susan hesitated a moment. "I don't know, I'll see if I've got time."

"Maybe the two of you would like to come to dinner one night?" Betty suggested. She turned to Dave. "We could repay you for your help with the car."

"I'd love to," Dave replied.

"So would I," Trent added.

"So, tell us, what delayed you in Independence?" Betty asked.

"Me. I drank too much beer last night, way too much beer. Trent saved me from the worst hangover I ever had. Gave me some kind of herbal stuff and did somethin' with his hands."

Trent glared at Dave.

"Oh, sorry, I wasn't supposed to mention the cure."

"What was it?" Susan asked.

"Ah, just an old Indian hangover remedy." Trent continued to glare at Dave.

"I didn't think Old Native American's drank alcohol. Why would they need a cure?"

"You're right. Not until the White Man came and brought their firewater." Trent turned to Susan. "Not many people remember that."

"I'm an anthropology major, Western Pre-Columbian tribes my specialty."

"My mother was Shoshone Paiute." Trent said. "From Independence."

"Why didn't you say somethin'?" Dave asked. "We could've stayed longer."

"I don't have any relatives there any more."

"Will there be anything else?" the waitress asked as she prepared to present the check.

Dave quickly grabbed it. "Let me treat you lovely ladies."

"Well, thank you." Betty politely accepted.

Betty took a business card out of her purse and gave it to Dave. "Give me a call when you get to town. We'll have dinner."

"I sure will."

"I hate to eat and run," Betty looked at her watch, "but we have a lot of driving to do."

"How far are you going today?" Dave asked.

"We plan to stay in Reno tonight." Betty answered. "And you?"

"Carson City, I hope," Dave said as he stood.

Susan and Trent went on ahead, Betty turned back to Dave and put out her hand. "Well, good luck, it was nice seeing you again." As Dave took her hand, she added, "I meant it, I would really like to have you come for dinner." She paused for a moment and looked into his eyes, before leaving.

As Dave waited at the register to pay the bill, he saw movement reflected in the glass of the window. It was the Indian, but this time he didn't frighten him. As he watched, the Indian turned, looked at him and smiled, then vanished.

When he exited the diner, Trent was leaning against the pickup waiting.

"That was a smooth move," Trent said, frowning. "I was going to pay for lunch."

"Yeah, well." As he was about to put Betty's business card in his shirt pocket he read it, *Betty's Cupboard, Candles, Aromatherapy and Metaphysical Gifts. Oh Jesus, a weirdo store, should of known it was too good to be true.*

Trent got in and waited for Dave. "Something Wrong?"

"Naw," Dave finally climbed in the cab. *Oh well, dinner is dinner.* He thought as they returned to the open road.

*   *   *

Betty drove in silence, a radiant smile on her face.

"What are you grinning about?" Susan asked.

"Oh nothing, just thinking."

"About Dave?"

"As a matter of fact, yes."

"I really didn't think he's your type."

Betty didn't answer. She just smiled as she drove leaving Susan to wonder what her mother was thinking.

"Did you happen to notice Trent's face?" Susan asked, breaking the silence. "His face, his skin is flawless. I looked to see if he was wearing makeup."

"Was he?" Betty gave Susan a quick questioning glance.

"I don't think so. But I've known a couple of guys in school with looks like that. They are so into themselves they make you sick."

"Trent didn't seem to be like that."

"We'll see, but I'm not holding my breath."

"So a cute guy can't be genuine?"

"Not in my book, not that cute."

"Well if I were your age, I'd sure give a second look."

"Mother, what's gotten in to you?"

*   *   *

Dave started whistling, 'Good-night Irene' with an up beat tempo. After several choruses he stopped. "That Susan's kinda cute, don't ya think?"

"I guess."

"Guess? She sure put a wiggle in your walk." Dave giggled then started to whistle again.

"Well, I noticed a spring in your step too."

Dave just whistled.

Out of the blue Trent asked, "Why don't you want to marry again?"

Dave stopped whistling and glanced a Trent. "A thunderstorm and a hurricane."

"What?"

"A thunderstorm and a hurricane."

"What are you talking about?"

"Why I don't want to get married again, my two marriages, one was like a thunderstorm and the other like a hurricane."

"Oh, all right, I'm not going to touch that."

"Ya see it's like this, my first marriage was like a thunderstorm, hot, full of flash and fury, passionate, but short. It hardly made it past the honeymoon. She couldn't get it through her head, that getting married meant giving up her old boyfriends. There isn't room for three in a marriage bed."

"I guess it depends on who's counting. So what happened?"

"Yeah know, sex clouds a man's mind. Well a lot of sex will make a man crazy and we had lots of sex, nothing but. I was a damn fool, not twenty-two yet, I knew her for less than six weeks. One night we ended up in Reno, married. Did you know it takes six minutes to get married and six months to get a divorce. And a whole lot of dough." Dave laughed.

"The second marriage," Dave continued. "I took it slow. We met at work. I was twenty-eight by then and workin' for a newspaper in San Jose, head Advertising Account Executive, a big name for an advertising salesman. Hurricane Joann was a columnist and workin' on her law degree. We dated two years before gettin' married. We had two kids, boys, the youngest is about your age. After she passed the Bar, she got a job with a hotshot L.A., law firm and was gone all the time. So we moved south and I went to work selling advertising for a big agency on Wilshire Boulevard. At first, I put the extra time into my work, then I started somthin' I shouldn't of with a gal at work. I got found out the night I won the Clio. Don't ever screw around on a lawyer, cause they will fuck you real good. She nailed my balls to the wall. That's why I don't plan on ever getting tied up again with another woman. Dave smiled, and then went back to his whistling.

"Maybe you just never found you're life's partner, or what some call a soul mate."

"Shit kid, you're a dreamer. my soul mate's in hell, where I belong."

"No, I'll bet there's someone out there, waiting just for you. Maybe Betty."

"No way kid. It just doesn't happen that way."

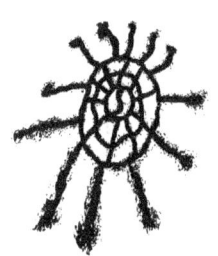

CHAPTER 11

"Go ahead and hit me if you're so tough." The fat bastard taunted, as sweat dripped from his red face. "You asked for it. You know you want it."

Dave clinched and unclenched his fist as O'Doul taunted him, but he couldn't strike. All the frighten kid could do was run away.

The sun was high and intense. Dave pushed the flash of memory back to his subconscious; he had thought he was free of it. It hadn't surfaced for at least twenty years. He drove in silence with a toothpick left over from lunch stuck out of the corner of his mouth. Trent had his eyes closed, but Dave could tell he wasn't asleep.

"We are makin' good time, I expect to make Carson City by dinner," Dave broke the quiet. Dave rolled down the window and tossed the toothpick out. A blast of scorching air reminded him how hot it was. As he started to whistle 'Good-night Irene', fragments of memories moved through his head, like the lyrics of a song you can't quite remember.

In the past twenty-four hours he had recounted most of his life to the stranger he picked up at the gas station. Now the parts of his life he had tried so desperately to forget were trying to be heard. It made Dave uneasy. Although all the effects of the hangover were gone, he couldn't help but believe that something in the herbs Trent gave him was causing the flashbacks. Try as he might he couldn't shake off the ominous feeling that had come over him since they had left Bishop.

Trent's head was tilted against the window now, the relaxed look of sleep on his face. Dave couldn't help wonder what made him think he looked like Joe. Trent's belt buckle glistened in the sun and Dave thought of the old man at the gas station.

Suddenly, Dave felt as if a hand was on his shoulder. Fear gripped him. He fought to keep control of the pickup. It was Mr. O'Doul, his sophomore math teacher. He blinked and stared at the road ahead. The feel of O'Doul's clammy fingers lingered on his shoulder.

Dave wet his lips and continued to whistle softly, but he couldn't shake the feeling and the memories that came with it. O'Doul's hand moved across his chest, the smell of the hot, rancid tobacco stench breath. The feeling of his trusted teacher's whiskered cheek brush against his neck when he kissed him. The image of the fat sweaty man terrified him. All the fear of that moment raced through is mind. He remembered wondering, *What is he doing?* Then he knew.

Dave shook his head to clear his thoughts and looked over at Trent sleeping. He looked back to the road and yawned. Immediately the memories returned. O'Doul clung to him. His huge hand sliding down Dave's shirt to his pants. He felt his fingers.

The tires roared as they hit the shoulder. Dave fought to correct his course. He wrestled the pickup to a pullout and came to a stop. The near mishap jarred Trent awake.

"I think I need to stretch my legs a bit." Dave killed the engine and bolted from the pickup.

After a short time Trent got out and approached him. "Are you okay?"

94

"That stuff you gave me to drink, are you sure it doesn't have any side effects?"

"What do you mean?"

"Yeah know, like hallucinations?"

"No."

"Are you sure?" Dave's brow wrinkled questioningly.

"Yes, why?"

"Oh, nothin'. Just wondering." Dave hung on the word wondering a moment.

There was a faint path that led down from the road to an outcropping of rocks a couple of hundred of yards from where they stood. Dave started down the path and Trent followed at a distance. When they came to the first of several large rocks, Trent found a comfortable place to sit in the shade of an overhang. Dave walked on down the path until it ended abruptly at a ravine. He picked up a handful of small stones and tossed them one at a time at an old bottle that laid half buried in the sand.

The darkness came over him again. Dave remembered how he froze. All the thoughts of what his teacher, mentor and friend had done rushed through his head and he couldn't stop them. He wasn't just remembering, but reliving the moment in detail.

The screech of a ring-tailed hawk startled Dave back to the present. He wanted to vomit. The hawk screeched again. Dave stood for a long time trying not to think about what his teacher had done. With a deep breath, he turned and started back up the path.

Trent's eyes were closed as Dave approached. "Good walk?" he asked without opening them.

"Yeah." Dave leaned against the rock Trent was sitting on. He was trembling. He folded and unfolded his arms and then hung his thumbs from his jeans' pockets. "No, I need to talk."

"The last couple of hours I've been having some pretty vivid flashbacks or an incident I thought I'd put behind me." He began slowly. "That's why I asked about that stuff you gave me."

"I can assure you, the stuff I gave you won't cause such things."

"Well, what I'm seein'—rememberin', well, I've never told anyone about it." Dave kicked at the dirt with his boot. "Not even

Joe." He made a line in the dirt with the toe of his boot and then smoothed it over again. His shoulders rounded as he drew in a breath.

"When I was in High School, I had this teacher, Mr. O'Doul. I thought he was a great guy, kind of a second father to me, made up for my dad bein' dead. He helped me with homework and things after school, a man I could talk too. One afternoon, I was helping him get some stuff out of a storage room. It was dim, close and hot. The next thing I knew he was touching me, trying to feel me, you know. I didn't know what to do, so I didn't do anything." Dave started pacing. He didn't look up.

"He kissed my neck, I felt his whiskery face against my skin, his mouth, lips, tongue . . . ." Dave closed his eyes. "I couldn't move, I wanted to slug the bastard but couldn't. I just stood there and let him . . . touch me." Dave sat back on the rock. "Finally when I realized he wasn't going to stop, I ran. Once I got home, I stayed in the shower until all the hot water was gone." He looked up at Trent for a moment and then looked away. "I never told anyone what happened."

Trent stared into space.

"I stayed home the rest of the week. The following Monday when I went back to school the fat bastard acted like nothing ever happen. It was a few weeks before the end of the school year. The next year he wasn't there. All I ever found out is he moved back east somewhere. I was glad he was gone."

"You need to let go."

"I can't."

"Why not?"

"Because, I . . . ."

"Because you froze. Because you didn't do anything to stop him. Or is it that you wonder if you might have wanted it?"

Dave stood with his back to Trent. His stature slowly rose, his back straightened and his shoulders squared. Dave spun around on his heals toward Trent.

"Who are you? JUST WHO THE HELL ARE YOU?"

"Nobody! A friend! A fellow traveler."

"A FELLOW TRAVELER, BULLSHIT!" YOU'RE SOMETHING ALL RIGHT! Why am I telling you all this shit? You make me see things, and tell you things I don't want too." Dave started for his pickup.

Trent grabbed Dave's sleeve. "Because you need—"

"Shut-up!" Dave pulled away and raised his fist. His vision blurred, for a moment Trent looked like O'Doul.

"Go ahead and hit me if you're so tough." Trent taunted, but it wasn't Trent. Somehow Trent became O'Doul. "You asked for it. You know you want it."

Dave clinched and unclenched his fist as his confusion grew. He was in the cramped storeroom with O'Doul.

"You've been flaunting your tight little ass at me for months you little cock-sucker." O'Doul's voice cracked. "I know what you want."

Dave swung his fist with the pent-up anger and emotions of thirty-eight years and struck O'Doul square in the mouth, the force knocked him to the ground. Dave stood over O'Doul and shouted, "Shut-up. Goddamn you!"

Then before his eyes O'Doul became Trent.

"What the hell." Dave stood a second before he charged up the hill. He couldn't process what just happen, all he could do was get away. He got in his pickup and sped off.

He struggled to gain control of his emotions as he drove. *Goddamn kid! Let him find some other asshole to give him a ride.*

Dave looked at the empty seat and saw Trent's buckskin bag. He pulled off the road and slammed on his brakes. The pickup's wheels locked and slid in the dirt. He jumped out of the pickup and into the cloud of dust, flailing his fists at the sky.

"Goddamn it!" He shouted. "Dammit! Dammit!" He threw his hat on the ground in anger. "He did it on purpose, damn him. He left that fuckin' bag on purpose." Dave kicked the dirt until he exhausted his anger and then dropped to his knees. Finally he began to laugh.

He sat on his heals laughing for a long time before he got up, dusted himself off, picked up his hat and got back in his pickup.

When he got back to the turnout where he had left him, Trent was sitting on a rock by the side of the road. Dave pulled off the road and turned around, Trent nodded and tipped his hat as Dave drove up. He held a bloody white handkerchief to his mouth.

"Go for a little drive?" He joked as he climbed in the pickup.

"Not a word." Dave said. "Not one Goddamn word, do you hear?"

They had traveled for a half-hour in silence, Dave hadn't even whistled. Trent sat straight-backed, his eyes on the road. When Dave's right hand began to ache, he looked at it for the first time since he had struck Trent, it was swollen and bloody from both Trent's lip and a laceration on his knuckles, apparently from Trent's teeth. He looked over at Trent, his lower lip and jaw were swollen.

"All right Goddamn it," Dave said coolly. "I'm sorry . . . ."

CHAPTER 12

"I love you Betty and I want to be with you forever," Dave whispered.

"I love you too." Her lips vibrated against his face.

The faint but intoxicating smell of her perfume gave him the sense of springtime. He felt the warmth of her body next to his. In each other's arms they swayed in a tender lover's dance; their bodies moving as one.

He felt her breathing quicken when his hand found its way under her blouse and cupped her breast. A fire burned deep in his loins as her gentle fingers undid the buttons of his shirt. Each touch of her soft fingers to his exposed skin sent waves of pleasure through his body. They shed their clothes and found their way to the bed. The fire she kindled begged to be fanned and he obliged.

She anticipated his every want and desire. When her hand gently encompassed his swollen passion he moaned with pleas-

ure. He kissed her, their tongues entwined as her fingers guided him into her.

"Are you all right?" Trent asked.

Oh shit! With an agonizing jolt, the bungee cord of his mind snapped Dave back to their motel room in Carson City. Refusing to open his eyes he rolled to his stomach hoping that any physical results of his dream weren't obvious.

"Yeah!" He answered. *A bad boy caught by his grandmother in an awkward moment in the cellar.*

"Were you dreaming about Betty?"

Dave refused to give up the pleasant memory and pressed into the mattress. "What makes you think that?" As if he didn't know.

"You were moaning like a cheap whore."

"You know about cheap whores, hum?" Dave said, attempting to change the subject.

Trent didn't dignify him with an answer.

Dave opened one eye to see Trent place his book on the nightstand. Amazingly the swelling in the kids lip was gone and the only sign of the afternoon's altercation was a small scab.

"It's not too late for you, you know." Trent folded his hands behind his head and stared at the ceiling.

"You're fucked, I've been a bottom feeder so long I've nothing to offer anyone. I couldn't ask someone like Betty to lower herself to my level."

"But you weren't always, maybe it's time to start lifting yourself up."

"I'm too old and too tired."

"With the right motivation you might be surprised. Remember what I said about a life partner. The right woman could do wonders."

"Right, here I'm, a sexually frustrated old man, listening to a kid explain true love and life partners." Dave sat up. "You don't understand kid. From the time of my second divorce my life has gone to hell. Not that it was much before that. The longest I've held a job since I left advertising was two years as a maintenance man. Oh it was fun at first, shirking responsibility's, but now its become a trap."

Dave wished there was some of the Old Turkey left, but settled for the remains of Trent's soda. "Not counting jobs that lasted less then a month, I've had more than twenty. Most of which I ended up getting my ass fired from. Everything I own, beside the piece of ground in Mystique, is in the back of that pick-up. And, all the money I have is in my wallet. I'm damn near fifty-three, what the hell do I have to offer anybody."

Trent sat up, their knees almost touch. "I'm telling you, Betty is not interested in what you don't have or what you haven't done. She is interested in you."

"Shit, kid, lunch with someone at a hamburger joint doesn't make a love affair. You just don't get it, do you?"

"No, Dave, it's you who doesn't get it. When the right woman comes along, your past won't mean a thing."

Dave fell back on the bed. "You are a damn fool, a god-damned dreamer."

"Yeah, maybe you're right." Trent stood. "But what if I'm right, and what if what I say is true?" He took a couple of steps then turned back. "Then it will be you who's surprised."

"I'd sure as hell . . . forget it." Dave pulled on his boots. "I'm getting hungry. How are your funds holdin' out?"

"I have more than sufficient, why do you ask?"

"Thought we'd go Dutch tonight."

"Our agreement was, you pay for the room . . . ."

" . . . and I buy dinner." Dave mimicked Trent. "Suit yourself."

*　　　*　　　*

They left the restaurant after a quiet dinner. Trent avoided any further mention of Betty and Dave refrained from beer.

"It's still pretty warm." Dave observed.

They walked across the parking lot and side street, toward the dark alley that led back to their motel.

"Oh no, I left my bag in the booth." The unflappable Trent panicked. "It'll only be a second. Go on, I'll catch up with you." He yelled, as he ran back toward the restaurant."

Dave walked on slowly, enjoying the night air. As he turned the corner and started up the alley, he was aware of movement in the shadows. When his eyes adjusted to the darkness he saw people standing in a doorway. He tried to stay as inconspicuous as possible when he realized there were four men, making what appeared to be a drug deal. Before he could decide whether to go on to the motel or go back and warn Trent, they spotted him. He continued in the direction of the motel and hoped they would ignore him. No such luck, they started toward him. He was afraid that if he ran they might have guns and shoot. When they caught up to him and cut him off, he raised his hands.

"I didn't see anything." Dave said. He knew it was a stupid thing to say, but didn't know what else to do in the situation.

A short stocky man with a red bandana tied around his head stepped in front of Dave. "How do I know what kind of eyesight you've got?"

"Trust me, it's bad."

"How bad?" A skinny guy with a shaved head asked. He wore a dark tee shirt stretched tight around the biceps of his tattooed covered arms.

"Real bad."

At this point he was surrounded. "Got any money?" One of them asked.

"Now, do I look like I've got money?"

"You look like you've got shit for brains." The one in the red bandana said with a push that slammed Dave to the wall. "You look like you might have a few bucks too."

"Listen, I don't have any money and I didn't see anything, I'm just walkin' back to my cheap motel down the street. I don't want any trouble."

Another man with a shaved head and shirtless, with skulls and a swastika tattooed on his chest, grabbed Dave by the shoulder. "Maybe you've already got trouble."

The other two grabbed Dave from each side and started checking his pockets. The creep with the red bandana pulled Dave's wallet out of his pocket and opened it. "Fuck man, he's loaded. This don't look like; no money!" He started hitting Dave in the face with the wallet forcing him back to the wall.

A forth man, thin and wearing a dark polo shirt, stepped in front of Dave. "So, you lied."

"I forgot."

Something hit Dave's gut so fast he thought he'd been stabbed. The pain so intense Dave dropped to the ground in a ball as he fought to breathe.

The guy in the polo shirt motioned to the others. They yanked Dave to his feet and slammed his back to the wall. Dave sucked in a breath and looked down at his stomach. *No blood, it wasn't a knife.*

They held him up against the corrugated-tin wall. A fist hit him in the mouth, his head banged on the tin. Dave tasted his own blood. Out of the darkness a second fist hit his face and his nose cracked, the tin resonated and he felt his blood begin to drip from his chin.

"Maybe this will help improve your memory."

A fist hit low on the left side of his jaw. Lights flashed as his head twisted, slamming his ear against the metal.

"Is your memory improving?"

"Yeah," Dave spit a mouthful of blood. "I'm beginning to remember you all real well." He said in a moment of insanity, knowing he was going to regret his words.

A knee found Dave's groin, the force lifted him in the air. He felt as if he had been split in half. White hot pain rose up and forced every bit of air out of his lungs, and then like a sack of potatoes he dropped to the ground in a heap.

His mind dulled by the pain, unable to even lift his face out of the dirt. He lay helpless fighting to breathe. There was silence, but Dave knew they weren't finished? *Oh God, let it be over.* Struggling for breath he held his groin, the pain began to throb. With his other hand he tried to lift himself from the filthy pavement.

A strange rhythmic pounding began. He strained to see. With his face still in the dirt he saw shoes and heavy motorcycle boots rise and stamp the ground inches from his broken nose. They surrounded him, thud, thud, thud.

"It's time for a little boot schoolin', for ol' stupid." One of them said with a laugh.

The skinhead with the tattoos lifted Dave by the hair to make sure he was conscious. "Yea awake? Don't want ya ta miss anythin'."

"Please don't do this." Dave begged for his life. Their stamping feet vibrated through the ground. The toe of a boot, slammed into the side of his head, his ear caught fire. "Please . . . you've got my money. You can have my pickup. Everything." Dave reached out for mercy, still unable to raise his head. He saw a boot, as if in slow motion, rise high and then come smashing down on his hand, his fingers crushed into the pavement, bones splintered. There was a delay before the pain registered, then momentary blackness.

The sound came again as he regained consciousness. Dave knew he was about to die. "Fast, do it fast," his plea bubbled from his mouth in his blood on the dirty pavement. He was helpless, knowing he was about to be stomped into eternity. *Where's the tunnel of light? Where are the angels to carry me to heaven? Blackness, blackness and pain are all I get to accompany me into death. Oh God help me, help me.*

In his vague fog of awareness, boots struck him from all sides. His mind refused to surrender to the peace of unconsciousness and his body refused to die.

A scream, the horrid yell of a banshee, pierced the night. *At last the Angel of Death has come for me.*

The screaming Angel of Death landed with its feet on either side of Dave. The boots stopped. The angel reached down with a hand of reassurance.

"Who's there?" Dave asked at the touch.

"Trent. Lay still." He straddled Dave. His sudden screaming appearance had stopped the men for only a moment.

"Get out of here." Dave cried. He could only open one eye to see the blurry figure of Trent standing over him. "Run damn it, run."

"What's this?" The guy in the polo shirt asked. "Some kid's gonna save old shit-head?

"A fairy! The shirtless skinhead yelled. A fuckin' queer with a purse, shit." The shirtless skinhead laughed.

Their taunting rose as they prepare to beat the crap out of the lone idiot that dare challenge them. Dave looked up through the blur to Trent with what strength he had left. He knew the kid didn't stand a chance. In his dire circumstance he found comfort in Trent's heroics, futile as he knew they were.

The men began to make catcalls and kissing sounds. Yelling, "pussy and queer." They took the kid with a purse for easy sport. Trent slowly assumed a low marshal-arts posture. He appeared fearless, ready to take on all four men at once. He lowered his buckskin bag to the ground. Dave drew it to his chest. *The gun.* Dave struggled to open the bag, but couldn't with only one hand.

The ape with the tattooed arms rushed forward. Trent extended his hand in a thrust and knocked the man to the ground. Dave didn't see the hit, but knew it had to be hard by the way the guy hit the ground.

"Shit, did you see that?" The shirtless skinhead yelled.

"I didn't see nothing!" The punk in the polo shirt growled. "What the hell's a matter with you guys? Get him."

Two of the men dove at Trent, he spiraled and the men were knocked on their backs. The tattooed ape got to his feet and ran at Trent. Trent turned, deflected his attack and flipped him high into the air. The goon landed head first on the pavement, crushing his face into the asphalt under his own weight.

"Hold it right there." The punk in the polo shirt stood a couple of feet behind Trent with a handgun pointed at his head. Trent turned and looked down the barrel. Dave could see a grin come to Trent's lips. The gunman's hand shook, as the two faced-off. Then the gun fired as Trent dropped, the bullet struck the guy with the red bandana in the forehead. Trent's foot struck the gunman's wrist. Dave could hear the bone crack. The gun flew into the darkness.

A yell from behind alerted Trent. The shirtless skinhead leaped high in the air and Trent flipped him up over his head. Dave saw the terror in the gunman's eyes the instant before the skinhead's head smashed into the gunman's face. They both hit the ground. There was a hollow sound like a pumpkin splitting, and then all was still.

In the silence, Trent calmly picked up Dave's wallet and his own bag. He knelt, touched Dave's shoulder and looked up. "Why did it have to be this brutal?" Trent whispered and then looked at Dave and asked. "Can you stand?"

"I don't know."

"Try, pull yourself up on me."

Dave found the strength, with Trent's help, to stand. Trent maneuvered Dave over his shoulder and carried him to the end of the alley.

"Stop, can't take any more."

Trent let him gently to the ground. "I'll get help."

"No! Don't leave me."

"I'll call an ambulance."

"No, can't do that." Dave struggled back to his feet. "Walk—me—room. Let me hold on."

Dave hooked his arm over Trent's shoulder. Together they covered the last two hundred feet to the motel room.

Dave lowered himself on the bed and looked up at Trent. "Promise you won't call an ambulance. I'm dying. Take my cash and get away. The police will never believe you." He implored. "The state can bury me. You save yourself." Dave faded into unconsciousness.

*   *   *

The touch of a cool wet towel to his forehead brought him back. Dave tried to focus.

"I need to get you help." Trent sat on the bed and wiped the blood from Dave's throbbing face. "I'm not going to let you die."

"You do the . . . your stuff."

"I can't. You need more than what I can do. Let me take you to the hospital."

"NO! No insurance. They'll take everything. You got to do it."

"I can't."

Dave took a hold of Trent's arm. "Please."

Trent hesitated for a minute. "There are some people, a couple of hour's drive from here, if you can make it, they might help. They are healers, my people, not doctors."

Dave nodded his consent and began to fade out.

"Drink some water, it will help keep you from going into shock." Trent handed Dave a bottle of water. "I'm going to the office for a minute."

*   *   *

Dave found himself in the pickup. Apparently Trent had carried him there. He was wrapped in a blanket from the motel room. His left hand had been wrapped in layers of motel towels.

"Here we go." Trent got in the driver seat and started the pickup. "I told the night clerk you had fallen and injured your hand, and that I was taking you to your doctor in Sacramento. I paid him extra for the blanket and towels." Trent backed up and then started for the highway. "When he wasn't looking I grabbed the registration card. We don't need anyone nosing around."

Dave's jaw had swollen to the point he could no longer speak. He nodded in pain, closed his eyes, and drifted into blackness.

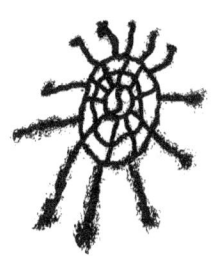

CHAPTER 13

"Guilty! Murder in the first degree. I sentence you Trent Salvador to hang by the neck until dead," the Judge yelled from his high bench.

Two bailiffs grabbed Trent and dragged him out of the bizarre courtroom. Outside, the gallows were already prepared. The people laughed as they hauled Trent to the gallows. With his hands cuffed behind him he slowly ascended the thirteen steps. A masked hangman put the noose around his neck and placed a hood over the terrified Trent's head.

Dave struggled, trying to fight his way through the crowd. Just as he reached the foot of the gallows with the evidence to prove Trent's innocence the trapdoor opened. Trent dropped in front of him and was jerked at the end of the rope a few feet from the ground. Dave collapsed in anguish at Trent's feet.

A bump on the road brought Dave around. The remnant of his hellish dream faded. His vision was blurred. Yellow, red and orange lights flashed. He turned his head toward Trent. "Where . . . ?" His voice was faint and labored.

"Doing okay?"

Dave nodded a doubtful affirmative.

"We're in Reno. We've got another hour or so. You're going to make it."

Dave could make out Trent at the wheel. He tried to ask where he was taking him, but the words wouldn't come.

"Drink some water."

"Cold . . . I'm cold."

"I'll turn on the heat. You rest." Trent turned up the heat then handed Dave an open bottle of water. "Drink some."

Dave took a sip of water and then closed his eyes. He felt the warm air from the heater on his face.

*   *   *

Dave woke when the pickup slowed and turned onto an unpaved road. He looked at Trent. "We're heading east, I turned off 445 a half hour north of Reno on a county road. Don't know the name. We've come to the end of the pavement, but we've got another twenty miles of dirt road to go. Hang on. We'll make it?

Dave nodded. His face throbbed as he drifted back to sleep only to wake again when the pickup finally pulled to a stop.

They were in the middle of nowhere. A yard light illuminated two small flattop houses that sat thirty feet apart. A four-foot high chain link fence encircled the two houses. Trent got out and approached one of the dark houses. A pack of dogs put up a racket and a light turned on in the house on the left. The face of a man peered out of the window. Trent had stopped under the mercury vapor yard light and waved. The porch light turned on and a man stepped out. Dave cracked the window open so he could hear.

"Who's there?" the man asked.

"Trent."

"Who?"

"Trent. Trent Salvador, Silvia's son."

There was silence. Trent stood at a distance and waited as a second man joined the first. The two men talked quietly, then one of the men said, "Come."

Trent approached and the three men talked. Dave couldn't hear what was being said. Trent pointed to the pickup, the men looked distressed and they appeared to argue. After a couple of minutes, Trent turned and walked toward the pickup. One of the men followed him, the other waited at the gate. As they approached the pickup the man looked through the window at Dave. The trip had taken its toll on Dave and he shivered from the early stages of shock.

"Why have you brought this white man here?"

"He is my friend and he needs your help."

"Take him to the hospital."

"No, I can't." Trent insisted. "Have you become like them?" The old man didn't answer. "He has a good heart and he is in need. You can't refuse."

"Are you his keeper?"

"Yes, I have saved his life and now I am his keeper."

"So be it, bring him in. But I can tell you, you bring trouble with this white man."

The old man returned to the house as Trent opened the pickup door, took Dave in his arms and followed. Dave felt safe in Trent's strong arms. The old man held the screen door as Trent carried him into the house.

Trent held Dave in his arms as the taller man pushed the two recliners from the middle of the modest living room to one side. The older man brought a mat and blankets, and placed them on the concrete floor. Trent gently placed Dave on the mat and covered him with the blanket. Dave's body shook.

"Shock, not good." The tall man said. "Must elevate feet." He left the room for a moment and returned with a couple of pillows which he placed under Dave's feet. Then the tall man knelt beside Dave and Trent knelt on the opposite side. Dave felt him place the tips of his index fingers on his forehead. The man closed his eyes as he ran his fingers slowly to Dave's temples, then over his face. "Dislocated jaw. Broken nose." He ran a finger in Dave's mouth. "Teeth okay."

Dave struggled to hear the rest of what was wrong with him, but he couldn't stay awake.

*   *   *

Dave could smell a heavy, sweet, grassy smoke and tried to focus. There was a steady beat from a drum being played by a man sitting on the floor in the corner. Shadowy figures on each side of him chanted. A candle on a low table to his right was the only source of light.

The figure on his left started to chant louder in a strange language and shook a rattle over him. It was the tall man, but now his shirt was gone and there were red, black and yellow painted marks on his face and chest, a necklace of claws and feathers dangled from around his neck and he wore a strange woven basket with feathers as a headdress.

The figure on his right joined the chant. Smoke came from a large abalone shell held in his hand and he fanned the smoke toward Dave with feathers. Dave recognized it was Trent, shirtless and painted too, with several strands of beads around his neck.

In the haze of confusion, Dave realized the pain had subsided to a dull throbbing ache. All of his clothes had been removed and only a small blanket was across his midsection. There was some kind of splint on his left hand, and when he tried to move it, a sharp pain told him not to.

Dave became aware of several other people in the room. They sat on the floor around him. He tried to ask Trent where he was, but couldn't open his mouth. When he tried harder the pain returned and the room went black.

*   *   *

He faded in and out of consciousness several times. When at last the fog began to lift, the room seemed empty. Light leaked in around the heavy drape on the window. *It must be day.*

Someone was sitting on the floor near his feet. By the hair and baggy clothes he couldn't tell if it was a man or a woman. Whoever it was, they were applying compresses to his right leg with a warm damp cloth. They dipped the cloth in a pan of liquid, rung it out and then pressed it gently to another area of his leg. The area where the cloth was placed felt warm at first, then hot and then finally a pleasant tingling cool. After they finished his right leg, they did the same to his left. From there they moved to his right arm and then chest, but when they started to remove his only covering, Dave protested. A swirl of pain ended his objection as he faded out.

*   *   *

Dave was suddenly outdoors. He lay on a large, low flat rock. Above him were stars, but around him was a strange dim light. He could see he was in the middle of a desert surrounded by dark hills. The sky beyond the hills was crimson and it bled into the black starry night. He was alone.

In the distance he could hear a drum. It played a slow mournful beat like a death march. A small woven cloth crossed his loins. He could not move, held by some mysterious force. He imagined himself as a helpless victim of an Aztec priest about to have his heart carved out of his chest and was gripped with fear. When would it come? He lay waiting. The drum he heard was his own heart beating. The longer he waited to meet his fate the faster his heart beat. What kind of cruel torture was this, he wondered. "Let me die," he cried to the twinkling sky. "Let me die."

"You shall not die," a voice answered.

A dark figure stood at his feet. It was the Indian from the basement.

"What do you want?" Dave asked. "Why are you harassing me?"

"It is you who called me."

"It can't be, I don't even know who you are."

"You will remember."

Lightning flashed across the sky with a loud crack and then all went black.

*   *   *

He wasn't sure of what were dreams and what was real. He was aware of various strangers' hovering over him, their chants, the constant drum and repeated applications of the odd warm liquid to every part of his body. The passing of time was apparent, but not relevant. He didn't know how much time had passed, hours, days or weeks, but with each bout of consciousness he felt himself getting stronger.

Dave woke to someone's touch. Trent knelt at his side. Across from him sat the stranger applying the warm compresses to his right arm and chest. "What is that?" Dave was surprised he could speak.

"Welcome back. Feel better today?" Trent asked.

"Yes." Dave looked at the stranger. "What are you doing?"

"Cheyenne is giving you a treatment. It's part of what saved your life. Herbs and other things have been applied every two hours around the clock."

"How long have I been here?"

"Eleven days."

"Eleven days? You are kidding."

"Afraid not."

"Where are we?"

"Nevada, Virginia Mountains, the backside of Pyramid Lake, Indian lands."

"Are these people friends or family?"

"Both."

Dave looked up at the person who knelt beside him applying the warm compresses to his chest. A large hooked nose dominated the long skinny face framed by long black hair. A large denim shirt hung over the slender frame. Dave still couldn't distinguish if it was a man or a woman.

"Who's that at the table?"

"That's Willy, this is his house."

Cheyenne continued to meticulously dip the cloth in the pan of hot water and herbs, wring it out and pressing it to Dave's chest and arm.

"Can I get up?"

"No, not until Harold gets back," Trent explained. "He's the boss, our Medicine Man. He'll be back in a couple of hours."

Cheyenne had finished with the application to Dave's arm, and started to remove the cover across his midsection.

"You're not gonna do that?"

"It's part of the treatment," Trent said.

"Well you can end the treatments right now."

"White men are all alike, bitch, bitch, bitch." Willy said with a disgusted look. "A week and a half ago you came here near dead. We took you in and nursed you back to life. Now you start feeling better and you start to bitch."

"I didn't mean . . . I just . . . it's embarrassing."

"Embarrassing? Four men tried to take your life and you almost let them, now that's embarrassing. You've lain on my living room floor naked and we all nursed you, now you feel better and you're embarrassed. It is too late to be modest. Modesty is incidental when your life is at stake."

"Dave, this is my uncle Willy." Trent said.

"Willy. This is got to be the worst introduction I've ever had."

"Should I be offended?" Willy was now standing over him.

"I mean, me lying here like this, this is not the way I like to be introduced. I'd like to shake your hand, but I think it will have to wait.

"Shaking hands makes introductions good? White men are all alike." Willy found his way to one of the recliners, sat and began to laugh, a deep hardy laugh that seem to shake the room.

Dave realized a little dignity was a small price to pay for what these people had done for him. Dave turned to Cheyenne. "Ok, go ahead."

Trent had moved to the recliner next to Willy.

"You guys gonna just sit there and watch?"

"We've been doing it for days," Willy answered.

When Cheyenne finished, the treatment, he replaced Dave's cover and took the pan to the kitchen.

"Trent, what happens if I need to take a piss?"

Cheyenne came from the kitchen and placed an old glass milk bottle on the floor beside Dave.

"Aim carefully," Trent said.

Dave looked at Trent trying to hold back a smile. "Don't make me laugh."

Cheyenne spoke in a quiet gentle voice. "I'm glad to see you are doing better."

"Me, too."

Just then the backdoor opened and an older woman came in with a basket of eggs.

"Dave, this is June, Willy's wife." Trent made the introduction.

June nodded and slipped around the corner to the kitchen.

Dave lay quietly, and took as deep of a breath as he could. *God, it's good to be alive.*

*   *   *

Dave woke at the sound of the door. The tall man walked straight to him and knelt. "How are you doing?"

Trent came over and knelt on the other side of him. "Dave this is Harold. He's our Shaman. He patched you up and has supervised your recovery."

"Glad to meet you. Thank you." Dave lifted his good hand and Harold took hold of it.

"You were in bad shape. Jaw dislocated, nose broken."

Dave touched the bandage across his nose and then the left side of his sore face.

"Broken ribs here and here." He pointed to both sides of Dave's ribcage. Then he placed the flat of his hand gently on Dave's belly. "Gut was bad, very bruised inside, very hot, but cool now. Good sign." He lifted and looked under the blanket. "Gonads bruised bad but not ruptured, we save them for you. You're still a man.

"Thanks. I guess I've been the floorshow for the last several days."

Harold laughed. "Humor coming back. Good sign."

"Can I sit-up?"

"Try, we'll help."

With Harold and Trent's help Dave sat up. "Whoa!"

"When you're ready we'll put you in a chair."

It was several minutes before Dave thought he was ready to try the chair. The men helped him stand and put on a pair of sweat pants. Then they sat him on a kitchen chair. June fixed him a bowl of scrambled eggs. Encouraged by the men and with the aid of a little catsup, he slowly downed the meal and hoped it would stay there. He sat for a while then Trent walked him to a small bedroom down the hall from the living room. The room had two single beds, a night stand between them and a diminutive chest-of-draws. "This is our room." Trent said as he helped Dave into bed. "Get some sleep. The bathroom is down the hall. If you need help call, or you can use the bottle on the nightstand."

"Trent." Dave grabbed his hand. "That Cheyenne, he's a he?

"Yes, and he has nursed you most of the time. Fed you, bathed you and cleaned you up when you soiled yourself. We all helped, but he did most of it, hardly sleeping."

"Oh." Dave let go of Trent. "What time is it?"

"A little after four in the afternoon."

"Thanks. I owe you big time."

"We're not out of here yet."

"What do you mean?"

"We'll talk about it later. Now rest."

*   *   *

"Dammit no. He's my nephew I won't let it happen."

Dave woke to Willy's booming voice coming from the other room. By the angle and color of the sunlight coming through the window Dave figured it was near sunset. Willy and Harold seemed to be arguing.

"There are two men dead," Harold continued. "The third's not expected to live, and Trent was the cause of it."

"But he wasn't, and nobody knows who—"

"There's a witness."

"But the witness is one of them," Willy insisted. "We must help them."

"But the white eyes is not one of us, he's one of them too and he's trouble. Your nephew will get himself hung, if not all of us. "

"You exaggerate, Trent is blood, and the white eyes is his friend."

"Have it your way dammit, but Vince has the final word "

Dave heard footsteps and the door slam.

Where's Trent when I need him. Dave tried to get up but was too weak. He lay back to wait for Trent, but sleep came first.

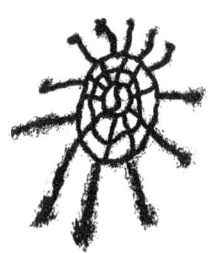

CHAPTER 14

A single young Indian brave rode hard. His near naked body glistened in the desert sun and his painted pony was lathered with sweat. The tired brave urged his equally exhausted mount down the embankment onto the dry arroyo. In the sand, the horse faltered and slowed to a forced walk, then stopped, unable to go on. The brave dismounted and in the shade of a cottonwood tree growing on the bank, dug feverishly into a patch of damp sand and soon the hole began to fill with water. He led his exhausted pony to the water and let him drink his fill.

Just as the brave bent down to drink, someone shouted. He jumped up, but it was too late. He was surrounded by the posse of cowboys who had been chasing him for days. With their guns drawn, there was no place for the brave to run, so he simply lowered his head and raised his hands in surrender. One of the men took his rope and slid off his horse. "Tie his hands together behind his back and hoist him up Ted." Ted tied the brave's hands as instructed and threw the other end of the rope over a branch of the cottonwood tree. Mercilessly, he hoisted the young Indian up until his shoulders twisted and he bent from the waist. He pulled on the rope until his captive's feet barely touched the sand, and then tied off the rope.

The oldest of the group, a crusty old man with a tin sheriffs badge on his vest, got off his horse, took hold of the brave's hair and lifted his head. "Okay Frank, this the one that stole your horse and beat up your boys?"

"Think so. They all look a like, even half-breeds."

"Good enough," The sheriff declared. "The only good Indian is a dead one," he said and spit in the Indian's face.

Then the sheriff backhanded the brave in the face, causing him to swing from the force of the blow. As he danced to regain his footing, the men laughed.

"Have at him boys." The sheriff said as he walked away.

After the cowboys had their fun, the sheriff called for them to stop. The brave hung limp, unable to stand.

"Okay," the sheriff commanded, " let's string him up so he can really dance for us."

"Nah, that's too fast." Ted protested. "Let's cut him first."

"No. He's a tuff son-of-a-bitch, we'll string him up slow and he'll dance for a half-hour. You know how Frank, slow like they do in England. Do it."

Frank tossed his rope over a higher branch of the cottonwood and tied a noose that wouldn't tighten. He tied the other end to his saddle horn.

Ted stood in front of the brave with his knife drawn, leering, tossing the knife from hand to hand, occasionally slicing at the brave's groin. "Come on boss, let me cut him first."

"No. Okay Frank, hoist him up."

Frank walked his horse back slowly, lifting the brave high into the air. He tensed and tighten his neck against the rope. Frank tied him off. He hung motionless from the tree.

"See, ya should a let me cut him. I'd of made him dance."

"Shut-up," the sheriff shouted. "He'll dance."

The torturous form of execution gradually started to take effect. The brave began to involuntarily jerk in a death dance, delighting the men.

The Sheriff started to repeat, "The only good Ind—." A single arrow struck him in the neck and protruded out the other side. Silenced, he fell from his horse as the others looked on in shock.

Before they knew what was happening, a hail of arrows fell on the men and in less than a minute they were all dead, except for Ted, who managed to duck into a hole at the base of the cottonwood tree. The small war party quickly rescued their brother and as two of the band tended him, the rest set about stripping and scalping the bodies.

There was laughter when the band found and dragged Ted from his hole. They had sport with him as they made him strip. When they were ready, they brought the brave to him. One of the band handed the young brave Ted's knife. He looked in Ted's eyes and began to toss the knife from hand to hand. Terror gripped Ted. He began to weep like a baby and plead. "No, no, please for God sake, no . . . ." He crumpled to his knees.

The brave stood for a second, grinned and then roughly cut off a lock of Ted's hair..

The war party quickly mounted up, taking all the men's horses, clothes and gear, leaving Ted, crying naked in the sand to die in the desert, a slow but certain death.

*   *   *

By the light Dave could tell it was morning. His head slowly cleared of the cobwebs as he concentrated on where he was. Trent's bed was unmade, his jeans lay across the foot and the door was ajar. He mustered all his strength, got out of his bed, pulled on sweat pants and slowly made his way down the hall. In the empty living room, the recliners had been put back in the middle of the room, aimed at the TV. Joan was doing dishes and looked up when he stepped around the corner.

"Good morning. Ready for breakfast?"

"Morning, I was looking for Trent."

"He's with the others. Out back in the sweat lodge, they are making prayers for you."

"Oh." Dave hung onto the wall.

"I've got fresh coffee."

"I need to use the bathroom first."

"It's down the hall to the right."

The face that looked back at him from the mirror shocked Dave. *Good God they did a number on you.* It was the first time he'd seen himself since his beating. Blue pee-holes, peered out of black puffy eyes sockets. The whole left side of his face was blue and swollen from his nose to his ear. A white bandage clung to a sausage of a nose and his lower lip hung like an old lady's purse on the way to bingo. The rest of his face was dotted by several abrasions that glistened from a thick ointment that covered them. *You're a beauty.*

Dave returned to the kitchen and lowered himself onto a chair.

"Here's your coffee. Milk and sugar?"

"No, thanks, I drink it black." Dave sipped at what he was sure was the best coffee he had ever tasted. "Thank you. You said that Trent and the others were in the sweat lodge. I don't understand."

"They should be finished soon, I'll let them explain."

*   *   *

Dave was wiping up the last bit of egg with a corner of toast when the backdoor opened. Willy, followed by Harold and two other older gentleman Dave didn't know, came through the door. The men were wearing loincloths, all but Willy, who wore shorts. Their bodies glistened with sweat. Willy, followed by the two men, nodded at Dave as they made their way down the hall. Harold stopped at the table.

"Good to see you up and eating."

"Thanks" Dave answered as he looked up at Harold.

"I'm going to change, then I'll check you over.

Moments later Trent came through the door. "Hey, how are you doing," he asked.

"I think I'm gonna make it." Dave looked him over. He too wore a loincloth, but his was buckskin and tied around his waist with a red sash. A strand of shell and turquoise beads circled his neck. Seeing Trent, Dave knew the young Indian brave in his nightmare was Trent. Relieved and amused, Dave fought to keep his amusement under check. Knowing full well that, even an inappropriate smile could insult the man who saved his life, he kept silent.

"More coffee?" Joan asked.

"Please."

Joan cleared the table and started washing the dishes.

"I really want to thank you for your hospitality." Dave said to Joan.

"You're welcome. Now if you will excuse me I need to feed the animals."

Dave waited until Joan was gone then grabbed Trent's hand. "I heard Willy and Harold argue last night. It was about me, you and the mess in Carson City. What's goin' on?"

Trent handed Dave a newspaper. The headline read, 'Two Men Dead and One In Critical Condition After Gang Confrontation in Carson City.'

"Is this about us? I can't read the small print." He pushed the paper back to Trent. "Read it to me?"

"Let's see, it says, 'Gang violence erupts in Carson City, Thursday night, leaving two men dead, one man in critical condition and another in custody. Allegedly Angel Sanchez killed Jessie Vasquez with a single shot to the head. Both men were from Reno. Sanchez was in turn bludgeoned to death allegedly by Ryan Dukes. A third man, Ron Scott of Carson City, is in critical condition from head trauma suffered in the altercation. Ryan Dukes, also of Carson City has been charged with second degree murder'."

Dave touched Trent's hand. "What really happened?"

"Let me finish, 'the incident is believed gang related. All four men are members of two rival gangs operating in the Reno and Carson City areas.

Sergeant Jones of C.C.P.D., says he believes that it was a drug deal gone sour that sparked the incident. Dukes' claims two other men started the conflict and are responsible for the injuries to Scott and the death of Vasquez and Sanchez. When asked to explain the teeth and bone fragment found imbedded in his scalp, Dukes replied, "A Man in Black levitated me and used my head to kill Sanchez." Dukes' is being held for psychiatric evaluation at the state mental facility in Carson City, his arraignment is pending.

Jones is seeking more information about the two men, believed to be from the Sacramento area'."

"You killed two Men?"

"No, Dave, they killed each other."

"But I saw, I thought I saw, what Dukes said—"

"Dave when I got there you were surrounded by four men, kicking the shit out of you. I yelled and they stopped and then started at me."

"I remember that."

"The first guy, the one with tattoos all over his arms, jumped me, I countered, used his own energy to knock him on his ass.

"I saw that, but how? I didn't see you touch him"

"I didn't, I just reflected his energy. The same thing to the guy with the red bandana and the skinhead with no shirt, I guess that was Dukes. It doesn't take much, get them off balance, they flipped themselves. There's no levitation, just self-defense. When I turned to check on you, the guy with the tattoos jumped at me again, I stood up and he fell over my back and landed on his head. That must have been Scott"

"Yeah, I think I remember that, then there was the gun, I remember a gunshot."

"The guy in a blue polo shirt, that must've been Angel, pulled a gun. He sure didn't live up to his name. He fired just as I crouched. I guess the bullet hit Vasquez. I kicked the gun out of his hand, and then the Dukes guy dove at me. I flipped him like the Scott guy. He landed head first on Sanchez. That was it. Then I carried you out of there."

"Don't you think we should go back to Carson City and tell the story to the police?"

"No!" Harold's voice rang from behind Dave. He had returned as Trent was telling the story. "White men still don't believe Indians. You and Trent are not responsible for what happened. Those fools did it to each other. Look what they did to you."

Dave looked at Trent as he tried to justify Harold's logic. The fog began to roll back in his head.

"You okay?" Trent asked.

"Feeling a little woozy."

"You need to rest." Harold said. "Tomorrow we sweat, finish your healing, then you can go, but not to the cops." Harold took a cup from the dish rack and filled it with a brown brew he poured from a pot that was sitting on the stove. "Here, now that you're up and your strength is come back, drink this."

Dave took the cup and tasted the brew. "Oh God, that's terrible."

"It's strong medicine, but will make you heal fast. Drink. Remember, no cops."

Dave looked at Trent's eyes, as he watched Harold go out the door. "What does he mean, we sweat?"

"You have been invited to the sweat lodge."

"You're going to have to explain."

"Drink up. I'll walk you back to bed, then I'll explain."

Dave forced down the thick brown nasty tasting brew. Trent waited, and then helped him to their room.

Dave stood beside the bed and looked at the wrapped splint on his hand. It was starting to throb. His lips were tingling and the effects of the medicine were kicking in. The tape on his ribs pulled as Trent helped him into bed.

"Trent, sit down here beside me. I want you close, to talk." Dave patted the bed and Trent sat down beside him. "Thank you. You and your friends have saved my life. I can never thank you enough, but I'm worried about you and the mess in Carson City."

"Nobody knows who we are or where we are. Harold feels if I go back to Carson City it will stir up nothing but problems."

"I think Harold is right. I've been having terrible dreams about you. Dreams of you being hung."

"Don't worry about it, they are not premonitions."

"How do you know?"

"Trust me, I know."

"One more question, how did you do what you did, to those guys?"

"I've studied marshal arts since I was four, a form of Kung Fu. I used their chi energy and turned their attacks back upon them."

"Okay. I think you might have to explain that again when my head is a little clearer." Dave paused. "These people. Who are they?"

"Willy is my mother's brother. Harold is a healer, a Shaman, and our spiritual leader."

"I don't know how Harold and the others did what they did, but I've become a believer in his medicine. Cheyenne is he . . . I mean, he seems different, is he?"

"He is what we call, of two spirits."

"What does that mean?" Dave was puzzled.

"In our beliefs, some among us are of two spirits. They have a special place in our culture. Some have psychic powers and can see the future, others bring healing or possess wisdom."

"But, what are the two spirits?"

"They are both male and female."

"Queer?"

"In your society they are called that and looked down on as freaks. Our people accept them for who they are and what they bring to humankind."

"I guess there is a lot I don't understand about your people. What about this sweat tomorrow?"

"A sweat is both a healing and spiritual ritual. It takes place in an Indian version of a sauna. A group of us will go into the sweat lodge. Heated rocks will be placed in the center and the doorway closed. There will be a leader, who will lead some chants and prayers. Water will be poured on the rocks to make steam. We sweat for a purpose, as in your case healing, also wisdom, answers to prayer and things like that."

"That sounds simple, but do I have to wear a loincloth?"

"We call it a breechcloth. Some of the men wear shorts or swim trunks, but I recommend you wear a breechcloth. We'll have one for you in the morning."

Dave took Trent's hand. "I thought I was going to give you a ride, instead you've taken me on the trip of a lifetime and some how, I don't think it's over."

Trent reassuringly held Dave's hand to his chest, as Dave aided by the medicine, drifted off to sleep.

*   *   *

The sound of someone working in the kitchen woke Dave. He looked around the room to orientate himself. By the light he felt it must have been getting near evening. Most of his pain had changed to soreness. His ribs had quit aching, the throbbing in his face was gone and there was only a dull pressure in his gut and groin. His hand only hurt when he tried to move it. Dave rose to his feet. His suitcase was open on a stand at the foot of the bed. With his shaving kit in hand, he headed to the bathroom.

He took a good look at himself in the mirror. The change from that morning was nothing less the miraculous. The bruises had lightened and his face was no longer swollen.

Returning to his bedroom he tried to put on a shirt but realized he couldn't get his splinted hand through the sleeve. Without help he couldn't dress himself. He sat on the bed defeated. *How in the hell did I get in this mess?*

The door crept open. "Good, you are awake, I brought you something." Dave looked at the large glass of iced brown liquid Trent held, suspiciously. "It's ice tea."

"Thanks." Dave took a sip and was surprised to find that it really was ice tea. "I can't find a shirt I can get on." There was desperation in Dave's voice.

"You can go without."

"That's alright for you, but I'd scare the natives. Oh no, I didn't mean it to come out that way."

"Let me see if I can find something." Trent left. Dave finished his drink. He returned shortly with a muslin shirt without sleeves and held it for Dave to slip on. "It's uncle Willy's." The loose-fitting garment had no buttons, only a cord that tied across the chest. The muslin shirt was soft and frayed from countless washings. "Come with me I want you to meet some people before dinner."

Trent led Dave to the yard. As they passed the kitchen, Joan and another woman were busy. Willy, Harold, Cheyenne and two other men sat on handmade stools under the shade of a single huge poplar. Dave stepped carefully over the barren ground in his bare feet.

"This is Vince Youngblood, he lives next-door." Trent made the introduction. He's our Headman, like a Chief, and this is

Johnny, his son. Vince's wife Mary is in the kitchen helping June. And you know Cheyenne."

Dave shook each men's hand, and then used Vince's support to lower himself into a wooden chair. "Pleased to meet all of you." Dave made himself comfortable. Being outdoors felt good. He turned to Harold. "Thanks again for saving my life."

"Thank everyone here, they all took part."

"Thank you all for taking me in and helping me under such circumstances. Trent has explained your reluctance, I understand."

"How are you feeling?" Vince asked. "You are looking better."

"I'm weak and sore all over, but doing better."

Joan came from the house with a plastic pitcher and refreshed their drinks.

"You're on your way to Mystique?" Harold asked.

"Yes." Dave realized there was likely to be a long wait before the next question. *Somebody needs to turn on some music.*

"Nice place." The pace of the conversation was so slow Dave had to think for a moment to remember that Harold was referring to Mystique.

"I haven't been there in almost forty years."

Dave rested his head back and let his mind wander. He had enough of a dull throbbing headache that he was glad that the conversation was slow.

"Vince was in Carson City this morning." Trent began.

A cold chill went up Dave's back.

"The third man is dead." Vince continued. "Dukes is in a padded cell. Carson City police are still interested in finding you two, if you exist, but aren't doing much about it. Reno police are involved as well, since two of the men were from there. The attitude is mixed, is seems that all four men were nothing but trouble, police records a mile long. I think the whole thing will be forgotten in a week or two."

"I disagree with you Vince." Harold stood. "They should leave now. If they trace them here, there will be hell to pay."

"We are a sovereign nation, the police have no rights here."

"But he's a white man."

"He's my brother." Trent stood.

"He is our brother." Vince said. "Now both of you sit down. We have saved his life, now he is all our responsibility. Tomorrow we sweat, I will make my decision then."

They all sat in silence.

Joan and Mary began carrying food to the picnic table. When dinner was ready the men took their stools to the table. Vince helped Dave and sat next to him. Before them were heaps of fried chicken, boiled pinto beans and fry-bread.

Their joy returned as they broke bread together.

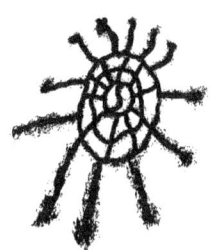

CHAPTER 15

"That damn white eyes will get us all killed, you're a fool for bringing him here."

Dave woke with the sound of voices from the yard. A red glow of morning light filtered through the bedroom window. Dave got up and looked out the window to find the source of the voices. Trent, in a breechcloth, stood near the poplar tree. A large bonfire near the back of the house cast an eerie light in the dim morning. Around Trent stood several men, all in breechcloths and many had paint on their faces and bodies. The younger men wore headbands and the older men wore an array of headdresses and other adornments.

"I brought him here because he needed our help." Trent was on the defensive.

"Since when has a white men needed an Indian's help?" Harold asked.

"You are overreacting," Vince said. "It might bring problems, but it's not a matter of life or death."

"It can be if the cops try to come on our land."

"I'm chief. It's my decision and my responsibility. Today he is one of us. We will take him into our sweat as a brother. Tomorrow Trent will take him away and we will forget he was ever here. That is my decision."

One of the young men spotted Dave at the window. "The white eyes is spying on us."

"His name is Dave." Trent walked away.

*   *   *

The bedroom door opened. "We are waiting for you."

"I heard."

"Please, our people have suffered greatly, you must forgive their suspicions."

"I understand. I am so thankful for their help I don't want to cause any problems. Maybe we should just go now."

"No, Vince has spoken. We will have the sweat. You are our brother." Trent held out a woven breechcloth.

"Is this necessary?"

"It's traditional. The bathroom's free, Get ready. I'll wait."

In the bathroom, Dave was astonished at the healing that had taken place overnight. The black eyes were reduced to dark circles around his eyes. The swelling was all gone and except for the bandage over the bridge of his nose, he looked as if he may have simply had a bad night.

He washed his face in cold water, then slid off his sweatpants, and attempted to put on the breechcloth, but after several failed tries, he peeked out of the bathroom door at Trent.

"I need some help."

Trent laughed as he entered the bathroom.

"I don't think I can get this on without both hands."

"It's simple, fold a third of the cloth over the sash, the short part to the back, place it behind you and tie the sash around your waist." Trent put the sash around Dave's waist and tied it over his hips. "Now reach down between you legs and pull the long end of the cloth up. Push it up under the sash and out and adjust it."

"I feel like a nut."

By the time they emerged from the house the group of men had started around the back of Vince's house, Dave and Trent followed, tenderfoot Dave stepped lightly. There, at the back of the house was the sweat lodge, a small domed structure dug into the ground and covered with brush. Two younger men tended the large open fire that Dave could see from the window.

The group gathered around a tub of ice, filled with bottled water. Each took a bottle and began to drink as they stood around and talked.

"Everything is traditional if not authentic." Trent opened a bottle of water and handed it to Dave. "The two older gentlemen next to Harold and Cheyenne are Dan and Julian, they are elders.

"Pleased to meet you." Dave nodded at the men.

"Over here is Sam and his son Travis."

"Sam, Travis, pleasure to meet you."

"So you've come to sweat with us today." Travis a stocky young man slapped Dave on the back. "Welcome."

"The young studs tending the fire are Jerry and Wounded Bear."

Dave waved to the young men. "You mean someone has an Indian name?"

"He prefers that to Grumpy," Travis joked, "but his wife just calls him Tripping Dumb-Dumb."

Harold came over to Dave. "You look even better today brother. Are you ready for the sweat?"

"I guess so." *Brother, that's a change.*

"Good. Trent will you lead the way." Harold pointed to the opening. "He'll take your water for you."

Trent stooped to his hands and knees at the entrance of the lodge and crawled through the door, Dave followed. The lodge opened up inside, but not enough to stand upright. Trent and Dave worked there way around the rock circle to a spot opposite the door and sat cross-legged on the mat that covered the earth floor. Vince's son Johnny sat next to Dave. The lodge was already warm from the sun. The only light came from the open door. Dave studied the branches that bowed from the ground to overhead. A black plastic tarp cover the wood frame and was apparently held in place by layers of brush on the outside.

"It would have been skins in the old days." Trent whispered, as he watched Dave examine the inside of the lodge. "And we would all be naked."

"And you pale eyes, only your scalp would have been allowed in," Johnny joked.

"I'm glad you are a little more liberal now day's."

"Who said? It's not over yet."

"Harold will prepare a pipe of tobacco," Trent continued. "Everyone will smoke as it is passed to the left, the way of the spirit wind."

"I don't smoke."

"It is a native tobacco, and you will smoke it. And don't just puff, inhale. The pipe is carved from a piece of red soapstone from South Dakota." Dave didn't argue. "After that the attendants will bring in the hot rocks and place them in the center."

"How long will the sweat last?"

"Longer than you think you can endure."

By the time everyone was in the lodge, they were pressed against each other and the outside wall.

Harold was the last to enter. He sat by the door and prepared the pipe with the assistance from one of the attendants, chanting in his native tongue as he worked. The pipe was shorter than Dave expected, plain with a short wooden mouthpiece. The attendant brought Harold a burning twig and soon he puffed swirls of blue-white smoke that lingered above his head. He passed the lit pipe to the next man.

"Take a good drag before you pass it on." Trent said in a shushed voice. "The pipe will be passed around the lodge three times as the stones are brought in. Take at least one good drag each time it comes around. And don't let it go out or I'll have your scalp."

Dave's head turned to Trent with a snap.

"I'm joking." Trent smiled. "About the scalping, but don't let the pipe go out. Once the hot stones are in place, Harold and the attendant that stays inside will pour water on the rocks and place sage, sweet grass and cedar on the stones. The door flap will be closed and the sweat begins. You must not talk. Understand?"

"I think so." Dave looked around the lodge. "What do we do in the dark?"

"Start by asking the Great Spirit to heal your body and mind. Then you may ask for a glimpse into your future or wisdom or what ever knowledge you seek. The dark and heat, it is like sensory deprivation and sensory overload all at the same time. You may see visions or just sense the answers."

"How will I know when it's over?"

"When Harold says it's time."

"What if you need somthin' or need to . . . ?"

"You wait."

Trent passed the pipe to Dave. He examined it quickly then swallowed and put the mouthpiece to his lips. He drew smoke into his mouth, it tasted sweet, he allowed it to pass over his tongue and finally into his lungs. He coughed. After a moment he lifted the pipe a second time and drew the smoke a little deeper into his lungs and held it as long as possible, as he passed the pipe to Johnny.

With each stone the heat intensified, it felt good against his beaten face. The pipe was passed to him again. He inhaled two drags and passed it on. The tobacco or the heat made his head swim. By the time the pipe reached him the third time the heat was so intense Dave's back was pushed hard to the outside wall.

A loud hiss accompanied the blast of steam and then the smell of sage. Dave realized he was breathing through his nose, the first time since Carson City.

The flap folded closed over the opening and plunged them into total darkness, except for a dull red glow from the stones in the center of the lodge.

In the darkness, unbearable heat and stifling steam, claustrophobia set-in. He began to panic and reached out into the blackness. His hand found Trent's leg and his fingers dug into his flesh. When Trent's hand touched the back of his, he grabbed hold of it and the panic began to subside.

Thank God for Trent. He was truly thankful to be alive and to have Trent by his side. He pulled Trent's hand tight to his chest and began to weep, not for sadness, fear or pain, but joy and the feeling of being a part of the group.

I can make it with Trent here at my side. I know I can make it. Another hiss, Dave jumped. There was the press of more steam and a whiff of cedar. *God help me to understand what's going on.*

Instantly the lodge seemed to expand in all directions. He felt completely alone. In the darkness he stood naked. As his eyes adjusted he found himself in a pool of light somewhere between earth and sky. After sometime his sons approached out of the darkness with gifts in their hands. They were grown men in business suits and they carried gold boxes. His oldest son opened the box, took out a small gold dagger, raised it in the air and stabbed it into Dave's heart. He felt the sharp pain and at the same time, black liquid began to trickle down his chest. His second son stepped forward and also plunged another dagger into Dave's chest.

Then his ex-wife came and stood between the boys. With a grin, she grabbed his testicles and castrated him with a huge gold scissors as the boys looked on and laughed. Gold coins started dropping out the gaping hole in his groin. She filled buckets with the coins and handed them to their sons. When the flow of coins started to slow down, she punched Dave in the belly to make more coins fall. When he was drained dry, she reached into the hole. He felt her fingers groping around in his gut. She finally pulled out one last coin and held it up to his face and the three began to laugh.

*   *   *

The hiss of water on the hot rocks momentarily brought Dave back to the sweat lodge, his hand still in Trent's. He felt Trent and Johnny pressed against him. Their breathing was slow and steady. Their strong young bodies were, hot, sweaty and masculine. A fiery energy began to flow from them and into Dave like hot lava.

Dave turned toward Trent and he was immediately back in his vision. He saw Trent reach up, pull the daggers from his chest and throw them on the hot stones. Sparks flew into the air as the glowing gold melted and disappeared between the stones. Then Trent's strong fingers wrapped around Dave's heart. He squeezed, there was intense, breath stopping pain. Dave tried to cry out but couldn't. Trent squeezed until all the thick black liquid was gone and the pain stopped.

Suddenly Dave stood alone again in the pool of light, somewhere in the vast darkness. He looked down to see that his genitals had grown back, virile and turgid.

Hot fluids filled his insides, rising up and through his stomach, heart, chest and lungs. He was young again and sitting with Joe by a campfire. Joe rose, took Dave's hand, and pulled him to his feet. He led him out onto a thick green meadow, to a pool of deep blue water and pointed. In the pool Dave saw Joe in a doctors office, an x-ray of a head hung from a lighted viewing box. The doctor pointed to a large mass in the brain, the words inoperable malignant brain tumor was written on the x-ray.

Suddenly he saw Joe bend and hold his head and scream in pain. He saw Joe with his face distorted in pain, take a rope and throw it in the air. He tied the rope around his neck and jumped. When the rope tightened Joe was instantly transformed, freed and running across a meadow. Donny and Gary joined him; the three looked at Dave for a moment then turned their backs and ran into the meadow.

Dave started to follow after them, but ran into a high chain-link fence with razor wire coils along the top. He stood and watched his three best friends run across the meadow. They stopped at the edge of a grove of trees and looked back then disappeared into the grove. Dave stood at the fence, his hand reached out to them in a plea to follow.

Once again he was back in the sweat lodge. Short of breath, he labored to breathe. In the dark, he became aware he still held Trent's hand. He struggled to orientate himself. From somewhere in the lodge came the sound of a rhythmic rattle and a voice started to chant. He turned to Trent but it wasn't him holding his hand. In the dim he saw he was holding the hand of the Indian from the basement. Before he could pull away, the Indian took Dave's hand and placed it in another's, a soft feminine hand.

Out of the darkness Betty rose slowly, like Venus rising out of the sea. Their naked bodies floated in the warmth. Her kiss drew him to her, their bodies fuse and he grew large in her. They danced a lover's dance, slow, ever so slowly they move toward pulsating orgasmic rapture, true paradise. They became one with the universe, bathed in wave after wave of warm sensual pleasure, ecstasy beyond any he ever dreamed, beyond his comprehension they road on into infinite oneness.

*   *   *

Brilliant sunlight and cool fresh air rushed into the sweat lodge at the lifting of the flap. *Over so soon?* Dave fell back to reality like the last reluctant fall leaf of an aspen descending to the earth. His hand was still wrapped in Trent's. With gratitude, he squeezed it. Savoring the sweat to the end, he was in no hurry to depart the lodge. When his time came, he emerged fresh as a new born.

A bucket of cool water dumped over his head heightened the senses. Light headed and giddy, Dave could not find words to express his gratefulness at being included in the sweat. Hugs were exchanged with everyone.

When everyone except Harold, Willy and Trent were gone the four men walked to the house. By then they were dry in the warm desert wind.

"You did well." Harold told Dave when they reached the backdoor. "After you shower, I will change your bandages."

Bandages? Dave had forgotten his bandages, the beating, the terrifying moment when he faced his mortality and didn't want to be reminded of them. He wanted only to hold to this moment of happiness, his new friends, the sweat and most of all, Betty.

CHAPTER 16

"Ouch! You're peeling off my skin."

"Grin and bear it."

"Geeze!" He complained as Harold ripped off the last piece of adhesive tape that clung to his chest. Dave sat at the dinette in his jeans, his hair was still damp from the shower.

"You're lucky," Harold said. "You're like Indians, not hairy. Some white men are hairy like bears." Dave winced as Harold probed with his finger the faded bruises on the sides of his ribs that marked where Dave had received repeated kicks. "I think you will be all right now without tape. Just take it easy for awhile. No fights."

"You don't have to tell me that."

"Keep the bandage on your nose a few more days, you don't want it to look like mine."

"I'm amazed how fast I've healed."

"Indian medicine works fast, we didn't have HMO's. Now let's look at that hand." Harold removed the dressing that held the splint with a bandage scissors. Once free from the tape and splint, he started to examine each finger. "Bend your fingers, make a fist."

"Awh . . . I can't do any more than that." Dave could only bend his fingers a little.

Harold took Dave's hand and started to bend and probe his thumb with his skilled fingers. "How's this?"

"Not bad." Dave watched as he took his index finger and started to move it. "Oh Christ! don't . . . don't!" Harold worked with the finger until Dave was able to curl and extend it by himself. Dave was able to curl and extend his middle finger without pain. "At least I can flip the bird."

"A talent likely to get you another black eye. Now this might hurt, try curling your ring finger."

Dave's ring finger was still swollen and dark. "I can't bend it."

Harold worked the tips of his fingers lightly over Dave's ring finger with his eyes closed. "We can see the bone without x-rays." He stopped to probe a spot. This might hurt." He took hold of Dave's ring finger with both his hands. "Need to reset the bone." Without giving Dave a chance to brace himself, Harold gave the finger a twisting yank.

"Awww . . . Damn." Dave heard a crack and felt the bones shift. His finger ignited, he was about to pass out with pain. "Ouch shit!" More pain, another crack. Harold let go of his hand and the pain began to subside.

"Sorry it was not straight. Try making a fist again."

Dave bit his lower lip as his fingers curled slightly. "Oh God." He muttered as he struggled to make a fist, it closed more than the first time. "That's it, that's all I can do."

"Your hand will get better now."

"That hurt more than when they stomped on it."

"Indians know how to make pain for white men. I'll splint it now."

Trent came down the hall fresh from his shower, in his usual jeans and tee shirt, but with the addition of moccasins instead of his boots.

"Where were you when I needed you?"

"I didn't want to see you cry?"

Harold began to apply a new splint to Dave's hand as Trent sat across the table and watched.

"How's it going?" Trent asked.

"Hurts like hell. Indian torture," Dave responded.

"If you think that's torture, you should try being staked to an ant hill." Trent continued. "They go for your eyes and your balls first. Take you apart mouthful by mouthful and when the juicy parts are gone the keep going until your nothing but bones. It might take two or three days to die."

"That's comforting."

"Thought it might be." Trent grinned. "Will he be ready to travel tomorrow?"

"He's ready now." Harold answered.

Dave looked at Trent then back at Harold. "Can I ask you some questions about the sweat while you work?"

"Go ahead."

"I saw some strange things in the sweat lodge this morning."

"The spirits talk to you in the Sweat." Harold spoke without looking up from his work. "They answer questions."

"I'm figuring out what some of the images meant, and I know more understanding will come, but they're a couple of things that have me real confused."

"What's that?"

"Well I know the sweat lodge is suppose to be a holy place, but this wasn't very religious."

"Religious is what white men think, the Great Spirit is sacred not religious. What is your question?"

"Well, when I saw myself in the sweat lodge I was naked, and so were most of the others."

"You were seeing in the spirit."

"Why were we naked?"

"You were as the Great Spirit created you. The Great Spirit didn't make clothes."

"Okay . . . Now this it's a little embarrassing." Dave paused.

"Go on."

"There was a point where I saw this woman, someone I met on the trip, Betty. Well this woman was there and she was naked and I was naked too, and we were together . . . and, well we made love."

"Naked people sometimes do that."

"It was in the air, like in heaven, and it was the best sex I ever experienced. The orgasm went on and on. It was real, the orgasm."

"That's not uncommon. Doesn't your white man's religion teach that God is Love. What is love? Orgasm. Isn't that the ultimate expression of love? Orgasm is God's gift to his creation. Being one with the Great Spirit, being in heaven is like orgasm, totally consuming."

"If that's what heaven is like . . . Wow!"

"There, you hand is done. You must keep it splinted for three to four more weeks."

Harold gathered up his things and took them to the bathroom. Dave looked up at Trent, embarrassed about his confession. Before Dave could speak, Vince came in the back door with a folded newspaper in his hand and put it on the table in front of Trent.

"Where's Harold?"

"Down the hall, in his room."

"You need to read that." Vince handed Trent the paper and headed down the hall to find Harold.

Trent picked up the paper and read it to himself as Dave put on his blue short sleeve shirt, carefully maneuvering his splinted hand through the sleeve. Trent lowered the paper with a concerned look on his face.

"What does it say?" Dave asked.

"The Reno police are getting more involved in the investigation. Another witness has come forward, said she saw the fight from her window."

"Witness? Witness to what?"

"Let me read it to you. 'Authorities want to question two men believed to be involved in the incident. An older Caucasian male in his fifties, six-foot, medium build, graying brown hair, possibly injured, believed the victim of an attempted robbery. The second man is in his twenties, dark hair, tall, six-foot plus, slender with a muscular build. They were last seen driving a dark colored

142

Ford Ranger pickup, possibly black or dark blue with California plates and matching camper-shell. It is believed the men are still in the area." Trent put down the paper.

"Holy shit," Dave exclaimed. "Well we are gettin' out of here tomorrow, period."

"I think I'll go back to Carson City."

"Like hell you will. It's like Harold said, you didn't do anything wrong, but if they can stick it on someone, especially an Indian, they will. We'll head up to Mystique, lay low a couple of weeks and see what happens. Then you can head on up to Oregon."

"That's probably a good idea." Vince had returned and had been listening to their conversation.

"I've got to think. I'm gonna take a walk." Trent grabbed his buckskin bag and headed out the back door.

"Wait let's talk this out." Dave grabbed for Trent to stop him, but it was too late, the screen door slammed and he was gone.

"He will talk it out by himself. Some say Trent walks to a different drumbeat, but Trent walks to the very heartbeat of the Great Spirit," Vince said as he and Harold went out to the backyard.

"What do you mean by that . . . ." The screen door banged closed leaving Dave alone.

Dave moved to one of the recliners. New concerns whirled in his head After several minutes of worry his eyes grew heavy. He was about to fall asleep when Cheyenne came through the back door, in his usual oversized shirt and what looked like pajama bottoms and moccasins, and sat in the recliner next to Dave. "I watched you in the sweat lodge," he said.

"Oh?" *It was total darkness in there. What could he have seen?*

Dave didn't know what to say. He didn't want to be rude, but with his concern about Trent, his mind went blank when he tried to speak.

"I won't bite."

"Sorry, just a little fussy. Harold had to reset the bone in my finger."

"Are you okay, can I get you something?"

"No thanks, I'm fine.

"Your sons are angry with you because you failed them and blamed their mother for your mistakes. Then, instead of facing your responsibility, you cowered away and shirked your obligation. The daggers were symbolic of their anger."

Dave's heart sank. The truth stung. He wondered how Cheyenne could have known what went on in his head in the sweat lodge. *Did Trent tell him about the marriage and divorce or did he guess or is he psychic? I haven't told anybody about the daggers.* He had no comments.

"But before that, you had turned your back on your best friends because you were too busy, but the truth was you were to fearful to help. You blame their deaths on the military yet you could have intervened and helped all of them."

Dave broke down and began to sob uncontrollably. Cheyenne stood, moved to behind Dave's chair and put his hands on his shoulders. "What is past, is past. You cannot change it. You have been given a second chance."

Cheyenne began to massage Dave's neck and shoulders as he softly sang a Native chant. Dave closed his eyes and felt himself relax, soon he began to drift.

Dave found himself in an open forested area of oaks and pines. The sun shone through the canopy to green and tan grasses on the floor, casting patterns of light and dark. As he descended the gentle slope, the place seemed familiar yet he couldn't place it, and though he couldn't see it, he knew there was a clearing just ahead. When he emerged into the open sunlight, he stopped and stood by a stream. To his right the stream curved and formed a deep pool, then it spread out before him onto a shallow stretch of rocks, causing the water to dance and shimmer in the sun to its own music. The birds sang in harmony with the burbling waters as it turned away from him to his left and disappeared into the trees' shadows.

He followed the bank downstream until he saw a man sitting on a log at the water's edge. There was a strange recognition as he approached, then the man turned and said, "Hello Dave."

"Donny?" The name escaped Dave's lips. There was no doubt who it was, yet Dave never saw Donny look like this, he

was somewhere in this thirties, healthy and strong, but without the flair.

"I've been waiting for you," Donny said in his strong but velvety gentle voice.

"Me? Where are we?"

"It's not important. Come sit."

Dave sat on the log beside him. "You look well."

"I am." Donny answered as he took Dave's hand. "You look well too."

"But I thought you were . . . ."

"I am dead, in your world."

"I'm confused, really confused. Am I dreaming?"

"No, you aren't dreaming, you're journeying."

"Will I get back?"

"Of course. Trent will explain."

"You know Trent?"

"Yes, we sent him. In the future you will understand, right now our time is limited. First I want to thank you for coming to visit me at my time of crossing. You were the only one who wasn't afraid."

"Time of crossing?"

"Shush, just listen. I need to tell you about me and Gary."

"I know. He came and told me. I was a little pie-eyed, but I think it was him."

"There is more. Gary is a great man, he knew I was gay before I did. It was in our freshmen year, we were in gym together. One day he came up to me in the showers and said, 'If I looked at the other guys the way I looked at him, I'd end up with a mouth full of fist or worse.' Up until then I didn't understand my feelings. I realized that I was excited and aroused by other guys, not girls. He knew the truth and was the only one I could talk to. No, he wasn't gay, but his older brother was, and he understood me and wasn't threatened by me. In our redneck high school, being gay was not an option. If anyone suspected, Gary would assure them I was straight. Nobody questioned Gary. I tried dating girls but it didn't work.

I never had sex with guys from our high school, too risky. There were plenty of men available in town, older guys, usually.

Gary taught me how to act straight and gave me the stories to tell about my sex life. None of it was true."

"So, why didn't you tell me?"

"You, chicken little? You're still homophobic. When will you understand it's not contagious? Beside you had your own problems. I'm proud of you finally standing up to that old O'Doul, even if you hit the wrong man. You weren't the only one O'Doul took into the storage closet, it was a busy place for years. The week after your experience, he tried it with Travis, the cowboy kid they all called the Goat-roper. He flattened old man O'Doul on the spot, then told his father. He wasn't ashamed like everyone else. His father told O'Doul that if he wasn't gone by the end of the school year, he'd rope him and castrate him himself. When O'Doul moved east, Travis' father put the word out and O'Doul ended up getting arrested. He never taught school again. If you and the others he molested before Travis hadn't been so insecure about your own sexuality and spoke-up, he would have never gotten away with it. But that was what he counted on."

"He didn't molest me."

"What do you call it? He kissed you and fondled you against your will. That's molestation and rape, even the attempt, even the intent is."

"I'm beginning to understand."

"More boys in the world are molested or sexually assaulted by men before they reach maturity than you can imagine. Most of them blame themselves for the assault and never tell anyone about it, believing they must have done something to cause the attack. Instead they live a life of hate, fear and self-doubt about their own sexuality. In a way it is worse than a girl being molested, in that they are usually attacked by a male and their sexuality is not put in question. If rape and sexual molestation were as prevalent among young women as it is among young men, there would be a huge outcry, but in some way it seems to be an unspoken part of a man's rite of passage. It is a silent crime and an outrage."

"Why are you telling me this now?"

"So you can understand yourself."

146

"But you never seemed gay to Joe or me? You never did anything in high school to make us think you were gay."

"I wasn't attracted to you two skinny-assed, hairless, tight-butts. I liked men like Gary, muscular and hairy with full round asses and thick cocks."

"Spare me the details."

"No, you've been spared the details long enough. I need to tell you the whole story. All through high school as much as I wanted to, I never tried anything with Gary, but that night at the castle things were about to change. Gary indicated that he might be willing to try, to experiment. We brought the beer and let you and Joe get drunk. When the two of you passed-out, we slipped off to the swimming hole. We got naked and swam for awhile. When at last things got intimate, he couldn't go through with it. When we got ready to go back to camp, Gary couldn't find his clothes, so he wrapped up in blankets and we sat by the fire, talked and drank beer until we too passed-out. You remember the next day."

Dave sat quietly and tossed stones into the stream. When there was a change in the sound and rhythm of the water, Donny stood. *"You've got to go back now. Follow the trail back up the hill."*

Dave rose and they embraced and then he started to leave, but he paused and turned back. *"Wait, is this place heaven?"*

"You can call it that."

"But isn't homosexuality a sin?"

"What sin is there in two consenting adults giving each other pleasure?"

"I have so many questions?"

"They will have to wait. Right now you have to go back."

Once again Dave started up the path, but after a few steps he turned back again to give Donny a wave good-bye. Donny was walking away and someone had joined him, it looked like Gary, but Dave wasn't sure. The two men walked together into the shadows and disappeared.

When Dave woke he was alone in the house. *What a weird dream.*

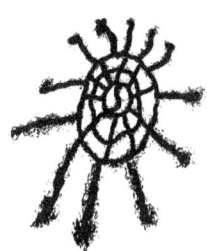

CHAPTER 17

Trent ran into the desert away from the setting sun.

He ran until he was exhausted and in the overtaking darkness, could no longer see the ground. He stopped, and on a small area of level ground, he bent down and felt around until he found a stick about three feet long. In the dark he sat, his eyes closed and held the stick with both hands and pointed one end into the sky and the other end he placed against his chest above his heart. He envisioned the tree from which the stick came, its leaves, its branches, and its trunk, down to its roots in the ground. Slowly he drew in his breath as if it came from the very center of the earth, held it deep in his lungs then slowly let it out. Without opening his eyes, he stood, took the stick and drew a circle in the desert sand. After he acknowledged the four directions from memory, he sat in the center of the circle, the only sound was that of his pounding heart. He began to beat the ground with the stick to the rhythm of his heart, moving it around until it struck a rock with a crisp clap.

He continued the sharp staccato rhythm, and began to chant. He continued his ritual until at last he felt a presence before him.

"Why have you summoned me,"

Trent with his eye still closed answered, "I need your counsel."

"What is it that you seek?"

"I am confused. I have started him on his voyage, but now there is an unforeseen diversion. I know Dave was to be tested, but the turn of events has gotten me confused. Others are involved, were they suppose to be part of the journey? I can't remember. And there has been deaths at my hands, I don't believe that it was intended. May I see the chart again?"

"No, that is not needed, you will remember when the time comes. You were starting to lead not guide, my son. Your knowledge of what is to come was getting in the way. You are to walk beside him and let him take the lead from now on. When the time of intervention comes again you will know. Now rest and be refreshed, Lady Leopard is here to comfort you."

At that, Trent felt the strong push of his old friend's head against his shoulder. He raised his hand, felt the fur of his totem and began stroking the great cats ear as he leaned his cheek to the animal's. He heard the sound of pleasure gurgle from deep within the animals throat.

"Hi lady love," he whispered. "I've missed you too." As they embraced, he felt the mystical creature change to its human form. He kissed her cheek as he lay down beside her and took her in his arms. "I love you."

Above them the stars glistened. How long they laid together he didn't know. When he opened his eyes, the waxing moon had risen and hung large above the eastern horizon. Warmed by the mystical lover in his embrace, he stared up at the night sky. Suddenly, to the north he realized that a huge chunk of the sky was black. At once he recognized the shape, "Winnedumah!" He fell prostrate before the monolith.

"You have done well so far my son. Now that you are refreshed, go and do what must be done. Your guidance will come when the time is right. The Council is watching over you."

*   *   *

They had waited dinner until after dark. Dave hoped nothing had happened to Trent, but the others didn't seem the least bit concerned. After dinner Dave waited up until the last one was ready to retire.

"What if he is lost?" Dave asked as he followed Willy down the hall.

"He's fine, don't worry. He'll be here by morning."

"How can you be so sure?"

"I know Trent." With that, Willy closed his bedroom door.

Dave stood in the hall for a minute then thought he had heard the back door. He checked, but there was no one. With a last look around he turned off the living room lights, leaving the porch light on and retired to his room. Standing beside Trent's empty bed, he looked out the window into the night and the rising moon. *At least there's a moon even if it's not full.* "Take care of him, I don't want to lose him now."

In the darkened room he watched the shadow of a cottonwood on the bedroom wall gently move in the night air. He watched the clock and pondered the bizarre dream he had had that afternoon and all that had occurred since he met the strange kid at Kramer's Junction.

*   *   *

Betty stood at her living room window and looked out at the rising moon.

"Are you all right?" Susan asked.

"Yes, just couldn't sleep. Why are you up?"

"I don't know, I couldn't sleep either. Shall I make some chamomile tea?"

"Sounds good, want me to help?" Betty asked.

"I can do it. I'll be back in a minute."

When Susan returned with a pot of tea, cups and plate of cookies, she saw that her mother had lit the candles on the coffee table, and was again standing, looking out the window.

"What's wrong mom, you've been moody for a week now?"

"Disappointed I guess.

"Is it because Dave hasn't shown up?"

"I expected to hear from him a couple of days after we got home, it's been over two weeks. I feel that something may have happened to them."

"Trent probably got a pimple and they had to go to the emergency, and now they are hanging out in some spa until he recovers."

"That's cruel. Why do you dislike him so much?"

"I don't, I just don't want to get my hopes up. Pretty Boys are usually pretty disappointing. I've been there. Trent's too perfect to be true, the guys got to be a jerk, or worse."

"You're too young to have such a low opinion of men."

"Not all men, just some. I've been in L.A., too long. You've got to be good-looking to get anywhere down there and the place is full of them, dumb blonde women and tall, dark and handsome men that haven't got a clue. Cookie cutter want-a-bes who can't think for themselves, all trying to make it big in Hollywood."

"But you don't even know him."

"I know his type. And I can't believe you are moping over a man you don't even know. Your handyman may have found a job along the way for all we know and pretty boy is long gone on his path to 'nowhere in particular'."

"Touché, maybe we both need to forget Dave and Trent."

"It's a deal."

*   *   *

"Three-twenty," Dave spoke the time. So far any meaningful sleep had eluded him. He drifted. Images of what could happen to a man alone at night in the desert pummeled his thoughts.

The latch of the door clicked as it slid off the strike plate. The door slowly opened. At last Trent had returned. Dave pretended he was asleep but he watched Trent slip off his jeans and tee-shirt and slide into bed. "I'm glad you're back."

"Did I wake you? I'm sorry, I hope you didn't worry."

"No. Just couldn't sleep." Dave paused. "What's your decision?"

"As you said, we'll go on to Mystique, then after a few days I will go on to Oregon."

"I think it's the right thing to do. It'll all blow over in a week or two."

"Okay dad, enough said, let's drop it."

After a long pause Dave asked, "What happen to your father?"

"He was killed a year after we moved to New Mexico."

"How was he killed. Auto accident?"

"He was a fireman, got trapped in a burning building. He saved three children. He thought the mother was still inside and went back to look for her, but she had made it to safety out the back. The roof collapsed on him. He didn't suffer. My mother grieved herself to death a couple of years later."

"Sorry."

There was another long silence. "What about your sons?" Trent asked. "You gonna have them come visit you in Mystique?"

"Fat chance. I haven't seen or heard from them for ten years. Their mother . . . ."

Dave remembered the vision in the sweat lodge and Cheyenne's words. "I guess I let them down pretty bad. I don't think there's much of a chance at reconciliation."

There were no more words and Dave finally fell asleep.

*   *   *

Dave woke to a bump of the bed. *Trent must be getting dressed.* He buried his face in his pillow to saver a few more moments of his bed. *He must be anxious to get going, it isn't even daylight yet.* His thoughts strayed to Betty and the image of her in the sweat lodge. He felt him sit on the foot of his bed.

"You going to marry her?" he asked.

"Isn't that rushing it a bit?"

"Not if you love her."

"I've only met her twice."

"But you're in love with her."

"I don't know. I don't know if I've ever been in love."

"You love her. You know it. Every time you even think about her you get a hard-on."

"Isn't that getting a bit personal?" Dave turned and sat up. "What the fuck?"

The Indian from the basement sat on the bed.

Trent switched on the bedroom light as he entered. Dave sat staring at the foot of the bed.

"You okay? I heard you yell from the bathroom."

"That thing, that Indian thing sat on the bed and talked to me." Dave was shaken.

Trent sat on his bed. "Dave, that Indian is your Spirit Guide."

"What?"

"He is your Spirit Guide."

"Ah crap, I don't believe—"

"After all you've been through these past two weeks, isn't it obvious that there are things happening around you that are not all of this physical world?"

"I don't know. I'm trying to believe, but I'm not there yet."

"Just stay open-minded." Trent stood. "Get dressed, June is fixing breakfast. I've checked the pickup, we're ready to go.

*   *   *

Dave took the passengers seat of his pickup. The sun rose during breakfast to a gray and overcast morning. Trent hugged Harold, Vince and Willy a final goodbye, and then climbed in the drivers seat. The goodbyes had started at breakfast and lasted an hour. People Dave had never met, but apparently were part of the healing circle, came by to wish them well and send them on their way. Dave was not sure if they were happy or sad to see them go. He had started to feel comfortable with his new extended family, but there was still some distance between them, Dave chalked it up to him being a white man, but what ever it was, he was grateful for all they had done for him.

As Trent drove out of the yard and onto the dirt road, the dogs chased after them barking. The pack eventually stopped, gave a last bark and trotted, high tailed, back to the houses, proud that at last they had run off the intruders.

Dave was surprise by the distance off the paved road Willy actually lived. Once they reached pavement, Trent picked up some speed, but it was another half-hour drive before they reached the highway and headed north. The desert sun had consumed the thin cloud cover and in its victory spread its heat over the parched ground.

"They live a long way out."

"They like it like that."

Nothing more was said. Dave tried to sleep but couldn't, the words and image of the Indian sitting on his bed returned every time he closed his eyes.

"Okay dammit, tell me about this Spirit Guide."

Trent turned to Dave with a grin. "We all have them, Spirit Guides." Trent began. "They are with us our entire lives. Some people think they are their guardian angels, but, angels come and go. They are not your conscience either, as other people seem to think. They are separate spirit entities, humans spirit forms that have passed over and have come back to earth to help us."

"What do they want or do?"

"What the name implies, they guide us on our life's journey, convey spiritual knowledge, give us guidance and warn of danger."

"How do they do that?"

"Sometimes we hear their voice, but most of the time they speak to our spirit, and occasionally we see them."

"Are they all Indians?"

"No. They take on an appearance agreed upon before you are born. You will eventually understand the significance."

"If he's been with me all my life why did he take so long to reveal himself?"

"Why did you take so long to acknowledge him? Next time you sense his presence, speak to him. Ask him his name and what he wants to tell you."

"How do I talk to him?"

"Open your mouth and talk, just like you talk to me."

"That simple?"

"That simple, but I suggest you're alone."

"Got ya." Dave smiled as he digested Trent's words.

"Wait a minute. Why didn't he warn me about the guys in Carson City?"

"Maybe he did or was trying too."

"One more question, what's journeying?"

"Why do you ask?"

"I had a strange dream about Donny. I asked if I was dreaming and he said no, that I was journeying."

"Journeying is when your spirit travels to the spirit world. It's like astral travel only you can go to the lower world and the upper world."

"Like heaven."

"Yes, but we simply call it the other side."

"I've got a lot to think about." Dave settled against the door and closed his eyes. Suddenly he sat up. "Wait a minute, if everybody has a Spirit Guide then you have one, and if you are so tuned in, why didn't they warn you about Carson City?"

"I wasn't the one in danger."

"But you are now."

"I know, but what would you have me do, let those guys kill you?"

"I guess not." There was a long pause in the conversation then Dave asked. "You are human, aren't you?

"What do you mean?" Trent looked over at Dave.

"You and all this that's going on isn't something that's happening in my head is it? I'm not still back in the motel room in Independence having a nightmare, sleeping off a drunk?"

"No, it's real, all of it's real and I'm human, very human."

"It doesn't all add up, but I'm too tired to sort it out." Dave settled back against the door. "Shit, what a ride." Before long the hum of the road put him to sleep.

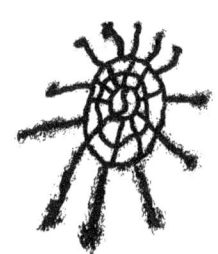

CHAPTER 18

"Where have you been?"

"Out walking." Trent answered and took a seat in one of the two chairs that accompanied a small table in the otherwise sparse motel room at the Mystique Lodge.

"I figured so." Dave had been awake a short time, and had assumed Trent had gone out for one of his usual walks. He was in no hurry to get out of bed as it had been a long ride to Mystique and even though Trent drove, he was exhausted by the time they got into town the night before.

"What time is it?"

"A little after ten." Trent looked at the morning newspaper he brought in with him. "Have a hard night?"

"My hand hurt. Kept me awake a lot. Hope I didn't disturb you."

"No, but I could tell you weren't sleeping well."

"Let me use the room, then you can tell me what you saw."

While he was in the bathroom, Dave put on some coffee in the mini coffee pot. He returned and sat back on his bed. "So tell me, you meet anyone we know?

"Hardly."

"So what's the town like? I presume that's where you went walking."

"It's nice."

"Come on kid, give me a break. Tell me what you saw."

"Well it's a nice, pleasant little town. The business district isn't more than three blocks. There's a grocery and department store, hardware store and a feed and western wear store in a shopping center on the north end of town and a small strip mall on this end. There are a few restaurants, gifts stores and several antique shops scattered in between. Most of the buildings are made to look older than they are, an attempt to make the town look Old West, I would guess. To the west of Main Street is a group of medical buildings with assorted doctors, dentists and what have you. The rest is residential. Oh, on the far end of town is a large park with a stream."

"You should try for a job at the Chamber of Commerce. What about Betty's place?"

"Let me think; it's a gift shop. Cute little stand-alone building with lots of gingerbread."

"What does she sell? Its not a kook joint full of weird stuff is it?"

"I bet Betty would like to hear your description. She could use it on a brochure. Kook-House full of weirdo stuff."

"I didn't mean it like that. It's just that in L.A., anything connected to metaphysical meant weirdo."

"Her place is very nice, not full of voodoo dolls and witch-craft if that's what you mean. She sells candles and incenses, essential oils, figurines of angels, crystals and other beautiful things. She even handles some Native America things made locally."

"I don't know if I believe in all that stuff and I don't want to be pushed."

"Nobody's asking you to believe anything or do anything. Get dressed and go down there and see for yourself, just don't be an asshole."

"Sorry."

"I think your coffee's ready."

*　　　*　　　*

Dave walked the block and a half from the motel to Betty's shop. He stayed across the street and slowly passed the shop and then turned and walked back again before crossing the street on his final approach. He stopped at the window and examined the crystal dolphins, owls and other animals displayed in the window. A stream of sunlight reflected miniature rainbows onto the shelf. Beyond the window display, he could see Betty in the rear of the shop. He felt a rush of excitement. Betty was busy ringing up a customer, and he was sure she hadn't seen him. He decided to wait outside.

*　　　*　　　*

Susan stood in the doorway between the main part of the shop and the back office, and peered through the beaded curtain. She had heard Lorelei come in and now wondered what had taken so long to make up her mind on her purchase. "There you are Lorelei." Betty handed her, her purchase in a gift bag then turned to Susan. "Don't you think that will make a perfect birthday gift for Lorelei's niece?"

"I guess so."

Betty stopped and looked out the window. Susan wondered what had caught her mother's interest. Her excitement was obvious.

"Thank you, dear," Lorelei chattered. "I'm so glad you got back from your trip. I knew you would know just the thing for Kelly."

As Lorelei pushed a lock of her stringy over bleached blonde hair out of her eyes. She too noticed Betty looking out the window, turned and looked to see what had captured her interest. "Did you find anything new or meet anyone interesting on your trip?"

"What? Oh yes," Betty seemed distracted. "I ordered something interesting, new aromatherapy candles, they're supposed to bring romance."

Susan went to the window and Dave stepped back.

"Oh, that's what we need, some romance." Lorelei could see Betty's concentration on something outside the window and turned. "Who is that?" she asked.

"A gentlemen I met on the drive home."

"Girl, you must have been burning one of those candles already? I'll take a half dozen, no make that a dozen.

"Oh Lorelei, don't be silly. I just ordered them."

"Well let me know when they get in." Lorelei said.

"I wonder if Pretty Boy is still with him?" Susan muttered on her way to the back room.

*　　　*　　　*

Obvious that he had been spotted, Dave took a deep breath and opened the door. He stood in the open door as a soft chime announced his arrival. Betty looked up and smiled. Their eyes met and he grinned. He felt an electric quiver through his body. He hoped Betty's curious customer hadn't noticed the silent exchange.

"I'll be with you in a moment." Betty blushed slightly then turned her attention back to her customer. "They'll be here in a week."

"Who? Oh candles. Well, thanks again, I'll see you later."

The elderly lady sashayed toward Dave. He stepped aside and held the door for her as she approached, but she stopped, turned and gave him a thorough once over. He smiled politely and tipped his hat as she stuck out her hand. "Hi I'm Lorelei, welcome to Mystique." Before Dave could say anything, she nodded her approval to Betty then quickly hurried away. Dave turned his attention back to Betty, an excitement burned in him, the likes of which he hadn't felt in years.

"Well, look who's here? Good morning. Welcome to Mystique."

Dave approached and his smile widen.

"Who gave you that?" She reached a hand toward his face.

"Had a little trouble along the way."

"Not Trent I hope."

"Quite the contrary, he saved my ass—" He caught himself. "No, it wasn't Trent."

"Are you all right?"

"Ya, just a little sore." He held up his left hand. "And this, a couple a broken fingers."

"How?"

"Will talk about it later."

"Is Trent still with you?"

"Yeah. He's staying on a few more days. We got in late last night, we've got a room at the Mystique Lodge."

"It seemed you've joined at the hip."

"Huh? Oh, ya, we've become good friends."

"I was kinda expecting you sooner, Now I understand. How is Trent?"

"He is fine. Nothing's happened to him. I've been resting up the last several days with some friends of his." He looked down at her face and wanted to take her in his arms and kiss her so bad he trembled. But instead, he took a step backward and started to look around the shop. "So, this is your shop?"

"Yes. Welcome to Betty's Cupboard."

"I never, ah . . . shop."

"Never shop?"

"Well, I . . . I mean this kind of place." He moved to the center of the shop and turned slowly.

"What do you mean? This kind of place?"

"Well you know . . . I'm kind of stupid about religious things."

"It's not religious. It's just spiritual. And, you're not stupid."

She moved closer to him and he shied away.

"Oh ya, I'm stupid."

"Don't put yourself down, I'll teach you—that's if you want to learn."

He moved slowly toward the door for safety, stopped and looked around again. *Why do I feel like this and why am I so damn tongue-tied?* When he got to the door, he turned as if he were about to speak, then started to turn away. *Hold on, you can do this.*

"You're looking good." She moved closer slowly. "Even with a black eye and that bandage on your nose. It's kind of sexy." He felt like a stray puppy who wanted to be petted and loved, but too afraid to let anyone near.

"I'm a little stiff . . . ." He turned back. *If she only knew how stiff, just thinking of her.* "So are you . . . looking good. I mean" He took a step toward her. "I've been thinking about you."

"Good thoughts, I hope."

"Oh, yes." The passion in his words betrayed him.

"Now, you're embarrassing me."

"I mean . . . Not like . . . ." He looked down with a blush. "I mean . . . I guess . . . a little like that. *I want to take you in my arms and make passionate love to you right here on the floor till our bodies quiver into oblivion.*

Dave looked at Betty, his cheeks dimpled in an uncontrollable smile. *Control yourself boy, she going to know what you're thinking and throw you out.* He could feel a blush of excitement. It embarrassed him and he blushed more. To hide the fire in his face, he turned to items on a shelf, touching them as he did. *You're making a fool of yourself. Calm down, you're not a teenager.* After what seemed an eternity, he gained control enough to speak, "Would you like some coffee?" He struggled to get the words out.

"What?"

"I said . . . ." He took a deep breath. "Would you like some coffee?" He turned. "Will you have a cup of coffee with me?"

"Now?"

"Yes, now." He pointed out the window. "There's a coffee shop right down the street, and . . . ."

"I thought you would never ask."

Dave was surprised and pleased by her answer. He smiled, then chuckled and finally started to laugh out loud. His laugh was infectious. "So did I."

"Let me tell Susan we're leaving."

She stepped through a beaded curtain to the backroom of the store, and Dave expelled a deep breath, as if he had forgot to breathe. He was pleased with himself. Shortly, Betty returned and took his arm. "Ready?"

The door closed with its usual chime. Dave looked back in the window as a silk butterfly fell from a top shelf and fluttered as if alive, then lit on a pink crystal rose in the window.

*   *   *

"Just then Trent let out a yell." Dave took another sip of coffee before he continued his story. "He used some kung foo kinda stuff and knocked three of the guys down. One of the guys tried to jump Trent from behind but the guy missed and face planted himself on the hardtop, knocking himself out cold. Then one of them pulled a gun and tried to shoot Trent."

"No! My God."

"The guy pulled the trigger but missed Trent and shot one of his own goons in the forehead and killed him. Finally the skinhead dove at Trent and smacked the gun man in the face with his head and it did a lot of damage, he died later."

"This sounds like a scene from a movie."

"It's all true, I swear. Then Trent dragged me off to get help."

"Did he take you to the hospital?"

"No, I don't have insurance. He took me to an Indian Medicine Man."

"That's some story."

The sensation of Betty stroking the back of his good hand as they talked began to overwhelm him. As he focused on the small movements of her fingertips on his skin it sent rivers of sensual pleasure up his arm. His whole body began to respond. Their gazes locked. He leaned forward and gently kissed her. When he started to pull back, her lips followed his. His eyes closed as he breathed in her scent, as delicate as a butterfly's touch. He was afraid to open them and end the dream. The continued stroking on the back of his hand was driving him wild. He began to tremble.

"Where are you?" Her lips whispered against his, the vibration ran through his body.

"On the other side of paradise."

The crash of a dropped cup shattered the atmosphere and his thoughts collapsed like a Las Vegas casino being demolished.

Dave blinked himself back to reality. It took him a moment to remember where he was. He looked at Betty and her soft eyes looked back. *You're moving too fast; you may be reading this all wrong. She's just concerned. You're making too much of it.* "Would you like to go for a walk?"

"Very much, but I would like to do something first."

"What?"

"My brother-in-law, my late husbands brother, is a doctor here in town. I would like him to check your injuries."

Dave hesitated. "We are on the family plan, professional courtesy, there would be no charge."

"Well, I guess it won't hurt."

"I'll call and make an appointment." She took her cell phone out of her purse. "Are you free tomorrow?"

"Yes, I guess so."

"This will just take a second."

"Excuse me, I'm going to use the restroom."

In the men's room he splashed cold water on his face. *Cool down boy, it's just her nurturing instincts. You're reading her wrong. You'll never get to first base. You'll strike out as soon as she gets to know what kind of loser you really are.* He ran a comb through his hair, then stopped and looked deep into the mirror. "So, got nothin' ta say? Some Spirit Guide." After a moment he tucked his comb back in his pocket and left. As he returned to the table, Betty stood.

"It's all set. He wants you to have and x-ray at eight tomorrow morning and he'll see you at one."

"X-ray? I don't know if—"

"It's all covered, besides it's doctor's orders."

"I don't know how to thank you."

"I'll find a way."

Dave took care of the bill, and they stepped out the door into the brilliant sunlight. The air was fresh, cool and clean.

"Which way?" Dave asked.

"Would you like to see the town or walk in the country?"

"I'd love a walk in the country."

"Then we'll go left to Knox Creek Park, there is a trailhead there that will take us up along the stream."

"Great, should we tell Susan?"

"She'll figure it out."

She took his right arm and he looked down at her face, he wanted to kiss her, but restrained his urge. They talked as they walked slowly toward the park. He decided to be up front with her and began telling her the assorted details of his life. As much as he desired her, he wasn't going to lie to get her.

At the west end of the park proper they took the Creek Side Trail, a well-marked path running alongside the small but swiftly running stream. When they came to a little clearing with a bench, they sat, and Dave finally ran out of words.

"You're suddenly quiet," She said breaking the silence.

"Just thinkin' . . . wondering if you're ready to go back to town, now that you know who I am."

She looked up at him and put her hand to his face and then kissed him. "Only if you do."

*   *   *

The afternoon had been quiet and Susan was taking advantage of it to start straightening the back room. She had just finished filing the stack of papers on her mother's desk when the chime announced a customer. It was Trent. She had expected a visit from him when she learned he and Dave had finally showed up.

"Can I help you?" she asked professionally.

"Just stopped by to say hello."

"Oh, well hello. We were expecting you sooner."

"We had some problems in Carson."

"You could have called, mom has lots of friends in the area."

"We stayed with some of my relatives, they live way out and don't have a phone."

"Oh." Susan picked up a feather duster from behind the counter and busied herself.

"I didn't know you would be concerned."

"I wasn't." She didn't know why she was annoyed, she just was. "It was mother, she was worried." She corrected herself. "Concerned."

"Oh. Do you know where Dave is?"

"He's with my mother and they should have been back by now." She said sharply, turning toward Trent. He was looking at the butterfly on the crystal rose, the late afternoon sun shown through the window, back lighting him in a golden aura as the rose sparkled miniature rainbows up on his face. *God he's beautiful.* She stared a moment then caught herself, determined not to be charmed.

"Good, I was getting concerned about him."

She could hear genuineness in his voice, as he turned and stepped toward her. He looked at her and smiled, his penetrating gaze caught her off guard. All she could do was stare.

"And you, how about you, how are you?"

Oh God no. She felt her heart melting.

"Could I interest you . . . ." He started to ask.

Could you ever.

" . . . in some dinner?"

*   *   *

Susan sat at the table and watched Trent as he placed the pizza order. He was pure eye candy, and she was going to indulge. There was nothing to lose, she thought, he was just passing through. And as he stood waiting to place their order, she couldn't help but admire the way he filled his tee-shirt and jeans. *Nothing's left to the imagination. He was a hunk.*

During dinner he told her about his childhood, his father's death and that his mother was a teacher at Albuquerque City College. And that he graduated high school when he was sixteen. But Susan didn't pay much attention to his words. He could be reading the want ads for all she cared. She was envisioning him in a much more intimate way.

I wonder if he's a noisy lover? She had to concentrate to keep from her fantasies. *I'll bet he's a quiet gentle lover, strong but gentle, French but part Native American too. Never made love to a Native American. Wonder if all those stories are true.*

"My mom died when I was a senior in high school." Trent continueed his story.

Mother dying? This guy isn't very romantic. Can't be much of a Latin lover.

"I made the promise on her death bed."

What promise? I missed it. What did he promise his mother on her death bed?

"So after I graduated from Fuller Seminary, I was the youngest minister to be ordained in the Native American Church of —"

"What? What did you say?" Susan didn't wait for an answer." *There's the rub. A Preacher, probably a celibate virgin too. I wonder if Dave knows what he's hooked up with.*

"Oh Look at the time." Susan stood. "I've got to run. I'm suppose to meet a friend. Thanks for the pizza. I'll see you around."

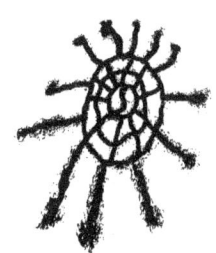

CHAPTER 19

"Where in the heck have you been?"

"Out walking," Dave answered. He tossed his hat on the bed and got himself a beer out of the refrigerator.

"It's after eight, I went down to the shop and Susan didn't know where you and her mother went."

"I'm a big boy."

"Susan and I were worried about the two of you."

"Sorry. We got talking and lost track of time."

"I hope not about the Carson City incident."

"I may have mentioned it," Dave said sheepishly.

"Well let's not broadcast it, we're not that far away from Carson City."

"Don't worry, Betty's not going to tell anybody. We are going to lunch tomorrow, I'll tell her to keep it to herself." Dave sat on his bed. "So you saw Susan, spend any time with her?"

"Some."

"What do you think, you two gonna hit it off?"

"I doubt it?"

"Too bad, I was hoping she might interest you in stayin' around a little longer, maybe even settle down?"

"I'll stay a week or two, but that's it."

"Okay. Now do you want to catch some dinner? I'm starved." Dave opened the door.

"I'll keep you company, but I've already eaten."

"Oh?"

"With Susan."

"Oh."

*　　*　　*

Dave opened the motel door slowly. He knew Trent would be wondering where he had slipped off to so early in the morning.

"Where have you been?"

Dave dreaded the inevitable question. "Betty insisted I have some X-rays."

"What! Why?" Trent sprung to his feet.

"Her brother-in-laws a doctor and she insisted."

"This is more serious than I thought."

"They won't connect anything with Carson City and I didn't mention Harold."

"No. I mean, one day and she has you in to see a doctor, checking you out before she invests any more time on you."

"No it isn't that way either."

Dave hesitated for a moment then caught Trent's telltale grin. "What are you pulling on me?"

"I called Susan this morning, she told me about the X-rays and your appointment this afternoon with her uncle. I think it's good."

"Then you're not mad."

"I wish the Carson City incident had been kept under wraps, but if you are at all serious about Betty, you can't start with a lie."

"I'm glad you understand. I won't say any more to the doctor than I have too."

"That's good." Trent picked up his hat. "I'm going to take Susan some lunch at the shop while you and Betty are out fooling around. I think we had a misunderstanding yesterday afternoon

170

and I want to talk to her some more. "Wanna walk down together?"

"It's a little early, do I detect some eagerness?"

Trent smiled. "Maybe."

"Well, let's go then."

*   *   *

Susan stood quietly as her mom greeted Dave and Trent. Dave and Betty didn't notice Susan's coolness toward Trent as they quickly said their goodbyes and left for the day. There was a long empty silence once the door closed.

"Well. You said you wanted to talk about something?" Susan stood behind the register with her arms folded.

"Would you like to sit down?"

"I'm comfortable. Speak your piece."

"I feel I might of said something last night that may have offended you."

"What makes you think that?" As handsome and charming as he was, Susan wasn't going to let her guard down, she knew what he was going to say. The religious fanatics of the town all had their say when her mom first opened the shop. Now it was only the stray passing-through fundamentalist that came in to preach.

"I kind of got that impression. I think I need to explain a little more about my beliefs."

"Listen. I don't want to hear about your beliefs. I heard enough from your type Pastor, Reverend or whatever your title is."

"That's just it. You gave me a title and assumed I'm someone I'm not. If you want to give me a title, call me a Pohagunt, a Shaman."

Susan's jaw dropped. "Shaman?" She had study shamanism and knew there was a growing renewal of the practice, but never new anyone that called themselves a Shaman.

"That's why I don't like titles. I was ordained so I could go into hospitals and prisons and minister. My degree is in Comparative Religion, because I have an interest in all beliefs and faiths. I'm not here to preach anything to you or anyone."

"Shaman. I—I don't know what to say."

*   *   *

"Where shall we go for lunch?" Dave asked as he and Betty left the shop.

Betty took his hand. "My friend Lorelei, you met her yesterday, has a little specialty restaurant just around the corner." They walked to the corner. "There it is, The Tea Cozy."

"Oh." Dave was a little hesitant.

"It's very good. I guarantee it."

"If you say so."

They crossed the large front porch of the Tea Cozy and Dave opened the door for Betty. Lorelei's teashop was a converted residential home, the front room served as the dining room with tables, each with four chairs, tucked into the four corners. Shelves with teas from all over the world and all kinds of teapots filled the rest of the room.

"Hello, you two, your table's waiting." Lorelei greeted them and showed them to a table in front of windows overlooking the side garden. Once they were seated she scurried to the back room.

"Lorelei lives in the back half of the house."

"Is there a menu?"

"No. Lorelei will make a suggestion. She has a sixth sense, you'll see."

Lorelei returned with two large glasses of ice tea. "Betty dear, I'm going to fix you an arugula salad with apple and pecans tossed with a raspberry vinaigrette dressing and topped with goat cheese."

"That sounds delightful."

"And for you handsome, I'm going to fix a roast beef sandwich on a Kaiser roll with homemade horseradish and red potato salad."

"Sounds good." Dave watched Lorelei duck out to the kitchen. "Is she all alone here?"

"Yes, she does it all herself. This is the oldest home in town."

"This isn't the old dump of a farm house that was falling down."

"Yes, you remember it?"

"Not by looking at it."

"Her parents owned it. When they sold the bait shop across the road, her father fixed up the old place and he moved the family from Susanville."

"I remember when I was a kid hearing stories about the old vacant house being haunted. That's why they called it Mystique Corners."

"Well, you do know the towns history. When Lorelei's parents passed on, she converted the front part to the teashop."

"Is all this stuff for sale?"

"She sells the tea, teapots and all kinds of things. During the warmer months, she rents out the garden for weddings and caters them as well."

"She sounds like a pretty busy lady."

"Oh, she is."

Lunch was every bit as good as promised, but Dave was so enchanted with Betty he hardly took noticed of the food. Lorelei had cleared the dishes and they lingered over their ice tea.

"So are you ready to go to the doctor?"

"I'd rather go for a walk."

"After you see the doctor."

Dave took a deep breath, he never cared much for doctors. "Thanks for suggesting this place," he said as he stood and held Betty's chair.

"I'm glad you liked it."

"Isn't she gonna bring a check?" Dave asked reaching for his wallet.

"I've taken care of it including the tip."

"Well, thank you."

"My pleasure." She took hold of his hand as they walked to the door.

*   *   *

The chime rang as Trent came through the door with two bags from the deli. "I got us veggie subs with provolone and ice tea."

"Bring them to the back, I'm just about finished." Susan had been working in the backroom when Trent and Dave arrived. After her shock at finding out Trent wasn't the religious fanatic she had thought he was, they talked and he helped her wait on customers and straighten the back room, before going to get their lunch.

They had sorted some seasonal decorations, wrapping paper and an odd collection of things her mother never wanted to part with but served no practical purpose, into boxes and put them on the upper shelves. She had one last box to put up and the job would be finished. As she struggled on tiptoes to slide the box on the shelf, Trent put their lunch on the desk and stepped up behind her to help. She felt the warmth of his body against hers as he lifted the box out of her hands and slid it effortlessly into its place. She closed her eyes as the touch of him took her breath away. In the past two hours, she had changed her opinion about him completely. She found him warm, kind and caring.

Suddenly, on impulse, she turned and with his hands still on the box, kissed him on the mouth. His arms fell around her as he kissed back. He pressed gently against her, the worktable to her back, she was caught in her own trap, gladly the prey.

Lost in his embrace, she tasted the fruit of his lips, inhaled his musk and felt him respond to her touch. She melted as she ran her fingers from his broad shoulders down to the small of his back. Slowly, her hands followed the waist of his jeans until they met at his belt buckel. She felt him move back so she could explore. Eagerly, she raised her hands up to his chest, then let them slowly drift down over his firm abs, over the waistband too . . . . The darn chime sounded, she pulled herself away without looking at him.

She stood patiently as the older couple looked over the collection of crystal animals. In her mind, her hands were still on Trent's body, remembering every detail. After twenty minutes the couple finally made their choice and the moment they left the store, she returned to the back room. Trent had set out their lunch.

"I thought we'd better eat lunch, before we got too distracted," he said standing by the desk.

"I agree." *Not really.* Susan wondered if she had moved too fast, but assured herself that he made no effort the stop her. They ate their lunch with only two interruptions.

Each time she looked at him, she could still feel his body in her hands. His muscles, his heat, his response to her touch, replayed over and over in her thoughts and with each replay, she wanted him more. She wondered if he wanted her as well? He was difficult to read.

Susan knew it was going to be a long afternoon.

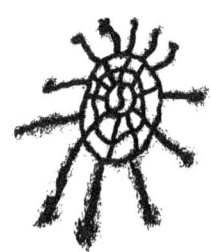

CHAPTER 20

Dave finished thumbing through the same magazine for the third time, put it down and looked at the clock. *Ten minutes? God it seem like we've been here an hour.* The door near the receptionist opened, "Mister Hoffsted?" a nurse asked. Dave and Betty stood and the nurse ushered them into an examining room, closed the door and started the routine of taking Dave's vital signs as she chatted with Betty.

"So, how was your trip to the big city?"

"Oh, fine." Betty answered. "Susan is home for the rest of the summer."

"The summer is going fast. I can't believe it's the end of July already." She grabbed a thermometer, "Open. We don't see much of Susan now that she's away at college and Cathy is married and moved to Chester. I'll simply have to have you and Susan over for dinner. I've got lots of pictures of the new granddaughter." She made some notes on a new chart. "Doctor will be with you in a minute," she said as she left.

"That was quick." Dave looked around the examining room. "Who's Cathy?"

"Her daughter. She and Susan are best friends."

He felt strange, This was the first time anyone had accompanied him to the doctor since he was a kid.

"You'll like Fred. He's a good doctor."

Just then there was a light knock on the door and it opened. Dr. Fred Lawrence was a big teddy bear of a man with white hair. He had a large x-ray folder and Dave's new chart in his hand. "Good morning Mr. Hoffsted. May I call you Dave? I'm Fred Lawrence." He greeted Dave with a pumping handshake. "And Sis, how are you doing?" Betty stood and they exchanged a hug and kiss.

"Fine Fred. Just wonderful."

"Well, Sis says you were ruffed up by some nasty hombres in Carson City."

Oh God did she tell him the whole story?

"Your lucky you're not in the hospital. Our Native American brothers patched you up well. The radiologist and I went over your x-rays. Let me show you." He pulled out the x-rays and clipped them up on the light box. "You have several cracked ribs, all are in place and show signs of healing properly. I would imagine they worked on your kidneys. Did you have any blood in your urine?"

"Not that I'm aware of, but I wasn't aware of much for several days."

"That's understandable, guys like that can do a lot of damage." The doctor switched x-rays. "You have two broken fingers. They have been set perfectly. The Native Americans are masters at setting bones. I'll look at your splint in a minute." The doctor switched out more film. "Your nasal cavity is okay. You're going to have a bump on your nose for a while, but it will straighten out eventually. If the bump doesn't go away in a year you might want to do a little plastic surgery."

"You mean a nose job," Dave said grinning.

"You can get rid of the bandage in a day or two, and I'll give you some ointment that will help heal the abrasion and prevent scarring. Now Sis, if you will excuse us a few minutes, I'll give our boy a look over. You can wait in my office."

"Check him out closely." Betty said with a wink. "See what makes him tick." She let herself out.

"Okay, if you will take off your shirt and lie back."

The doctor examined Dave thoroughly. After several minutes of pokes, prods and listening to his chest and abdomen with his stethoscope in silence, he said, "you can sit-up. Looks good, just take it easy, no heavy lifting or strenuous exercise for a couple of weeks."

"I don't plan on any."

"I'm going to give you a plastic splint. Does the hand give you any pain?"

"Aches a little at night."

"Take some aspirin, if that doesn't help I'll give you something stronger. I want you to keep it splinted for the next four weeks, but I want to see you in two. I'll give you some exercises and you can start taking the splint off when you shower. "Other than that you are in excellent physical shape—"

"For an old fart my age."

"For a man any age. We might want to do a blood panel soon. That's it. You can get dressed while I get the splint."

"You mean I don't have to cough?"

"Oh I almost forgot. Stand and drop your pants please."

Me and my big mouth.

*   *   *

When the doctor finished, Dave dressed quickly, anxious to get going. He stepped across the hall to the office to get Betty and say his goodbyes.

"I want to thank you for the checkup. Anything else I should know?"

"No, you're in fine shape. Here's the ointment for your nose and the splint. My nurse will make an appointment on your way out, I want to see you in two weeks. It has been a pleasure meeting you." He pumped Dave's hand goodbye. "Sis you've got a healthy guy here, treat him well."

"Oh, I intend too."

*   *   *

Dave held Betty's hand as they walked slowly on the same path as the day before. "I don't remember it being so green around here when I was a kid."

"A lot of things are nicer now than when we were young."

A gray squirrel joined them on the trail. It ran ahead then stopped and flicked its huge fluffy tail until they nearly caught up to him, then he ran ahead again.

She's right, things are nicer now than when I was young. The leisurely pace, the thrill of just holding hands, all so meaningless than when you're young. Ah maturity. There are a few good things about growing older.

They stopped where the stream made a bend and the trees opened to a view of Mystique, nestled in the valley. Betty looped her thumb in his back pocket. At first Dave paid little attention, but slowly became aware of her fingers gently raking across his buttock. Just an innocent gentle movement of her fingers, an unconscious act, he thought. Even through the layers of denim of his back pocket, it felt to Dave as if her fingers were lovingly caressing his bare skin. The touch sparked a fire in his groin. He was a kid again and the inferno of a first date burned in his jeans. All of the 'will she' and 'what ifs' of an adolescent suddenly swarmed through his head. *So where is maturity when it comes to passion?*

He turned and kissed her hard upon the lips. His tongue probed and found her willing, He wrapped his arm around her and pulled her close. Her fingers dug in and pulled him firmly against her. Her other hand ran up and down his back and finally rested at the back of his neck. He reached with his left hand and found it useless, wraped in its splint. He pulled away to look at her and she seemed to swoon slightly in his arms. "You okay?"

"I slipped."

He smiled. *It wasn't a slip.*

*   *   *

Throughout the rest of the afternoon Trent had been a perfect gentleman. He would find things to do when Susan waited on customers and they talked when she wasn't. The more she looked at him the more she wanted him and yet he made no move or said anything to indicate he felt the same. She'd even entertained the thought he might be gay, but remembered his response to her kiss earlier and knew he wasn't. Unable to find a good reason for his coolness, she decided she had moved to fast and started beating herself up about it, certain she had crossed some taboo.

It was late afternoon and the shop had been quiet for at least a half-an-hour. They were at the workbench wrapping an order, a wedding gift to be shipped back east. As Susan finished putting on the address label, Trent stepped up behind her and kissed her on the back of her neck. She had been waiting all afternoon for this. He reached under her arms and cupped her breasts in his hands then gently pulled her to him. She felt him fully against her back. He nibbled at her neck and gently rocked against her, like a slow dance. She pushed her hand behind her, and grasped the front of his jeans. Her body blazed, her fingers explored, her inhibitions abandoned, as he moaned with pleasure in her ear. At the feel of his response, she wanted him naked. Frustrated by her attempts to open his fly, backwards, she turned in his arms. Facing him, she unbuttoned his jeans as their lips met. Her fingers found what she wanted and her legs wrapped around his.

The door chime sounded, this time accompanied by a male voice. "Sis? Susan? Hello. Anybody here?"

Susan froze. "Uncle Allen." She gasped and felt Trent tense, this time not from pleasure. In one quick move she released Trent, adjusted herself and made her way through the beaded curtain to greet her uncle.

"Uncle Allen, you made it, moms out but should be back soon." She hugged him and his wife Dianna and greeted their boys as they came through the door.

"You okay Susie?" Allen asked. "You look a little flushed."

"Oh, I'm fine, I've been working in the back."

Just then Trent came through the beaded curtain with the package. "It's ready to go. I'll take it to the post office. If I hurry it will go out tonight."

"Ah, yes that would be great." *Good thinking.* "But before you go, meet my Uncle Allen, his wife Dianna and their two boys."

Susan made the introductions.

"Sorry to have to run," Trent said. "I need to get to the post office,"

"Maybe you can join us for pizza later." Allen graciously extended an invitation.

"Oh, I don't think so, I have some other errands to take care of." Trent turned toward the door. "Thanks for the invitation. Are you staying the night?"

"No, Allen said. "Unfortunately, we have to get back to Reno tonight."

"That's too bad," Trent told Allen. Then he looked at Susan and said, "I'll see you tomorrow. We can continue working in the back room,"

"Oh? Yes, maybe finish what we started."

"It's a promise," Trent said grinning, on his way to the door.

Susan felt a blush and prayed it didn't show.

*   *   *

Betty and Dave walked on, minus their furry escort. The trail looped over a wooden bridge before it returned back to the park. Below the bridge were several large boulders that created a cascade. They stopped a moment on the bridge and then Betty pulled away and ran toward a flat rock near the cascading water and sat, removed her shoes and put her feet in the water. "Come on."

Dave joined her. The clear swift water cooled his feet, but refused to quench the fire that smoldered in his loins. "Bet this creek is pretty good for fishing?"

"I don't know, but there are some good places a few miles north of here. My brother is up there now, fishing."

"I thought he lived in Reno."

"He does, but during the summer, he and his family come up as often as he can get away. They have been camping up there for the past few weeks, they left Reno the day after Susan and I stopped by their place on our way home from L.A.. I'm going to meet them in town for dinner in fact. They have to drive back to Reno this evening. Want to join us?

"I don't know. I don't want to intrude."

"You won't be intruding."

"Trent will be expecting me."

"He can join us too. I'm sure Susan would like that."

"Let's play it by ear."

He turned, aligning their gaze. The hunger for the taste of her lips gnawed in his belly. She leaned back in an unmistakable move. Dave leaned forward, ran his thumb gently across her lips and then lowered his mouth to taste them.

His hand brushed across her breast. Her mouth opened and her back arched, she beckoned his hand's return. He cupped her in his hand, her soft round breast responded to his touch.

She pushed her firming breasts to his chest and forcefully kissed him. His hand found its way under her blouse to the satin cup of her bra. His fingers felt her nipple. He rolled his thumb across it and felt it harden.

Her leg slid between his and he gave her permission. Her hand skimmed his jeans, the soft cotton fabric, the only separation. Her fingers trace the details beneath, sending him into ecstasy. *She wants me too.* His hand worked at the buttons of her blouse. Her fingers lost all restraint.

"Oh gross!" A prepubescent voice yelled from above followed by a round of laughter. The troupe of Boy Scouts out on a hike had taken temporary command of the bridge.

Dave and Betty froze as their passion fled like frighten birds. They laid still. Betty buried her face in Dave's chest as the scouts filed past, each one craned his neck in hopes for a little more education. Dave met each passing gawk with a defiant glare. *Do they have a merit badge for Sex Ed? A few minutes later and they would have got a real education.*

When all the boys were a safe distance down the trail Betty raised her head. Her face was beet red. He smiled at her and knew his grin gave her comfort.

"You enjoy being an exhibitionist." She gave him a pretend hit on his arm.

"I enjoy what led up to it."

"So was I." She sat up a straightened her hair.

"I hope I wasn't moving too fast."

She began putting on her shoes without an answer.

Dave sat up and put on his socks and boots. *Well the party's over.*

"Things were moving a little fast." She finally said as she stood. "However, not necessarily in a wrong direction." With a smile she held out her hands. "Come-on, we've got to get back, I want you to meet my brother."

*   *   *

The chime signaled their return. Coming through the beaded curtain from the back room, Susan greeted them. "I was just about ready to send a search party out after you."

"Hello dear." Betty kissed Susan on the cheek.

A tall man with a military style haircut stepped from the backroom. "Hi Sis." The touch of gray at the temples placed him possibly in his late thirties.

"Hello Allen." She kissed him on the cheek. "Allen I want you to meet Dave, he is half of the team that rescued us. Dave this is my baby brother, Captain Allen Ross."

"Pleased to meet you." Dave extended his hand.

Allen's handshake was like warm steel in a soft leather glove, firm, not a test of masculinity or power, but genuine sincerity. "It's my pleasure. I met your friend Trent earlier this afternoon."

"Where are Dianna and the kids?" Betty asked as she checked the back room.

"The boys got restless, so she took them to the pizza parlor where they could play some video games. Three weeks of camping and they think they're deprived."

"Captain? Are you in the military?" Dave asked. He had never been introduced to anyone with the title of Captain.

"No." Betty patted Allen's chest, "He's one of Reno's finest."

Her words didn't register with Dave at first. He looked to Allen for clarification.

"I'm with the Reno Police Department."

Oh shit! Dave's stomach turned.

"What's wrong?" Betty saw the obviously strained look on Dave's face.

"Oh nothing." *Don't do something stupid.*

184

"So, Dave, you gonna join us for dinner?" Allen asked as he looked out the window.

"No ah . . . I kinda got an upset stomach. Something I must have eaten."

"Well that's too bad."

"You gonna be all right?" Betty asked.

"Yeah, just need to lay down for a while."

"Can I call you later?"

"Sure, room fourteen. Sorry to miss dinner, have a good time." Dave worked his way to the door.

"Nice meeting you. Too bad you're not feeling well." Allen took a couple of steps toward Dave. "Lookout for swinging doors."

"Huh?" Dave was confused.

Allen put his finger to his nose, then made a fist and jabbed the air. *He knows it was a fight.* Dave's heart sank. He actually was sick to his stomach as he dashed from the shop.

*   *   *

Dave slammed the motel room door.

"What's a matter with you?" Trent asked as he sat up. "You look like you've seen a ghost?"

"Worse, I met Betty's brother."

"So did I. He wasn't that frightening. Of coarse I'm not hot to trot for his sister either."

"He's a fuckin cop! Captain. Reno Police."

"Oh shit! I see what you mean. Susan didn't mention that." Dave sat on the bed. "I feel sick."

Trent started to pace then stopped and turned toward Dave. "He's been camping. They left the morning after the encounter, and he probably doesn't know anything about Carson City."

"He's a police captain, he'll find out when he gets back." Dave got a glass of water. "I need a real drink. Wait a minute, how did you meet him?"

"I was at the shop with Susan when the family came in."

"Does she know about Carson City?"

"Yes, seems someone told her mother all about it." Trent gave Dave a harsh look.

"Oh. I'm sorry." Dave sat back on the bed and shook his head. "I guess I told Betty everything."

"Everything? Even about Uncle Willy and Harold?"

"I don't know. I might have. It just kinda came out."

"Holy shit, we're fucked." Trent sat on the bed next to Dave.

"I didn't think I'd hear words like that out of you." There was a long silence then Dave jumped to his feet. "Well maybe Betty won't say anything about it. Cops don't like to talk shop when they're off duty. Besides he won't even be back to work until Monday, that will give us three days."

"I suspect we will be the topic of their dinner, hopefully Carson City won't."

"I don't know about that." Dave's hopes suddenly diminished. "He made a remark about bar doors as I left. Pointed to his nose and hinted I looked like I'd been in a barroom brawl." He sat back on the bed. "Sorry about my big mouth. I'm sure he'll ask Betty what happened to my nose and hand."

"We'll just have to play it by ear."

"I guess I should have gone for pizza with them when he invited me."

"No, you said enough already."

"I'll talk to Betty tomorrow, see if the subject of Carson City even came up.

"I'll feel out Susan, see what she knows."

"You two are getting chummy."

"We've talked a while. Talk about getting chummy. You've been with Betty two afternoons."

Dave lay back on his bed and stared at the ceiling. *Why did her brother have to be a cop?*

"You gonna be ready to snag a burger?"

"I don't want any dinner. Just bring me back a vanilla milkshake." He pulled out his wallet and handed Trent a couple of bucks.

Trent laid the money on the table as he started out the door.

"You sure are a bullheaded Indian."

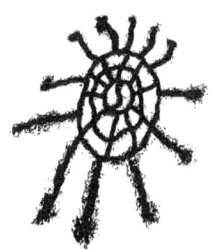

CHAPTER 21

Trent stood on the Knox Creek Bridge and peered into the water below. "You know I don't like this. Why do you hide it from me? How can I help him if I can't remember?"

"You must let him take the lead." The voice of the water spoke. "This is his test not yours. If you knew what he must do, you could influence his decisions. That is why the veil has been drawn. It will be removed when the time comes and you will know what to do then. It is you and Susan that should concern you. Remember your calling."

*   *   *

At the sound of the door Dave sat up in bed with a start and threw back the covers. "Where're you goin'?" Sleep still clouded his thoughts as he tried to quickly orient himself. Assured he was still in Mystique, still at the Mystique Lodge and still facing the Carson City mess, he knew he didn't have a clue of what to do next. For the first time in years, he realized he cared about someone other than himself, the future and the consequences of his actions.

"I'm coming in." Trent answered, startled by Dave's confused reaction.

"What time is it?" The alarm clock on the nightstand was obscured by Dave's carelessly tossed hat.

"It's after ten." Trent sat. "You were asleep when I left."

"Oh shit." Dave jumped out of bed and headed for the bathroom. "Where've you been?"

"I had breakfast with Susan."

"Did you learn anything?" The toilet flushed.

"Apparently the subject of Carson City never came up."

"That's good." Dave slid into his jeans. "What's on your agenda for today?"

"Hangin' out. What's on yours?"

"Tryin' to figure out what to do about you and this Carson City mess. And I wish you wouldn't use the word hangin'."

"I'll take care of myself, but thanks for the concern."

"It's because of me you are in this mess." Dave started a pot of coffee.

"The plan was not to say anything, remember. Now is not the time to over react, we have time to think things out, Allen won't be back in the office until Monday. We have time. The key's not to do something stupid." Trent opened the door. "I'll see you later."

Dave felt uneasy, but trusted Trent's judgment. When he finished dressing, he poured some coffee and sat on the bed to pull on his boots. He couldn't help but worry and wonder how he could help keep Trent out of facing murder charges. He wasn't going to let him down no matter what, not like he did his friends in the past.

Finally, he stood to check himself. In the dresser mirror was the now familiar figure, the Indian. Like several times before, he stood behind Dave, but this time Dave didn't turn, he stood still, looked in the mirror, and studied the tall lean figure in a buckskin breechcloth. Attached to a woven cord at his waist was a leather pouch hung from one side and a sheathed knife on the other. A beaded medallion hung from around his neck along with a necklace of claws and black feathers. Beside his painted face, a single large feather hung, braided into his thick gleaming black hair. Dave was mesmerized by the image, especially the eyes, brown eyes that glowed in a soul-piercing stare.

"Who are you?" Dave asked softly.

I am Silverhawk.

"What do you want?"

I am here for you.

"Is it gonna be okay? Trent, he's not in danger is he?"

He is. Will you stand with him?

"Of course I will." He promised.

Even if you face the same charges as he and receive the same punishment?

"Punishment?"

You could be facing murder charges too.

"But he didn't do anything wrong."

Can you prove that?

"No. Oh! What can I do?"

Stand with him no matter what the cost.

The image faded. "Wait. Don't go. What should I do?"

Dave was alone.

*   *   *

All during their leisurely two-hour walk about the town, Dave wanted to tell Betty about Trent and Silverhawk and ask what her brother might know about Carson City. Somewhere along the way, he stopped worrying and now, as they found themselves near Knox Creek, his thoughts were only for Betty. At the bridge, they took the less traveled branch of the trail west and followed the stream up toward the mountains. They left the trail, crossed the creek and found a secluded clearing where, in each other's arms they melted onto a bed of soft grasses and leaves.

Talk had given way to a quiet communication of a more physical kind. Dave lay on his back with Betty cuddled in his arm, as they watched lazy clouds pass overhead between the open spaces in the trees.

Her hand caressed the soft cotton of his shirt. The thin fabric separated her fingers from his skin. He found the contours of her neck, while she slowly unbuttoned his shirt and slipped her hand inside. Her fingers made lazy outlines of his bare chest. For the first time in his life arousal was coming from his heart and not just his crotch.

Her finger and thumb found a small hard nipple and pinched it, which sent electric pulses through his body. She rose and nipped his other nipple between her teeth and quivers of pleasure chased the electric current.

His fingers found the hooks of her bra and maneuvered them free. She lifted her body to allow his hand to cup her bare firming breasts. He worked his hand methodically between breasts until they begin to harden. He unbuttoned her blouse and pushed her bra aside. Slowly, gently, leisurely he savored each moment, each touch, each pleasure.

He rose above her, swallowed and drew a deep breath. The sight of her uncovered breasts fueled his excitement. She looked up at him and smiled. He moved closer until his lips touched her breast. She lifted herself to him as his lips found her nipple, it tightened hard as he teased it with his tongue. His hand found the nub of her other nipple and he fondled it with the pad of his thumb. She responded. Her response stoked his passion.

The rippling of his flesh beneath her touch followed her fingers to the waistband of his jeans. *Will she?* He wondered. *Am I moving too fast?* She unbuttoned it. *No.* He answered himself as she slid his zipper down. Beneath the sheer weave of his brief he responded as he felt her fingers explore the hard curves and ridges of his firmness, it throbbed as it hardened even more to her touch. Then she slipped her hand beneath the elastic band and traversed his vee of curly hair. He trembled at her touch as his veins flooded with fire. He gnawed at her wanton breasts hungrily, coaxing them to peaks. His primal fires raced like a speeding train.

Exploring his hardness, her fingertips stroked from his soft velvet sack at its base, along the length of his hot hard sensitive shaft to its ridged silky tip, each trip of her finger shot jolts of pleasure up his back. When her fingers encircled his shaft and slowly slid back to its root, he saw in his mind, himself a sleek and powerful steam locomotive engine, and with each trip of her fingers up and down his steaming ramrod she sent him racing toward his destination. He wanted to slow down but couldn't, in her hands he was helpless. That train, his train had passed the mountain's curves and now sped up as it crossed the open plains and headed full steam straight to its glory or demise. He had lost all control of himself and willingly let it go.

Dave's head swam with each stroke, each passionate touch stoked his boiler nearer its inevitable explosion. There was suddenly music in the air as the mighty locomotive past over the last trestle. Unstoppable the stoked engine sped.

The melody repeated. He felt Betty's body tense and her fingers retreat. *Oh God NO . . . .* His body winced with spasm at the first twinge of orgasm.

"I've got to answer," she said as she slid away from him. "Susan wouldn't call if it wasn't an emergency." She sat up and began to dig in her purse for the source of the melodic strains."

The mighty locomotive derailed all alone on the empty plane and spilled its molten hot load. Dave crumpled.

"What's wrong . . . ? Oh, it's you Allen . . . ."

Allen? What a kick in the nuts. His head cleared quickly.

She started adjusting herself with her free hand as if her brother could see her through the cell phone.

"Allen." An icy knife of fear cut through Dave, castrating him of the last lingering remains of passion. *What the hell does he want?* He sat up. The harsh light of humility glared at him as he quickly tried to cover the aftermath of his derailment.

"Yes. Okay. He's right here." She held out her cell phone. "Allen wants to talk to you."

"Me?" he took the phone. "Hello."

"Hello David, this is Allen. I hope I didn't interrupt anything."

"No. Ah, we were just—"

"The reason I called is, we are investigating an incident here in Nevada that happen a few weeks ago in Carson City."

The hair on the back of Dave's neck stood up.

"I'm wondering if you know anything about it."

Oh shit, if I lie he'll know and I'll ruin it with Betty, but if I tell the truth what will happen to Trent? "I don't know, possibly."

"I'd like to come up there tomorrow and talk to you and Trent. I'll meet you before noon, at Betty's store, be there at say eleven and make sure Trent is with you."

"Ah, okay." Dave trembled. The sudden swing of the pendulum so complete in just seconds, his thoughts were nothing but a thick fog. A cold chill embraced him.

"Well, have a good afternoon, I'll let you get back to what ever you were doing. Goodbye and say goodbye to Sis for me."

Dave folded the phone and handed it back to Betty. She had already reassembled herself.

"Are you okay?" she asked.

"Yeah sure."

"You can't fool me. What's wrong?"

"Your brother is coming up tomorrow to talk to Trent and me about what happened in Carson City."

"That's strange."

"The thought of your brother's official visit is a little unnerving to say the least."

"It'll be okay, just tell him what you told me and everything will work out fine."

"He sounded so authoritative. I'm concerned for Trent."

"He doesn't have good phone manners . . . . It'll work out fine, trust me, you'll see."

"I hope so." Dave still sat with his back toward Betty.

"I was enjoying myself before the interruption." She put her hand on his shoulder.

"So was I . . . maybe a little too much."

"Things were moving a little fast."

Too fast to stop some things. "Excuse me." He stood, faced away, adjusted himself and zipped up. He left his shirttail out to cover his obvious spilt load.

"Sorry." She stood and kissed him tenderly on the lips. "Forgive me, I must seem forward."

"Not at all, I was enjoying every moment." Dave smiled.

She looked away. "Now I'm embarrassed."

"You can never enjoy that too much, and it's me that's embarrassed."

"Don't be." She handed him his hat and took his hand. "The next time we won't be interrupted, I promise." She kissed him and they started back toward town.

*   *   *

192

The motel door flew open and slammed against the wall. Trent jumped.

"We got to get you out of town." Dave's voice crackled. "Get your stuff packed."

"What? What are you talking about?"

"Allen has connected the dots. He's coming here tomorrow to question us about the Carson City mess. I'm not gonna let you take a wrap for saving my life. I'll drive you to Susanville tonight so you can get a bus to God knows where."

"But I don't want—"

"I don't care what you want, I'm not gonna let them get you. Now call Greyhound and see if there's a bus out tonight. I've gotta take a shower."

"What about dinner? Susan made reservations."

"Oh shit!" Dave stood for a moment to think. "Call her and make up something, we don't want to create suspicion, but we can't stay around here any longer."

"Do you think you can calm down enough to drive?"

"Let me get a shower. I'll make it. Now call Greyhound and Susan."

Dave grabbed a change of clothing and headed for the shower.

CHAPTER 22

Ahead the lights of Susanville came into view. Dave had calmed, but wouldn't be content until he knew Trent was safely on a bus and putting distance between him and Allen. "If I remember right the Greyhound pick-up was near Denny's?"

"You're right. That's what they said on the phone, next to Denny's. It's just a stop. I pay on the bus."

"I see a yellow sign. Is that Denny's or MacDonald's?"

"Denny's. You can drop me off. The bus won't be here for an hour and a half."

"I'll stay and keep you company."

"You've got a long drive back. I'll be all right. I'll get something at Denny's and wait."

"Are you Sure?"

"Positive."

Dave made a turn into the parking lot and stopped. Trent unbuckled his seatbelt and put the strap of his bag over his shoulder.

"I'm gonna miss you kid."

"Gonna miss you too."

"I was hopin' you could stay in Mystique."

"It's not in the cards."

Dave grabbed Trent by the back of the neck and pulled his head to his chest. "Good luck." He held him until Trent finally pulled away and opened the door to get out. "Wait." Dave pulled a roll of cash out of his shirt pocket. "Here, this will get you started."

"I can't take that."

"Then it's a lone. Two hundred bucks. When this blows over you can pay it back. Send it to me in care of Mystique general delivery."

"Thanks, thanks for everything."

Trent tucked the money in his jean pocket, closed the pickup door and got his backpack out of the back. He walked to the door, stopped, turned and gave Dave a wave. Dave watched him take a seat at the counter. A waitress came up to him and they started to talk. Dave slowly drove out of the parking lot. With a heavy heart he started the lonely drive back to Mystique.

Just out of town he passed the garish yellow-green lights of the state prison surrounded with its high mortar walls and wire fences. "Whatever it takes kid, I'm gonna keep you out of there. They'd kill you in a place like that." Soon the green haze that hung over the prison faded from his rearview mirror. The black road lay ahead, only the stars separated the earth from the sky.

After awhile he could feel a presence in the passengers seat and in the right-hand rearview mirror he saw the now familiar image. Although he could only see him in the mirror he knew Silverhawk was seated next to him. "Why aren't you with him."

You need me more. Dave wasn't sure if the voice was audible or in his head.

"Is Trent going to be all right?"

Yes.

"How long have you been with me?"

Since before your time on earth.

"And you're here to help?"

Yes I'm your Spirit Guide, I'm here for you.

"Then help me protect Trent. What should I tell Allen to-morrow."

The truth, tell Allen the truth.

The words rang in his head as he sensed the presence fade. As Dave approached Mystique, he was relieved to think that Trent was now safely on the bus to somewhere. When he reached town, he drove to Betty's house and stopped. The house was dark. He thought about their afternoon and savored the moments before Allen called. Would his actions tonight end their relationship? He wondered. Was the train wreck a bad omen or a promise of better things to come.

He drove to his motel and entered his empty room. He missed Trent already.

*   *   *

Dave stood outside the door of Betty's shop and took a deep breath. He hadn't slept all night and this morning had been the longest in his life. The chime announced his punctual arrival. Betty smiled and hurried to greet him with a kiss on the cheek. "Hi Hon."

Hon, that's a good sign. "Hi yourself . . . is Allen here?"

"He's waiting in my office."

"Wish me luck." Dave stepped through the beaded curtain. Allen, seated at Betty's desk, wore a navy blue polo shirt with an embroidered Reno Police Department badge over his heart and the name Ross on the right. The small gold bars on the collar that signified his rank flashed as he looked up from a yellow legal pad.

"Good morning David, glad you could make it." As Allen stood to great him, the revolver that hung from his service belt banged against the desk. He extended his hand, a steely cold handshake that chilled Dave. "Please sit. Would you like some water, coffee or soda?"

"Water." Dave settled in the chair facing the desk. He could hear his heart pounding as he realized how different Captain Ross was from the Allen he met two days before. There was no doubt he was a cop and meant business.

Allen got two bottles of water from the small office refrigerator and returned to his chair. He handed Dave a bottle, then opened the second for himself and took a drink. Still standing he looked down at Dave. There was no nonsense in his stare. He looked past Dave to the front of the store for a moment and then back at Dave before sitting, the nerve-racking service belt rattled and squeaked as he did.

Dave broke into a cold sweat.

"Where's Mister Salvador?"

"Who? Oh Trent. I don't know. He was gone when I woke up this morning." Dave looked down at his splinted hand to avoid Allen's scrutinizing gaze.

Tell him the truth. Dave jumped. There was comfort in knowing Silverhawk was present. He looked around the office in hopes that he might see his visual presence. He met Allen's gaze and drew in a deep breath. "Well . . . the truth is . . . I drove him to Susanville last night to get the bus. I don't know which bus or in what direction he went."

"That wasn't a wise move." Allen looked down at the note pad and turned a page. "So, how about you telling me exactly what happen that night in Carson City. You are not under oath, but this is an official statement. Remember you have the right to remain silent. Anything you say can and will be used against you in a court of law. You have the right to have an attorney present during questioning. If you cannot afford an attorney, one will be appointed for you. Do you understand these rights?'

"Yes."

"Now just tell me what happened in your own words. Take your time."

"Well," Dave's voice cracked. He took a drink of water. "It was like this. We finished dinner at a coffee shop a block from our motel in Carson City. When we started walking back, Trent realized he left his bag in the restaurant and went back for it."

"So you went on alone?"

"Yes. Through the alley." Dave took another drink and tried to relax. "I saw something in the shadows. At first I thought it was two men standing in a doorway, but it turned out to be four men in what appeared to be a drug deal. Before I could do anything I was surrounded.

"Can you describe them?"

"The first one was a short heavy Hispanic with a red bandana tied around his head. There was a real skinny one, tall six two or three, with a shaved head and tattoos covering his arms and neck. He had an iron cross, tattooed on the back of his head. There was another skinhead, shirtless with skulls and swastikas blazed on his chest, arms and back. He was a little heavier, about my height. The forth man was better looking. He wore a dark polo shirt like yours without the . . . ." Dave pointed to his own shirt where the embroidered badge was on Allen's.

"I tried to talk my way out of the situation. That didn't work. One of them grabbed my wallet when two others held me. Then something hit me in the gut so hard and fast I kinda blacked out. The next thing I knew I was on the ground trying to breathe. I remember thinking at first I had been stabbed, but I wasn't. Then they yanked me to my feet and slammed me up against a wall. It was metal and made lots of noise. I tried to fight but everything was happening so fast I couldn't do anything."

"Did they hit you?"

"Yes, repeatedly."

"With their fist or weapons?"

"Weapons?"

"Sticks, chains, tire irons?"

"I think it was their fists. In my face and gut, and then a knee to the groin. They let me fall to the ground after that and started kicking me. I thought that was it, thought I was going to die. They kept stomping their boots on the ground and taking turns kicking me. I begged for my life. They laughed and kicked me more."

"Did all of them kick you?"

"Yes."

"Were you conscious the entire time?"

"I don't know. I was in such pain. I think I may of blacked out when they stomped on my hand, but if I did, it wasn't for long."

"Is this before or after Mr. Salvador joined in?"

"Before, I heard this yell, then Trent was standing over me. They started calling him names, taunting him. I told him to run, leave me and run. He wouldn't. He saved my life."

"Okay." Allen made some notes. "So then what happened?"

"I'm a little fuzzy about what all happened and I could only see out of one eye."

"Do your best."

"The tattooed one started to move toward Trent, the next thing I know the man fell flat on his back on the ground.

"Did you see Trent hit him?"

"No."

"So what happen next?"

"Two of the men dove at Trent, he twisted, and they hit each other and fell backwards to the ground."

"Again, did you see Trent hit either of these two men?"

"No." I asked him later about it and he said he just used their energy on each other, some kind of marshal arts. That's when the tattooed guy got to his feet and ran at Trent. The guy dove at him and Trent turned and ducked. The guy flew right over the top of Trent and hit the pavement headfirst, it sounded like a smashing pumpkin.

"Did you see Trent touch this man?"

"No." Dave's voice cracked.

Allen flipped a page of his note pad. "Would you like some more water?"

"Yes, please."

Dave took a deep breath as Allen got him another bottle of water.

"Now tell me about the gun?"

He knows the whole story, Betty must have told him eve-rything. "I heard someone say, 'Hold it right there.' It was the guy in the polo shirt. He was standing a couple of feet from Trent with the gun pointed at Trent's head. They just looked at each other for a moment and then Trent dropped to the ground and the gun fired, the bullet hit the guy with the red bandana in the head. Trent kicked the gun out of the man's hand. That was the only time I saw him come in contact with anyone."

"Okay." Allen was writing feverishly. "So then what happened?"

"Trent jumped back to his feet. The guy crouched down holding his wrist. Then the skinhead, the one without a shirt, started running at Trent. Trent ducked like before and the guy went up over the top of Trent and smacked the gunman in the face with his head. They both went down. There was silence. Then Trent picked up his bag and my wallet and dragged me back to the motel. That's it."

Dave finished off the bottle of water and wiped his lips with the back of his hand as Allen continued to write on his pad. He finally looked up at Dave.

"I have a couple of more questions. It'll only take a few more minutes. First, do you know where Trent is from."

"No, he didn't have any identification in his wallet."

"You saw in his wallet?"

"I looked in his wallet when I went through his pants."

"You went through the man's pants?"

"It was the first evening we were together. He was in the shower, I checked his pockets."

"Anything unusual in his pockets?"

"No." *If he doesn't ask about the bag I'm not telling about the gun.* "So what else do you want to know?"

"My last question. Why would you risk the possibility of being charged with obstruction of justice, aiding and abetting and possibly murder, by protecting someone you've known for approximately three weeks?"

"First he saved my life, in more ways then one. He's the first real friend I've made since high school. I'll do whatever it takes to keep him out of trouble."

"Including lying?"

"No. Everything I've told you is the absolute truth, so help me God."

Allen continued to write for what seemed an eternity, checking back to other pages of his note pad from time to time. He finally took the handy-talky from his service belt. "Steve, you can come in." Allen closed over the pages of the note pad. "David, your actions last night could have put you and Trent in serious jeopardy. However, what you told me lines up perfectly with our eyewitness and Trent's statement."

"Trent's statement?"

"Yes, Trent called me yesterday afternoon. We picked him up this morning in Susanville and took his statement on the way here. I have no jurisdiction in California, but could have you and your friend expedited back to Nevada."

Dave's heart pounded and his field of vision narrowed, all he could see were Allen's lips as he spoke.

"The people involved all have criminal records. However the account is so bizarre, I had to get the whole story. We are not bringing charges against you or your friend." Allen looked up and nodded.

Dave heard a sound behind him and somebody coming through the beaded curtain. He turned to see Trent followed by a uniformed officer from the Reno Police Department walk in. Dave jumped to his feet and hugged him.

"You stinker, I ought to—"

"You ought to what, you might end up with your other hand in a splint." Trent said with a grin.

"Anyone for pizza?" Betty asked. She followed Susan into her office. "It's quitting time. We are closing early today."

"I need the bathroom first." Dave announced and made a beeline.

Dave washed his hands, splashed water in his face, and looked deeply into the mirror. "I get it, Silverhawk, the truth."

CHAPTER 23

"The next time you are in Reno stop by and I'll give you a tour of the station and our jail." Captain Allen said as he stood. He and Officer Steve had polished off most of the three pizzas they had ordered. Pete's Pizza's Saturday night crowd was in full swing.

"Are you leaving?" Betty asked.

"We've got to get on the road." Captain Allan explained. Trent and Dave stood. "No, no, you guys stay put. We know where we parked the car." Allen joked.

Dave extended his hand. "It's been a pleasure, but I don't know if I'm quite ready for a tour of any jail."

Trent and Dave shook hands with Officer Steve as Captain Allan kissed Betty and Susan his goodbyes and then with a salute from Allen, the two men left.

"I think we need at least one round of beer before we leave." Before anyone could answer, Dave headed for the bar and returned shortly with a pitcher of beer and four mugs."

"Dave's firewater" Trent said and winked at Susan.

"Right, my firewater." Dave poured a round of beers. "Here's to a goodbye to yesterday and Carson City and a hello to tomorrow."

They clicked mugs.

"Speaking about tomorrow," Betty began. "I'd like to have that dinner I promised."

"Oh, Mom." Susan turned to Trent, then back to her mother. "Trent and I kinda made some plans." She hesitated. "I was going to take him to Mono Rock, camping."

"Okay." Betty looked at Dave. "Then can I interest you in dinner tomorrow?"

"You sure can."

Pete's Pizza Parlor was still busy but their attention was no longer pizza, beer or conversation.

"I'd like to go for a walk," Trent announced.

"So would I," Susan agreed. "I'll see you later mom."

"Take care." Betty gave Susan a sideways glance. "First one in turns on the porch light."

Susan looked at her mother with a bit of surprise.

"Dave and I might go for a walk too, or a drive."

Susan and Trent made there way to the front door and faded into the evening.

"Well, we are alone." Betty looked at Dave and sipped her beer.

"Are you serious about going for a ride?" Dave looked up with a grin.

"I sure am."

"Well let's go."

They were out the door in no time. Dave's pickup was parked across the street. As they approached, he opened the door for her.

"Do you have a direction in mind?" Dave asked.

"Likely Canyon is nice."

A few miles out of town Dave realized where he was. "My property is along here on the left. I got the map from a realtor yesterday and planned to walk it Monday. Want to come?"

"I'd love to but I've got a full schedule for Monday, but you can show it to me later in the week. We can have a picnic."

"It's a date."

Two miles further they took the Likely Canyon turnoff.

"It's beautiful up here." Dave parked and marveled at the view.

"Come on, follow me." Betty got out of the pickup and started down a path that led them to an observation area, a simple concrete circle with three benches that overlooked the canyon.

"Oh wow!" Dave stepped up behind Betty and put his arm around her waist. She leaned back against him as they enjoy the view and each other's closeness.

The sky continued to darken. The moon was bright against the field of stars, turning the clouds silver. He kissed her tenderly on the neck and inhaled her scent. She turned her head and their lips met in a long gentle kiss. His veins filled with warmth. The sounds of the night filled the air.

He nuzzled his lips to her ear and whispered, "I'm falling in love with you." The words surprised him for they came directly from his heart.

"I love you," she whispered.

Her words took away his breath. He knew nothing in his life would ever be the same. He wanted her in every way possible, but just standing there at the top of the world with her in his arms satisfied his every need.

*   *   *

Trent walked Susan to the park, then up the path to where the street lights ended. In the twilight he could still see her beautiful smile. He took her in his arms. His body ached to have her. They kissed. Could he love her and leave her, he wondered? *I've got to slow this down.*

"I didn't know we had plans for tomorrow," he whispered.

"I'm going to take you camping at Mono Rock. Alone."

"What have you got in mind?"

"I plan on seeing you naked."

"Are we ready for that?"

Trent felt Susan tense. "You will have to promise me something first." He looked into her eyes. "When it's time for me to leave, you won't ask me to stay."

"When will that happen?"

"When my work here is done."

"What work?"

"I can't tell you right now, but you will know, and then I will have to go. But I can tell you it won't be more than a week." There was a long silence. "Promise?"

"Yes, but I won't promise I won't make your leaving hard on you."

"You have already."

"Good."

She reached up and kissed him, and he sampled the sweetness of her lips. He engulfed her in his arms and pulled her tight to him. He felt her warmth. Her soft round breasts pressed against him. He took a deep breath and felt her nipples against his chest. He felt her tongue probed and his mouth was willing. He felt her heart pounding like a native drum. She pulled his tee shirt free of his jeans and dug her fingers into the bare skin of his back. He kissed her forcibly as she raked her fingernails down to the small of his back.

"I still don't believe your just a mortal."

"I assure you I am."

"We'll see."

She slid her hands up under his tee shirt and dug her fingers into his chest. He couldn't contain himself and moaned with delight.

"And am I going to get to see you naked too!" He murmured. Knowing if he gave in to his passion it could destroy them both.

"You better believe it."

He trembled as she ran her finger slowly around his navel. *Do I go with her tomorrow and risk her hating me when I leave, or stop it now and let her hate me forever. What if I can't leave her? What would happen if I stay? Mortal? If she only knew how mortal I am. What can I live with?*

"You are going to have to prove your mortality." Her hands caressed his jeans. "I'm going to make it very hard."

*   *   *

Dave pulled up in front of Betty's house and killed the engine and lights. The porch light burned a soft yellow.

"It looks like Susan beat me home."

"I hope she isn't worried."

"Let it be her turn to worry a little," she said and turned to Dave with a smile.

"I enjoyed our drive." Dave didn't want the moment to end. "I'll see you tomorrow?"

"With bells on. What time?"

"Noon."

"Can I bring anything?"

"Your smile and a hearty appetite, I'll take care of the rest."

Dave walked Betty to the door then took her in his arms and gave her a long goodnight kiss. "I love you."

"I love you too." Their lips touched. "You better get a good nights rest." Her words vibrated against his mouth. "I'm fixing dinner, but I'm counting on you being desert."

"I'll be ready."

Before parting, he gave her one last kiss. He walked backward toward his pickup, gave her a last reluctant wave and then got in and drove away.

*   *   *

Susan could see Betty through the window leaned against the porch post and knew she was watching Dave's pickup's taillights fade. She glowed in a way Susan hadn't seen in years. She had no doubt that Dave had touched her mother's heart.

Susan opened the door and stepped out. "Well, it's about time."

"That is exactly what I have been thinking. It's about time." Betty took a seat in the porch swing. "Come sit."

"Mom . . . you like him?"

"When that lanky city cowboy swaggered up to us at the rest stop and asked, 'You ladies have a problem?' I fell in love with him."

"But he seems a little—"

"A little what?"

"Not your type."

"What is my type?"

"Well not him. He seems kind of lost and shallow."

"Lost perhaps, but shallow, never . . . hurt, more hurt . . . a wounded spirit. He's so different."

"He's different from—"

"Your dad? It's all right honey. You can say it. No, he's not like your father. I know." Betty ran her fingers through Susan's hair for a moment, and then looked in her face.

"I didn't think I would ever be interested in a man again." Betty continued. "When Dave and Trent stopped to help us, well at first I suspected something. A boy and an older man, you know. Then I looked into Dave's eyes, just a brief glance. I felt something, recognition. At first I thought is was just the loneliness in his eyes. But it's more, it was like I knew him. Then, when we were having lunch, and he said he use to live in Susanville, I thought, that's it, I knew him then. But when I thought about it, I realized I could never have met him there. We were never there at the same time."

"Maybe you met somewhere else?"

"Well that's what I thought . . . . But at the diner, when I took his hand, I knew I had held his hand before. And the other day, when we went for coffee and a walk, it was as if I've known him all of my life. I knew what he was going to say before he said it. And when he held me, I was safe and secure. I can't explain it. Even his smell is familiar, like cologne. When I asked him what cologne he was wearing, he said he wasn't wearing any. It's like I've known him from another lifetime."

"Like the stories about soulmates?"

"That's it, a life partner, someone I've shared a love with in another lifetime."

"Take it slow mom, please. Be wise."

"Wise hell, I'm gonna marry that man."

"Mom!"

"If he would have asked me I would have gone to Reno with him tonight, called Allen and said meet us at the wedding chapel, I'm gettin' married."

"Mom, please take it slow."

"Honey. I've been dead in the water for twelve years. It's time I start living again."

"Just be careful."

"I promise. I'll let him make the first move as long as he doesn't take too long." She smiled with a wicked little laugh. "We are having our dinner here tomorrow and who knows."

"I know, I'm gonna get lost. I'm taking Trent camping to Mono Rock. I have everything ready, we'll be back Monday morning."

"Now I'll tell you, to be wise, he's a drifter."

"I think it's to late. I know he's only passing through. He's a migrating butterfly to love and enjoy while it's here, but remember it cannot stay."

"Why can't he stay?"

"I don't understand completely. He said he has a job to do here in Mystique and when that's done he will have to leave. He's hinted that it is of a spiritual nature. He told me he was a Shaman."

"Be careful."

"Oh mom, I will, I know how to take care of myself—"

"Just make sure he's not feeding you a line of bull. I don't want you to get hurt. You know you can't make him stay."

"I know. But, I want to take him to the mountain and leave him there breathless and gasping for air. We will love each other completely and when it comes time to part, we will return all but a tiny part of each other's hearts. I want to be burned in his memory so powerfully that no matter what woman he is with, I will be the image he sees. I want to make it so difficult on him to leave I will know only God could part us."

"Dreamer." Betty kissed Susan's forehead. "Be careful in your fantasy," she whispered. "As difficult as you make it for him to leave, you will make his leaving harder on you."

"I know."

"I love you and don't want to see you hurt."

"Oh mom."

"Oh mom." Betty mocked. They laugh.

*   *   *

When Dave returned to the motel, Trent was just getting out of the shower. "Hey, I've got a bone to pick with you, get dressed and meet me in the cocktail lounge, we need to talk."

Dave left before Trent could say anything. He quickly crossed the courtyard to the lounge and found a quiet out of the way table. He ordered two shots of whiskey and waited for Trent. Within five minutes Trent walked in, spotted Dave and joined him.

"So what's up? It sounds serious."

"Cheers," Dave lifted a drink and pushed the other toward Trent.

"Cheers," Trent took it, held it for a moment and looked at Dave, then they downed the shots at the same time.

"Okay, speak to me, what the hell did you pull?"

"You wouldn't listen to me. When I called Greyhound they said the service to Susanville had been discontinued decades ago. So I decided the best thing to do would be talk to Captain Allen. While you were in the shower I called Susan and got his number. I called him; he said he didn't think there was going to be any trouble as long as our stories checked out. It was his idea to pick me up in Susanville and take my statement then yours, without you knowing he talked to me."

"So you knew there was no bus and you were going to meet Allen before we even left Mystique?"

"Yes." Trent looked at his shot glass. "I waited for you to head back to Mystique then met up with Captain Allen." Trent took the roll of money out of his shirt pocket and stuffed it in Dave's.

"No, you keep it."

"That's your money, I don't need it"

"I'm pissed with you." Dave waved to the waitress to bring another round. "You could have let me screw-up the whole thing."

"I had faith in you."

"So did someone else."

"Oh? Who?"

"Silverhawk."

"Who?"

"Silverhawk, that's his name, the face in the mirror, my Spirit Guide.

The bar maid brought them their drinks. Dave paid her and waited for her to leave.

"The other day I saw him in the mirror so I did what you said, I spoke to him. He said his name was Silverhawk, my Spirit Guide. Then, last night, on the way back from Susanville, I got the feeling I wasn't alone. I knew it was him in the pickup with me. I asked why he wasn't with you. He said I needed him more than you. I see why now. I had rehearsed a pretty good story about how you didn't have a thing to do with the deal in Carson City. I was gonna say I did it. Then Silverhawk told me, if I were to help you, I had to tell the truth."

"The truth is usually the best. I'm proud of you Dave."

"Something else I want to talk to you about since you started it."

"What's that?"

"I realized this evening that I'm in love with Betty. I think I'm going to ask her to marry me . . . tomorrow."

"That's quick."

"If she's my life partner, why should I wait?"

"Now I know you've been seeing things. Congratulations."

CHAPTER 24

"You have an hour yet," Trent said. "Will you sit down? You're driving me crazy."

Dave paced like a caged animal. He was on his third change of shirts and had combed his hair a half-dozen times.

"Oh God, I'm nervous. What if she doesn't feel the same about me?"

"She said she loved you. Calm down, relax and please sit."

He stopped and looked around, trying to decide where to sit. He finally parked on his bed. "Do you think she likes me? Oh, that's stupid."

"What's not to like?" Trent kidded. "You may not be much of a catch, but you're likable . . . most of the time."

"Seriously, what do you think, is it too late for a guy like me to really find someone, someone special?"

"You know what I believe."

"I don't want to screw this up."

"You will never know if you don't give it a chance. Go, spend the day, have dinner, it's just dinner."

"You're right, it's just dinner," Dave agreed.

"A nice quiet, romantic, candlelight dinner for two. Then afterwards, a little talk, a little dessert. Who knows? Maybe you'll get lucky."

"Oh shit." Dave jumped to his feet. "That's what I'm afraid of, getting lucky. I can't get lucky."

"Aren't you a little mixed up? Isn't getting lucky what you want?"

"Look." He sat beside Trent on his bed. "Can I be honest with you?"

"That's up to you."

"Well I sort of got this problem."

"Yeah, well?

"It's a guy thing.... It doesn't always work right, you know, downstairs. Sometimes lately it misfires, jumps the gun so to speak. Like the other day Betty barely touched me and *pow*! I creamed my jeans. And other times, over the past couple of years, I can't even get it out of the holster, if you know what I mean. I'm afraid if I get, *LUCKY,* I'll embarrass myself."

"Well what do you expect me to do about it?"

"I thought, with your stuff, your Indian concoctions in your bag, there might be something that would help."

"Sure, but you don't need it."

"Come on, give me something."

Trent took a packet of herbs out of his buckskin bag and put them in the coffee pot in the bathroom to brew. "It will take a few minutes."

Dave checked his watch. "I've got time."

"While it's doing its thing, let me give you some warnings."

"Warnings?"

"Yes, if you drink it and don't have sex by midnight, your dick will fall off."

"What?" Dave looked a Trent stunned, then saw his lips start to curl. "You're kidding me."

"Yes, but you will need to take some precautions. This will increase the blood supply to your penis, so be careful. If you have

214

an erection that lasts more than four hours, seek immediate medical help."

"You sound like a Viagra commercial."

"That's what you want isn't it?"

Yeah, but I thought that four hour business was just some tricky advertising gimmick, a four hour erection, who should be so lucky."

"I'm serious, everything in life comes with some risk."

"Well, if I have *that* problem I'll call you."

"I won't be around."

"Where are you going?"

"Susan and I are going camping . . . to a place she calls Mono Rock, near Eagle Lake."

"Eagle Lake? That's the same area where The Castle Rock is. . ."

"Your brew is ready." Trent poured the herb tea into a cup. "Are you sure you're ready for this?"

"I'm sure." Dave took the cup and held it for a moment. Wait a minute, how long does it take to work? I don't want a teepee in my pants all day."

"It will work when you need it and last quite a while, one dose is all an Indian ever needs."

"I'm not an Indian."

"Near enough. It will do the trick, I guarantee it,

Dave took a sip of the hot liquid and made a face. "It tastes like piss," he said and laughed. He finished the drink and gave Trent a thumbs-up sign. They both laughed.

Trent took a box of condoms from his bag and tossed it to Dave. "You will need these."

There was a knock at the door. Dave quickly tucked the box in his pocket as Trent opened the door. Susan stood ready for their camping trip.

"Hi. Come in." Trent welcomed her with a kiss as Dave took his empty cup to the bathroom.

"Are you ready?" Susan asked.

"You bet, let me grab my stuff." Trent put the strap of his bag over his shoulder and grabbed his backpack.

Dave followed them to the door. "You kids have fun."

"We will." Susan answered. "You too."

"Oh I plan on it," Dave responded.

"See you later. Remember what I said about four hours."

Dave blushed at Trent's repeated words of warning and closed the door.

Checking himself once more in the mirror, Dave glimpsed Silverhawk. "If your gonna follow me around all day today, I hope what I plan won't embarrass you."

It won't.

*   *   *

Dave fussed around the motel room for a half-hour after Trent left, drove the town and was still early when he pulled up and parked in front of Betty's home. He jaunted up to her front door with flowers in hand and rang the bell. His heart raced when he heard the latch and the door started to open.

"I hope I'm not too early." He handed her the flowers. "They couldn't wait; they needed water."

"Good morning." Betty, equally happy to see him, kissed him on the cheek and took the flowers. "How sweet. Come in."

He followed Betty through her country cottage style living room to the similarly decorative kitchen. She found a vase for the flowers and placed them on the dining table.

"Would you like some coffee or ice tea?"

"Ice tea would be fine."

"I made us a pitcher. It is such a beautiful day, let's go out on the patio." She handed Dave the glasses and took the pitcher from the refrigerator along with a bucket of ice and led him to the backyard with its canopy of mulberry trees.

"This is nice."

"The trees are wonderful, but the leaves get a little messy in the fall." Betty placed the ice on the table and filled their glasses. They sat together on the large yard swing. "There, isn't this comfy?"

"Perfecto." *Oh that was dumb.* With nowhere to set his drink, he sipped at it and awkwardly tried to hold her hand with his splinted hand. *Now what?*

*   *   *

Susan drove around the west side of Eagle Lake, then took a narrow paved road which eventually forked to the dirt road that led to Mono Rock. When she reached the clearing at the base of the large monolith, she parked. Trent got out of the SUV and quickly opened the door for her.

"How did you ever find this place?"

"My dad use to bring us here camping when I was little."

"You miss your dad?"

"Very much, but here I can sometimes feel his presence."

"There is a lot of energy in this place."

After several minutes they started to unpack and set up camp. Trent pitched the tent near an old rock fire ring, the only indication of previous campers. Fifty feet from the tent a stream babbled a constant song. Susan opened a camp table and chairs as Trent finished staking the tent and then he helped her with the ice chest. Together they inflated a large air mattress, positioned it in the tent and then opened the sleeping bags, which were already zipped together.

Trent headed out to collect firewood as Susan finished arranging the camp. He soon had stacked enough wood to last more than one night.

"Are you ready for a sandwich?" Susan asked. "I made avocado and cheese."

"That sounds great."

"After we eat we'll climb to the top of Mono. I want you to see the castle on top."

"Castle?"

"Yeah, the top is shaped like a stone castle. They sometimes call this The Castle."

"I'll be, Dave talked about going to a place called The Castle Rock when he was a kid living in Susanville. He said his last happy memories were of this place. I wonder if he knew your father?"

*   *   *

"So Susan took Trent camping." Dave said. "Mono Rock, I" don't think I've heard of it.

Betty had arranged a pair of TV trays for their drinks and plates of Hors d'Oeuvres, then snuggled back to Dave on the swing."

"Mono Rock, it's north of Susanville. The locals call it The Castle."

Dave stiffened. "The Castle?"

"Yes, do you know it?" Betty felt the alarm go through Dave's body. "Is there something wrong?"

"I use to go camping there with my buddies when I was a kid and lived in Susanville."

"That's where Jake, Susan's father was from."

"But I thought you were from San Francisco?"

"I was. I met Jake in college at Berkeley. He used to take us camping at the Castle when Susan was little. It's her favorite place. Did you go to high school in Susanville?"

"I sure did."

"Did you know Jake, Jake Lawrence?"

"The football player?" Dave questioned.

"Yes, he went to U. C. Berkeley on a football scholarship.

"I didn't know him personally, but I certainly knew of him. He was a couple of years ahead of me in school."

"Isn't that amazing. You both going to the same high school."

*   *   *

Trent took Susan in his arms as they stood together a top the monolith taking in the view. They looked out over the trees and vast valley beyond. The afternoon sun hung low in the sky behind them as huge white thunderheads built to the south.

"The world is in a better perspective when viewed from a place like this." Trent said softly.

They watched the billows of white clouds build one a top of another. "Do you think Dave is right for my mom?"

"No question."

"How can you be so sure?"

"I just know."

"I wish I could be so certain. He seems so lost and misguided."

"He was lost. He took a wrong turn nearly forty years ago. Believe it or not, many of his problems started at the base of this very rock. He has been trying to find his way back ever since."

"I don't know that my mother needs that."

"Your mother needs him. Since your father went to the other side, your mother has been alone except for you. Now you are getting ready to start your own journey. It's time for her to let go of you and start living her own life again."

"Your right, but I just don't know if he is Mr. Right."

"Their paths were charted to cross. They have in the past and now it's time they walk the same path. He has always needed her and now she needs him, as well. She is the only one who can help him find his way. Believe me."

"I don't know why, but I do believe you. You seem so positive."

"I am positive." He kissed her on the neck.

She turned and their gazes met. Her lips found his wanting, as she pressed herself against him. A gust of wind blew across the top of the monolith, bringing a chill and the smell of rain. She clung tight to his warmth.

"We better get down from here," Trent said. "It looks like we are in the path of that thunderstorm, and this is not a good spot to be in when it hits."

She heard Trent's words, but was reluctant to let go of the moment. "Darn rain. I wanted this to be perfect."

"Who says it won't be perfect? We have shelter." Another breath of cool wind brought the distant rumble of thunder. "We need to get down."

"Just another minute, please."

*   *   *

After dinner Dave helped Betty clear the table and then started to scrape the dishes and stack them in the dishwasher.

"That can wait 'til later."

"I don't mind helping," Dave insisted. "There's only a couple of things left. Besides, there may be better things to do later."

"You're right and I have a couple in mind."

Dave stacked the last of the utensils in the dishwasher as Betty wiped down the counters.

"There, that's it, kitchen is closed."

She ushered Dave toward the living room where the flames from a collection of colored candles on the coffee table dance at their movement. Dave sat on the sofa expecting Betty to join him, but instead, she disappeared down the hall.

She returned with a basket and rolled-up mat, sat the basket of colored bottles and crystals on the floor and unrolled the mat. Dave looked at her questioningly.

"I'm going to give you a massage," She informed him. "I'm going to change and while I do, I want you to take off your clothes and lay on the mat. Here's a towel to cover with."

"You want me to take off everything?"

"Everything, down to your birthday suit, then lay on your stomach, I'll be right back." She again disappeared down the hall.

Dave quickly undressed. When he was down to his briefs he checked the front door to make sure it was locked and hooked the safety chain. *Well Trent, it looks like I'm gonna get lucky, real lucky, I hope that concoction works.* He then slipped off his briefs, wrapped the towel around his waist and lay on the mat in anticipation of her reappearance.

Betty returned in a white silk robe. She turned out the lights, turned on the stereo and knelt at Dave's side. In the flicker of the candlelight, he was sure that she was naked under her robe. He felt her pull at the towel so it just lay across his butt.

"Comfy?" she asked.

"Un huh."

"I want you to completely relax."

He trembled as she poured warm lavender scented oil on his back and began the massage. The magical Indian elixir was rising to the occasion. "That feels Wonderful."

*　　*　　*

When Susan and Trent reached the foot of the monolith, a heavy rain started to fall. Susan was upset and cold, sure her great plans were ruined. They quickly covered everything in camp that might be damaged by the rain. There was a loud crack of thunder and the rain came harder. By the time they made it into the tent, they were soaked.

"I guess we won't need the firewood I gathered."

"Not for a while." Susan started to shiver.

"You need to get out of those wet clothes."

"I know, but all of our dry clothes are in the SUV."

"I'll go and get them."

"No. No need, I'll just slip in to my sleeping bag." Susan started to unbutton her blouse. "You need to get out of your wet clothes, too."

"If you insist." He stood, his head touched the top of the tent as he pulled off his tee shirt. The tent lit-up to the accompaniment of another crack of thunder, yet they hardly seemed to notice. He hung his shirt from a rib support of the tent then started to pull off his boots. Susan removed her blouse and Trent hung it with his shirt while she removed her shoes.

The tent was growing darker but in the dim light and the near constant flashes of lightning she watched Trent poke his socks into his boots and stuff them in the corner. She handed him the rest of her clothes, but didn't climb into her sleeping bag. When he finished hanging her things, he unhooked his belt buckle and she trembled, but this time not from the cold. He unzipped his jeans as the lightning brighten the interior of the tent. She watched him slide them off to the accompaniment of thunder and her veins flooded with warmth. Her body throbbed as she watched him slowly take in her nakedness. "Not fair, you were supposed to let me see you naked first."

He smiled, slid off his boxers and stood before her. The lightning flashed as it was her turn to inventory him.

"See anything interesting?" She didn't answer. "Is it what you anticipated?"

She couldn't speak. All of her expectations were surpassed as he stood before her, the most spectacular man she had ever seen. When her survey at last found its way to his face, their gazes align. Their escalating passion becoming evident as they caressed each other with their gaze. The lightning continued to flash; the thunder rolled and the rain beat against the nylon tent. Oblivious to the tempest, he came to her.

*   *   *

Betty moved to Dave's feet when she finished with his back and began to slowly work her skilled massaging hands up his legs until she reached the towel. When she did, she slid it away and whispered, "Turn over."

Dave hesitated for a moment, then with his eyes closed turned on his back. He felt more of the warm oil poured across his chest and down his belly. He opened his eyes to see Betty's smile in the flicker of the candlelight and as he felt her caress through the warm oil, he watched her eyes. He could see the apparent pleasure in her face at what she saw. Her fingers glided across the width of his chest on the oil, gently but firmly back and forth several times and then slowly down past his belly. He felt her lay beside him and when her fingers began to explore all of him, a high voltage shock of passion ripped through his body.

"Is this all right?" Her faint voice asked as her fingers slid over him.

"It's right."

"Are you sure?" Her hand encircled him. She stroked slowly, he was hard, harder than he could ever remember.

"Oh, I'm sure."

Her hand slid down and gently explored the soft pouch of his stones, gently squeezed and rolled them between her fingers until bolts of intense passionate pleasure shot through him. There in the candlelight, she came to him.

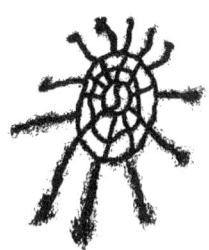

CHAPTER 25

Outside the tent Susan heard the storm's fury wane. Inside Trent slept as she lay cuddled in the crook of his arm. She had brought him camping to make love to him, so he could never forget her. She knew now the table had turned and it was she who could never forget him. In the darkness, her fingers trace and retraced every detail of his body. Softly and gently they moved as not to wake him. From his lips so soft and warm they moved to his strong rock solid chest, and when her fingers stopped and teased at a small hard point of a nipple, he moaned. She had brought him to the mountain and he took her to the stars and kept her there longer than she ever thought humanly possible. *Was he the mere mortal he claimed, or the angel she believed he was,* she wondered. *Would or could an angel make love like that?*

Her fingers traced and memorized every muscle and curve as they moved down across his abdomen. Ever turgid and flaccid curve of his body was forever burned in her memory, along with the images created by the lightning of his nakedness as he made love to her. *How can I be so in love with a man I've known such a short time? Did I cross the line? Can I let him go?*

Her fingers found and began to fondle the cradles of his seed, cloaked in their suede pouch. She felt their weight as she cupped them in her hand and remembered how cautious he was with the use of condoms to make sure he did not impregnate her. *What would a child be like that sprang from his loins? Will there ever come a day when he will be free to plant his seeds?* Images of what his children might be like passed through her thoughts.

He stirred; a soft tender sound of pleasure came from deep within his throat as he slept. "Arouse and arise you root of passion." She whispered as she took him in her hand. "Wake again my angel and take me once again to the stars," she prayed, as her fingers began to make love to her sleeping angel. "I don't care what future pain it might bring." When she felt his passion rise like a phoenix, she knew he was ripe and ready to be loved.

"Are you awake?" she asked.

"Yes."

*   *   *

Dave lay in Betty's bed, as she slept in his arm. The soft glow of a table lamp gently bathed the bedroom with warm light. The room revealed Betty's love of country style without being so feminine as to make Dave feel uncomfortable. The memory of the evening replayed in his head as he savored every moment.

Suddenly he sensed a movement in the room and opened his eyes. *Susan is home and I'm in her mother's bed.* His heart pounded. Then standing in the shadow just past the foot of the bed he saw the faint form of Silverhawk.

"How long have you been here?" he asked softly, not to wake Betty.

All evening.

"You mean when we were—I shouldn't of asked."

You did well.

"Trent's concoction worked. I've never had a night like this."

Maybe it wasn't the potion. Maybe you are in love.

"I'm in love, but I'm sure Trent's potion had more then a little to do with my performance."

Love is a remedy that cures a multitude of ills. It's love that made you perform the way you did tonight. It's love that makes you feel the way you do now. And it will be this love that you'll carry into eternity.

"I hope you're right."

I'm right. He faded.

Dave weighed the words his Spirit Guide had spoken. He remembered the sweat lodge and the experience of being with Betty there and then tonight and his body responded to his memory. *Is orgasm God, and heaven all rolled up into some Divine mystical spiritual forever?* Dave jerked as he bumped the edge of sleep. *Have I been dreaming?* he wondered.

His sudden movement had wakened Betty. She looked up at him and smiled. Her hand slid up his leg in a caress, that found him ready.

"Are you awake?" She asked.

"Yes."

*   *   *

"I brought you here, intending no strings attached." Susan spoke softly. In the dark tent as she clung to Trent. "Now I'm caught in a web I don't think I can escape. Can't I tempt you to stay?"

"You have tempted me more than you will ever know, but I have made a commitment. Someday I hope you will understand."

"When are you leaving?"

"Soon, when my work is done."

"You spoke of your work before, what work?"

"All I know is I am here for Dave, I don't know all the details so I can't influence the situation. I will know what I need to know when the time comes.

"Who do you work for?"

"I'm what some call, a Mystic Traveler."

"Why have you let me fall in love with you?"

"I warned you."

"I know."

"Trust me on this, everything happens for a reason."

"I try to believe that, but it's not always easy." Her fingers played across his chest as she tried to make sense of his words and her feelings. "I know I've asked you before, but are Dave and my mother really made for each other?"

"Yes."

"Is there a hesitation in your voice? What's wrong?"

"No matter what happens in the next few days you must believe it is their destiny to be together."

"You're frightening me."

"Don't be frightened."

*   *   *

"Will you marry me?" Dave blurted out the words. "There, I've been wanting to ask you that all day. In fact I've been wanting to ask you that ever since we had lunch in Bishop."

"I've been expecting you to."

"Well will you? I don't have much to offer other than love and a promise to work hard."

"What else could a woman ask for?"

"I've got some land, but no retirement or money in the—"

"Ssssh." She touched her finger to his lips. "I've been through that with Susan and my brother. Material possessions don't make a marriage."

"So you've been thinking about it too? What have you concluded?"

"I fell in love with the most incredible man I've ever met at a hot windy rest stop. I won't let anything keep me from him."

"What about Jake?"

"Jake was of another time. I'm not looking for another Jake. I have found the man I want to spend the rest of my life with. Yes, I'll marry you."

Dave's heart pounded. "I was so afraid you would say no." He leaned over her and kissed her. His hand ran over the soft skin to her breast and he cupped it gently in his hand. They lay cuddled in each other's arms. In his ear she whispered. "Don't be afraid."

A blissful calm settled over them. He closed his eyes and began to drift toward slumber, when suddenly his body jumped as it nudged the door of sleep.

"Are you okay?" Betty asked.

"Fine, just dozed off a bit. Must have been dreaming. I guess I should be going."

"Why?"

"I don't know. I just want to be proper I guess. Don't want the neighbors to talk, you know, my pickup parked out front all night."

"The neighbors will say it's about time. Lay down." Betty reached up and turned off the light then cuddled back to Dave.

"When should we get married?" he asked.

"Soon. Spring would be nice for a garden wedding."

"What do you have in mind?"

"Lorelei's garden. Her garden makes a perfect place. I always thought I would see Susan married there, I never thought it would be me.

*   *   *

Trent woke. Susan lay sleeping beside him. As not to wake her, he carefully maneuvered to the opening of the tent. In the dim misty moonlight he admired her beauty, the fire still burned in him. Gently he covered her nakedness with the sleeping bag and slipped out of the tent.

A strange ground fog had settled in after the rain. It glowed an iridescent blue under the full moon. As he stood, the mist surrounded him, cool and refreshing against his bare skin. He turned from the tent and walked into the fog. The dense vapor completely obscured the campsite, robbing Trent of any sense of direction. After several cautious blind steps, he could make out the trunk of a large pine tree. He stopped and spoke in a hushed voice. "Badger, guardian of the lower world. Awake, I need to speak with you."

In the damp mist he kept a vigilant watch at the base of the tree. After several minutes he repeated. "Badger, guardian of the lower world, I must speak with you. Awake." Finally, after standing motionless for several more minutes, Trent could perceive a movement at the base of the tree. Slowly, as if a part of the ground, a large round head began to lift. The leaves and grass parted and a sleepy-eyed creature rose up before him. Its fur more of earth than hair, the sleepy figure wiped his beady eyes and looked up at Trent.

"Who is it that disturbs my slumber?"

"It is I, Trent. I have need to talk to you."

"My counsel?"

The creature stepped forward and began to sniff closely at Trent's genitals. He could feel the hot breath snorted out during the intense personal scrutiny. At times he felt the creature's hot bulbous nose press against him, but he dare not move, because he knew that with one snap of its enormous mouth, he would be emasculated. He had called him and now he had to withstand the humiliation as Badger uncovered every secret moment of his night of passion with Susan.

"It seems you have been taking counsel of another kind." Finally the beast gave one last hefty snort and growled. "Sit down."

Without hesitation, Trent dropped, sitting cross legged on the ground. Badger looked him in the eyes, but did not speak for several more intense moments. Then the beast began to pace back and forth in front of him.

"You let her touch your heart. Do you wish to give up your work and resend your vows?"

"I don't know. That is why I called upon your counsel."

"It is you that will have to decide this matter, You have freewill."

"I know. But the veil has been pulled. Even now the fog obscures my course. I could love her the rest of my mortal life, but I can no longer see her chart, to see if she is to love another. I may have made a terrible mistake. I thought it was going to be a moment in the woods, now I am afraid I'm falling in love with her."

"You have been given great gifts and many talents to accomplish the work you have come to do." A ghoulish grin came across the beast's mouth. "Even that which hangs between your legs is a gift, but it is also a test. It's your test. A test of your mortal flesh. Only when you have past this test will the veil once again be lifted."

With that Badger stepped back to the base of the tree and returned to the lower world.

After awhile Trent stood. The fog that still surrounded him had began to take on the reddish glow of morning.

*   *   *

Dave stood in his briefs and looked out the bedroom window, examining the night sky. A nightstand light turned on.

"Is there something wrong?" Betty asked.

Dave turned to the light. "No, nothing, nothing in the world is wrong."

"What are you doing?

"Just looking at all the stars.

You haven't changed your mind? You're not sneaking out on me?"

"Oh, God no! You couldn't get rid of me with a stick."

"Then come back to bed."

She turned back the covers and patted the sheet. Dave returned to bed and pulled the sheet up to his waist. Betty ran her fingers across his chest as they talked. "Tell me what's wrong?"

"I woke-up a little bit ago. I was having this dream, strange dream. You were in it, but it was a different place and time. We were together, it seems we had a family, lots of children. Then it changed and I was fighting these men, like the other night in Carson City, but more and Trent wasn't there to help me. I was alone, I mean, there were you and the children, but I had to fight the men off by myself. To my surprise, I began to defeat them, one by one, all of them. But the men were really my fears and mistakes, and I conquered them, I conquered them all. And when they fell, they dissolved, turned to dust and blew away . . . . Then you came and took my hand, and we . . . . Well, it was like we could fly, and we soared to a mountaintop, and I could see everything. What I am to do with my life, my future, our future.

"Then I woke-up and the dream started to fade. I couldn't remember what I saw of the future . . . . I was lying there trying to remember and I could see the stars out the window. I saw a shooting star, so I got up to look. Until a couple of weeks ago, I forgot how many stars there are out here. You don't see many in L.A..

"It's the same night sky, but with all the glare of the light needed to live in the city you just can't see the stars."

"That's the way it is, sometimes you can't see the beauty of life for the glare of living. I've made lots of mistakes. I haven't made much of my life."

"There's always tomorrow."

"There weren't any tomorrow's for me, not for a long time . . . . I feel like I've awakened from a horrible dream. But now I'm not sure what's the dream and what's reality. Us, together, is this real?"

"It's real, I'm real."

"I don't like to admit this, but I'm confused and frightened."

"Maybe in each others arms we can both feel safe."

They embraced. As they kissed Betty reached over and turned out the light. The starry sky sparkled outside the window.

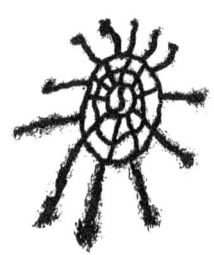

CHAPTER 26

The tent was empty and lit by a strange red light from outside. When Susan lifted the flap and looked out, she was in the middle of a vast barren desert. The sky glowed a dim red, but there was no sun or clouds or stars. A short distance from the tent Trent stood with his back to her. He was bent and stooped, not his normal posture. "Trent, what's happening?"

At the sound of her voice he swung around. His face was twisted and distorted with a wide garish grin that revealed snarled teeth and a long lizard like tongue that licked at his glowing yellow eyes. His deformed naked body was covered with open sores and scabs. His testicles were massive and hung to his knees. The skin of his scrotum was stretched paper-thin over undulating testes that seemed to be filled with teeming life forms. His penis was thin and long and hung to the ground resembling a snake. The end forked similar to a serpent's tongue and on each tip was a small human head.

As he leered at her, his penis, as if it had a life of its own, started to slither on the ground toward her. Susan tried to run but she couldn't move. When his slithering penis reached her the heads rose up into her face. The two heads were duplicates of Trent's distorted features. They peered menacingly at her through tiny yellow eyes and leered, as seman drooled from their gaping mouths. Slowly they began to slide down her bare chest. She felt cold dampness against her skin and looked down to see the heads sniff and examine her breasts. She was frozen. The two headed penis began to swell as it moved down her body. It enlarged and strengthened and when it reached her vagina, it began to prod, painfully, forcing itself into her, preparing to impregnate her with the progeny of the monster that stood before her. She felt the excruciating penetration deep in her flesh and screamed.

Her struggle to scream woke her. The horrifying image still fresh, she opened her eyes to the soft pink glow of dawn that filtered through the trees and into the tent. She was alone. Doubt and confusion gripped her as she tried to force the monster from her mind and replace it with the beautiful image of Trent standing before her last evening. Had the dream been a release of fear, she wondered, or a premonition? Could her beautiful angel really be the demon she saw in her dream? It took a long time for her to find peace.

She could hear the campfire crackle as she pushed the nightmare from her thoughts. Trent had placed her suitcase at the foot of her sleeping bag. She lingered to bask in the afterglow of last night as the horrific dream slowly faded.

The sound of a log being placed on the fire brought her back to the present. She looked out of the tent to see Trent tending the fire. She watched him through the flap of the tent without his knowledge. He was dressed in his jeans and tee shirt. She loved to watch him. She felt warm as she remembered him making love to her. Reluctantly she sat up and stared into the suitcase, she didn't want to dress, so she finally consented to pull on one of Trent's tee shirts and crawl out of the tent.

"Good morning beautiful." Trent greeted her with that mesmerizing smile. He sat by the fire and looked after a pot of coffee.

"Good morning to you too, beautiful."

He stood and greeted her with a kiss. She pushed herself tight to him as their arms encircled each other, their kiss lingered as her hand caressed the stubble of his unshaven face on its way to his ear.

There was a hiss from the fire. The neglected coffeepot had boiled over. Trent pulled it back from the flame.

"Coffee?" he asked.

"Please."

Two cups sat on a near by rock. "I'm not real good at making coffee, but it sounded like a good idea this morning."

"It smells wonderful, but I didn't think you drank coffee."

"I do sometimes. He poured the coffee and handed her a cup. Their gazes locked over the cups as they sipped the hot liquid. She saw a deep intensity in his eyes and wondered what he was thinking, but for now she would let it be a mystery.

"We are going to have to pack up." Susan broke the trance. "I promised mom we'd be back by ten."

"It's still early, we have some time, I want to show you something." Trent put his cup down. "Come with me."

"Wait, I don't have shoes." She grabbed a pair of thongs and steadied herself on his arm as she put them on her feet. They circled halfway around the huge monolith to a spot where the underbrush thinned. Trent led her under the limb of a young pine tree onto a faint path, to an open area at the base of the large stone. A shear hundred foot vertical wall stood before them and on it were dozens of names, dates and slogans, painted or scratched into the rock.

"Look, up there by the peace sign." He pointed.

She looked intently. "What am I supposed to see?"

"There, to the left of the peace sign, 'Jake L. '69 Spartans Rule.' I'll bet Jake L. was your dad."

"You think? I remember my dad said there was a place where everyone signed their names, but we could never find it."

"Now look over to the right and higher. 'David Hoffsted was here.' I know this is the place Dave came camping."

"My dad and Dave have both been here. Both wrote their names on the same wall, what a coincidence."

"Is it, a coincidence?" He moved close to the wall and pulled back a small bush that grew up against the rock. There were the words 'Dave Loves Betty', with a heart around them chipped into the stone.

"You've got to be kidding. Did you do that?"

"No. It's been here a very long time."

"Do you think?"

"That Dave and Betty? No, they didn't have anything to do with this. But I do know they are destined to be together."

"It gives me the chills."

Trent stepped up behind her and put his arms around her. She leaned into his warmth. They both stood for a moment and looked up at the names on the wall.

"Are you ready to head for home?" he asked.

"Not yet." Susan took comfort in his arms. "Can you see the future?" Susan asked, breaking the silence.

"Sometimes." He hesitated. "We are born into this world to experience and learn certain things. We chart our life's before we come, and there are options, including when we die. We have a Spirit Guide that helps along the way if we choose to listen. Our life is like the waters of a mighty river, it can flow freely on its course, speeding up and slowing down, dealing with obstacles, overcoming challenges and bring great benefits to all as it flows its riverbed to its destination. Or it can overflow its banks and flood, never to reach that destination or change its course and create a new riverbed and maybe never reach it's true destiny. Sometimes when someone gets off course, and there is someone waiting for them downstream that truly believes in them, messengers are sent to help guide them back to their intended course. Of course we all have freewill in the matter, all but one thing."

"What's that?"

"We have several departure points where we can shed this life and return home, however, one cannot avoid their final departure."

"Your work? You were sent to help Dave and my mother? Is there something bad going to happen?"

"You know I can't answer that."

Susan stared at the wall and pondered his words for a long time, then put out her hands and smiled. "I know the answer."

She took his hands and led him to the tent.

*   *   *

The mid-morning sun streamed through the window, found a mirror and began to tease Dave awake. He reached for Betty, but didn't find her. He sat up to discover himself alone, but she had left him a note on her pillow.

Dear Dave: You were sleeping so sound, I couldn't bare to wake you. I had to get to the shop. Clean towels are in the bathroom. Join me for coffee when you're ready. Love, Betty Irene.

"Irene? Good night." Dave looked around the room. All of his clothes were neatly folded on a chair. He looked at them and chuckled, then he lay back in the bed with his hands behind his head and grinned contentedly. His mind drifted back to Carson City and how he thought making love to Betty might be. Reality outshined any dream. He refused to let go of last night.

The antique wall clock in the living room began to strike the hour. At first he wasn't aware he was counting the soft gentle chime strikes. Seven, eight, nine, ten! *Oh Jesus.* He jumped to his feet and headed for the shower.

*   *   *

With a spring in his step and a grin, Dave reached the gift shop just as Susan and Trent emerged.

"Don't we look chipper today," Susan remarked.

"Good morning, good morning, you two look pretty chipper yourselves. Where are you off to today?"

"I have some errands to run for Mom, Trent's coming along. What are you up too?"

"I'm going out and take a look at the property." Dave looked at Trent arm in arm with Susan. "I was going to ask you to come along, but it looks like you're busy."

"Well kinda . . . ." Trent quickly overcame his momentary awkwardness. "How did things go last night, or do I need to ask?"

"Unbelievable, the pipes worked like new."

"I told you it was guaranteed."

"Lifetime, I hope."

Susan looked at Dave perplexed. "Did your have something fixed?"

"Yeah, a little plumbing problem, but with Trent's help everything was fixed." Dave struggled to keep from giggling.

"Trent's quite a fixer." Susan patted Trent's arm. "Maybe we can all check your plumbing repairs later."

The two men burst in to laughter. After a moment of confusion, Susan caught the euphemisms. "Oh, guy talk." She took hold of Trent's hand and told Dave. "No wonder Mom's all aglow."

Dave looked sheepish.

"You better get in there and rescue Mom, Lorelei is pumping her for all the details of last night." She reached out and adjusted a button on Dave's shirt. "By noon the whole town will know the condition of your plumbing. I swear that in her last life she must have been a publicist."

"Lorelei! Oh Gees."

Dave opened the door and stepped quickly past Lorelei, walked behind the counter, took Betty in his arm and gave her a passionate lingering kiss, then turned to Lorelei and asked, "Is the Tea Shop not open for lunch today?"

"Oh my," Lorelei looked at her watch. "Look at the time. I'll call you later." She turned to Dave, gave him a wink and headed for the door where she paused. "Congratulations you two," she said as she darted out the door.

"You told her we are getting married?"

"No! I haven't even had a chance to tell Susan."

"Are you getting cold feet?"

"No! Are you?"

"Never." He kissed her. "You shouldn't have let me sleep."

"But you were sleeping so peacefully. Besides, you had a very busy night."

"Ah, but so did you."

"Hummmm," She ran her finger across his lips then kissed them. "Ready for some coffee?"

"I guess it will have to do."

"I'm afraid so, for now." She led him to the back room. "I picked up some sweet-rolls at the German Bakery, thought you might be hungry."

"Great." He sat on the chair across from the desk and watched her every move as she served him.

"I'm going out to the property and look it over, want to come along?"

"Oh, I just sent Susan and Trent off to Alturas, otherwise I could have her cover for me."

"I just talked to them out front, they seem to be hitting it off."

"I've noticed."

"He's a good kid." Dave sipped his coffee. "I could wait till tomorrow."

"No, I think you better go on, or I won't get any of my work done." She tried her coffee. "I'd of thought you would have gone out there the first day you were in town."

"I didn't know how to find it. Dan Jackson at Country Real Estate looked it up and gave me a map. That, and I was a little distracted."

"Distracted, I don't know what may have distracted you." She smiled.

"Yeah, and I didn't want to be disappointed either. I have a lot of hopes for the place. If I remember right it's wooded with a creek that's usually dry by this time of year. There are several great building sites. I thought I might subdivide part of it and sell it off, then build a home for us."

Betty smiled and her eyes sparkled. "It's pretty around there," she assured him.

"It use to be, and peaceful too. I sure hope it's like I re-member, I'm tired of disappointments."

"I hope last night wasn't a disappointment."

"Oh God no, not for me, but I was afraid it might be for you."

"Dave, I don't think you could ever be a disappointment to me."

"You know, somehow, these things Trent's been saying, about life partners and stuff, it's different, I mean I'm beginning to see it differently."

"Trent's quite a young man."

"You're telling me, I don't know why I picked him up, I've never done that before, pick up a hitchhiker. After I did, it scared the shit—I mean, heck out of me.

"Why was that?"

"A guy thing. I was so drawn to him, it scared me, you know. You even thought something weird was up. Then I couldn't keep my mouth shut. Told him everything. Things about me I wouldn't of told anyone."

"I hope you can tell me someday."

"Telling those things to him, sort of freed me. There are no more secrets. Anything you want to know just ask."

"Sometimes the greatest gift someone can give, is just listening."

"But, he taught me things, showed me things too. He even took me to a sweat lodge, made me dress like an Indian and sit in the dark with a bunch of other Indians."

"I hope he'll stay awhile."

"I asked him too, he said he didn't want to over stay his welcome. He talked like he planned to move on by the end of the week."

"Plans can change. Well, look at the time, if you're going out to your property, you'd better shake a leg."

"You could close up and come with me."

"I'd love to, but I have deliveries coming in today."

"Then I'll be here to pick you up at five. I'm taking you to dinner."

"It depends on what's for dessert."

"What do you have in mind, reruns?"

"I love reruns, but we don't want to wear it out."

"I'll risk it," Dave said with a grin.

"You would." She gave him a kiss. "It's a date."

The chime on the front door rang as a customer entered. "You better scoot and let me get to work. I'll see you at five. Get here early and we can have a glass of wine while I lock up." Betty gave him a quick kiss then retreated through the beaded curtain to wait on her customer.

Dave transferred the rest of his coffee to a Styrofoam cup and grabbed a second sweet-roll before maneuvering through the curtain. "I'll see you about four." He told Betty. Then from behind the customer he mouthed, "I love you."

She grinned and hoped her blush wasn't noticed. Just then a cloud past in front of the sun and darkened the store. It made all take notice.

"That's strange, I didn't see any clouds when I came in." The dark-haired woman moved to the window and looked out. "One little cloud. Just one little cloud all by itself covering the sun, making everything turn dark."

Betty shivered noticeably as goose bumps formed on her arms. "Are you all right?" Dave asked.

"Yes, just a little chill. Now you get going."

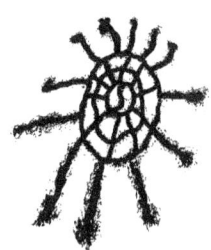

CHAPTER 27

Dave slowed then stopped in the middle of the infrequently used Old Mill Road, a paved county road that led west from Highway 395, a dozen miles north of town. He had driven a mile up the road when he spotted the small group of mailboxes indicated on the map the real estate agent had given him, drove another 300 feet, turned to his left off the paved road and onto a dirt road. He looked for any familiar landmarks that would lead him to his property. Aggravated, he stopped and started out on foot to find some sort of conformation that he may have located his property.

Frustrated after a lengthy search, he started back to his pickup when he tripped over a stake hidden in the grass. It was a surveyor's stake and the brass tag confirmed the parcel number. At last he had found his property.

Back in his pickup he followed the remnant of a road until it opened into a small clearing and he was instantly transported in his mind back to his childhood and the wonderful times he had spent at this place. He turned off the engine and sat for several minutes as whiffs of memories drifted by, Mom, Dad, the tent, a campfire in the afternoon with dinner in preparation, the smoke hanging in the still air as beams of light from the low sun streamed through the trees. When the memories finally faded, he stepped out of the pickup and stood. A shaft of sunlight fell on his face. He closed his eyes and let it caress him, renew his soul. After a deep breath that was close to a sigh, he got about his business. He grabbed his note pad, camera and canteen of water from the seat of the pickup, and started off in the direction he thought he would find the creek. Through the years, overgrowth blocked the old trail. He had to push his way forward blindly until he found a deer trail, and then followed it until it led to a clearing. There he stood for a moment and got his bearings. With new confidence, he headed out again, this time his memory served him well and he was soon at the creek.

The flow of water had recently stopped. A few stagnant pools between the boulders and sandbars provided life-giving water to the wildlife, evident by the abundant tracks. It took awhile for his ears to adjust to the quiet sounds of nature, a pleasant contrast to the sounds of civilization, slowly the tranquility settled on him like a favorite hat. Unhurriedly, Dave began to work his way up the creek bed, he savored every moment. He couldn't remember being so happy and was anxious to share his joy with Betty. *I'll go back early and we'll grab some dinner to-go and come back after she closes the shop. Maybe the kids will be back by then too.*

When he came to a particularly large flat bolder he sat, lifted his camera and snapped several pictures. Out of the corner of his eye he spotted a multicolored stone near his foot and picked it up to examine. Held to the light, it revealed it's prismatic quality. He gently placed it to his cheek and then took the stone in both hands, held it out before him and closed his eyes. Slowly he lifted the stone above his head on his fingertips. After a moment he looked around embarrassed by his actions. "He's got me doing it." He laughed, then placed the stone in his pants pocket and walked on.

At what he thought would be a possible building site; he stopped to sketch what he envision a home might look like on it. "Do you think you'll like it? Oh Betty, do you think we can make a go at it? Do I dare dream? Maybe this is all a dream . . . . No, it's no dream. For the first time in your life things are going your way, so don't screw it up."

As he walked, he examined every stone and plant he came across as if he had never seen any of it before. When he found a piece of red jasper in the shape of a heart with a vain of white quartz running through it, he got excited. "I'll polish it and make it into a necklace." He couldn't wait to share it with Betty as he pushed it in a pocket already full of new found treasures. It was after two when he reached the upper boundaries of his property, snapped some more pictures and then started back down the creek.

Climbing up over an area of boulders, he stepped over the rocks and moved from deep shade back into the brilliant sun. Before his eyes could adjust to the change of light he heard a loud buzz and the primal knowledge deep within him reacted before his mind connected to the sound.

With an instinctive jump back, he glimpsed the rattlesnake. His foot hung up on a rock and the force of his self-preservation recoil, shoved him backward. Helplessly he fell. With a twist of his body, he tried to throw himself away from the snake. He felt a sharp pain in his leg. In that brief moment before he landed, he tried in vain to protect himself, but his arms tangled in the camera strap and he could do little to lessen the impact. Face first, he smashed on the gravelly creek bed. Stunned, he was unable to even lift his face.

"No!" He yelled. "Hell, no . . . Betty hel . . . ." He drifted into unconsciousness.

*   *   *

The cell phone rang as Susan was driving. "Can you get that?"

"Hello." Trent answered. "Yes, just a moment, she's driving. It's your mom, she wants to talk to you. Sounds urgent."

"Tell her I've got to pull off," Susan said as she pulled to the side of the road.

"She'll be with you in a second." Trent handed Susan the phone as soon as she came to a stop.

"Mom, what's up?

"Susan? Is everything okay?"

"Yes everything is fine."

"Good, where are you?"

"On the road, we'll be there in about twenty minutes, is there something wrong?"

"No. Nothing. Just had a strange feeling and wondered where you were. See you soon. Got to run, got a customer, Bye." The phone went dead.

"That was weird."

"What?" Trent asked.

"Mom. She just doesn't call for nothing." She put the phone on the dash and they drove off. "That's just not like her."

*   *   *

The awareness of pain in his leg brought him around. His first thought was the rattlesnake bite. Lifting his face out of the dirt, he managed to sit up. With each movement the results of the fall became more evident.

"Stay calm," he reminded himself, "the worst thing for snakebite is panic." On closer examination of his leg, he realized it was not a snakebite at all, but just a deep gash, probably from the underbrush and by the looks of it, more painful than serious. The wound had already quit bleeding and by the scab, he estimated he must have been unconscious for at least a half-hour.

Oh God . . . what have you done to yourself? As he started to take stock of his other injuries, he became painfully aware that he couldn't move his left arm without excruciating pain in his shoulder. Using his right hand, he maneuvered his other hand to his lap.

"A dislocated shoulder," he assured himself. "Ahhhh! Shit. Damn it, I don't need this, not now." He sat awhile longer, and then took several sips from his canteen. "It's not that bad, get your ass up, you can't just sit here, you've got to get up. You've got to keep going."

Using all the motivation he could muster, he maneuvered up onto a rock where he could sit. "Hey Silverhawk, where the hell

244

were you when I needed you." Attempting to stand, he struggled with all his might to stay upright. "Some Spirit Guide you are. Let me fall on my face like this. All this spiritual stuff is just a bunch of shit."

He looked around to get his bearings and determine his direction back to the pickup. In pain, he took small slow steps up and over several rocks. "Damn kid is full of nonsense, I'll be glad to see him gone. Ahhhh!" With pain at every movement, he managed to struggle up the bank and out of the creek bed. Suddenly he felt everything around him begin to spin. "Oh God help me." He felt himself start to fall backward and grabbed for the sky. Falling hard, he felt a crack at the back of his head when he hit. He knew it was bad. His luck had run out. As he lay helpless on the rocks, he felt his life draining away.

*   *   *

Betty whorled around at the sound of the door, knocking several small figurines off a shelf, "Oh God, I'm glad your back."

"What's wrong?" Susan asked.

Betty put her finger to her lips and nodded toward Lorelei.

"Hello." Lorelei acknowledged Susan and Trent, but went right on with her chatter. "When you called to say my order was in, I had to rush right over." Lorelei watched Betty ring up her purchase. "Now just when did you say that delicious hunk of yours lived in Susanville?"

"Seventies, mid-seventies." Betty looked franticly at Susan.

"There wasn't a real town here in Mystique then, just my old place and the bait shop. That was even before I moved over from Susanville. Hoffsted, Hoffsted, let me think, oh yes, I remember now. His mother was Ruth Hoffsted. Little Davy, skinny blonde kid, wanted to be a writer or an artist or something, no . . . a poet, I remember. They used to print some of his poems in the Susanville Gazette. Little Davy, my, my, turned out to be a good-looking man, if you ask me."

"I don't think he would appreciate being called Little Davy. That will be $39.57."

Trent stepped to the counter.

"Yes, your probably right. Will you just put that on my bill, I didn't bring my purse."

Betty handed Lorelei her purchase and Trent graciously escorted her out the door.

"Dear woman, but sometimes."

"Mom, what's wrong?"

"I don't know. It's just I sense, something bad has happen to Dave. He went out alone to look over his property shortly after you left. Then this terrible sensation came over me."

"Is that why you called us?"

"Yes, look!" She pointed to the clock. "It's after five, he was suppose to be here at four. Something's wrong.

"Do you know where his property is?" Trent asked, as he stared at the flame of the violet pillar candle Betty always kept burning.

"I think so. I called Dan at Country Real Estate and got directions."

"Shouldn't we call someone?" Susan picked up her mother's anxiety."

"I started to, but who would I call to report a bad feeling. They would think I'm crazy. I don't have confirmation that anything is wrong. Oh, I wished I would have given him my cell-phone."

"I see it." Trent muttered, still looking at the candle. "I've got to go find him." Trent started for the door.

"Let me get my keys and purse." Betty grabbed her things from behind the counter, turned the closed sign and hurried out the door. As Betty locked the door, Susan saw the candle thru the window and froze, the flame fluttered and went out as if someone had blown it out.

"Hurry Susan."

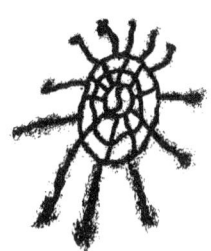

CHAPTER 28

"Dave. Dave, come to the light."

The voice in the darkness was familiar. *Silverhawk.* It was suddenly obvious to him that the voice that had always spoken to him in his head was Silverhawk's, but this time it was out there, speaking from the thick black empty envelope that surrounded him. He could feel nothing. The only sound was Silverhawk's voice, yet he was completely at peace.

"Come to the light." Silverhawk commanded.

Dave saw no light. He tried to speak but couldn't. *Where am I? Why can't I speak or move? Why can't I feel anything? What light?* The questions rocketed in his thoughts. *I'm dead.*

What at first appeared as a single star in the blackness, began to grow. As it steadily increased, he sensed himself begin to move towards the intensifying light, until it completely engulfed him, pure white light, infinite light with neither here nor there, up or down and without source or shadow, just light and in the midst of the light Dave stood alone, clothed in spotless, radiant white shirt and pants. In the empty space he felt as if he stood on something solid, but when he looked down he saw that his white boots stood on nothing but luminosity. He was suspended in space.

Out of the light as if from out of a fog, stepped the Old Man from Kramer Junction. He stood a short distance away and appeared just as he had at the gas station, except his clothes were pure white as well.

"Why have you interrupted his journey now?" The Old Man asked. He was expressionless and tranquil, his voice soft and near monotone as he spoke.

"He stopped his own journey long ago." A strong deep male voice answered.

"But you had sent me to help him find his way again." The Old Man argued. "Have I not done so?"

"You tell me, where is he going?" The Voice asked.

"To the higher ground."

"Why has he not gone there before?"

"He was bound. Bound by his past. He had to learn to let go of the past."

"Has he?"

"Yes."

The Old Man turned to his right. "What say you, Keepers of the Past?"

Gary and Donny appeared as they did in Dave's dream. Then Joe stepped up beside them, he too appeared not as he did at the time of his death, but appeared to be in his thirties, healthy and strong, and all were clothed in dazzling white. Dave was drawn to them, but could not move.

"He held us captive . . . " Joe began.

" . . . for many years . . . " Gary took over.

" . . . he kept us bound." Donny followed. They spoke one after the other in rounds, quickly, completing each other sentences in melodic phrases.

"We left our bodies . . . "

" . . . but we could not go on . . . "

" . . . and we found no peace because . . . "

" . . . he kept us bound . . . "

" . . . he kept us bound . . . " Gary echoed

" . . . he kept us bound . . . ." Donny repeated

"But he's come to terms with loosing them," the Old Man began to plead Dave's case as if he were before a judge. "He's let them go."

"Does he want to come with us now?" Joe asked.

"Come with us Dave," Gary said.

"Stay with us Davy." Donny pleaded.

"He has let you go." The Old Man stepped in front of Dave.

"Yes, he's let us go . . . "

" . . . he's let us all go . . . "

" . . . he's let us go and set us free . . . ."

"Yes, I've let them go." Dave assured The Voice, he at last found his own voice.

The three men disappeared.

"And what of his father?" The Voice asked.

Dave turned to the Old Man.

"He has forgiven him and let him go." The old man answered.

"And his mother?" The Voice continued to question.

"He has forgiven her and let her go."

"And what about his teacher, Mr. O'Doul?"

Dave grimaced; he felt a flash of fear at the mention of O'Doul's name. Then Mr. O'Doul appeared in front of Dave with his head bowed. Slowly he looked up at Dave and said, "I'm sorry."

"Has he forgiven him and let him go?" The Voice demanded.

"Can you, will you forgive me David?" O'Doul asked.

The fear in Dave faded, and he began to tear. At first he shook his head no, but then looked O'Doul in the eyes.

"Please David, for your own sake, you must forgive me."

Dave's stare was fixed on O'Doul for a long time as he slowly realized that he had been freed of the fear the day he had struck Trent; finally, a barely audible sound came from deep within him. "Yes, I forgive you."

"He has forgiven him." The Old Man shouted with exuberance and jumped into the air, then quickly regained his composure. "He has at last forgiven him and let him go."

"And all the others," The Voice asked in a quick demanding tone. "His wives . . . ."

"He's let them go . . . ." The Old Man answered back like a tolling bell.

"His bosses?"

"He's let them go."

"His fellow workers?"

"He's let them go."

"Has he let them all go?" The Voice rang a final demanding challenge.

"He has let them go, ALL GO . . . ." The Old Man's voice reverberated into a great chorus.

There was silence. Dave slowly turned and faced the Old Man and in a quiet voice he told him, "I've let them all go."

"They have all been freed." Silverhawk appeared, behind Dave and put his right hand on his shoulder.

"So, what of his way now my son?" The Voice boomed. "Has he found his course?"

"Yes, he again has stood upon the Mountain." Silverhawk answered.

"But has he seen?"

"He is learning to love." The Old man answered.

"But is he teachable?"

"He is teachable," Silverhawk stepped in front of Dave, "and he will love."

The Old Man turned to Silverhawk. "Can, he love?"

Silverhawk smiled and nodded to Dave and then turned back to the Old Man, but remained silent.

"Yes," Dave finally said with a raised voice, "I do love."

Dave took a deep breath and looked around. "I recognize where I am and I know the veil has not yet been lifted, so there is still a question, a chance. Three weeks ago I would not have cared. My life was over; it had been for quite some time. Then that morning at Kramer Junction, something happened, something changed. They were both there, they know. I met a young man and my life changed. He held a mirror up before me and I didn't like what I saw, but he offered hope. When I was being beaten in the alley, I prayed for death, but instead he rescued me. Since that night I've changed, I've fallen in love with the most wonderful person I've ever met. Right now I feel her tugging at my heart and I know without a shadow of a doubt, I love her. I realize before me here in this place is peace and bliss, and back there are the struggles of human existence. I care not what torments await me if I return or what future penalties I must face, I will confront hell to give Betty my love."

Dave looked at the Old Man, but said no more. Then he looked to Silverhawk questioningly, but he too was mute. Dave, Silverhawk and the Old Man waited for a response from The Voice, but none came.

After a long wait the Old Man said, "I must consult the Ancient Ones on your behalf," and disappeared into the light.

"What now?" Dave eventually asked Silverhawk.

"We must wait."

"How long?"

"As long as it takes."

"I wish Trent were here."

"He can't be here, he has other work."

"What do you think will happen?"

"What do you want to happen?"

Dave turned to look at Silverhawk and beside him was a full-length mirror. In its reflection Dave saw that he had been transformed, he was the age of his friends. That age we all see ourselves when there is no mirror.

"Is that what you want?" Silverhawk asked.

"I don't know."

A short distance away Dave saw Joe, Gary and Donny appear and behind them a meadow began to take form. It was green, lush and inviting and their clothing began to take on color until they were as brilliant as a rainbow. One by one each of the three men turned and started toward the meadow, as they did, they bid Dave to follow.

"Come on Dave," Joe began.

"You are home Dave," Gary continued.

"Come Dave." Donny beckoned.

*   *   *

"Dave, Dave, can you hear me? Are you all right?" Betty called, she jumped out of the vehicle before Trent had pulled to a complete stop behind Dave's pickup. He sounded several long blasts on the horn before getting out and opening the back of the SUV.

"You guided us right to it." Trent said.

"By Dan's description, I had a pretty good idea of where it was." Betty took a few steps and called again, "DAVE."

"What should we do?" Susan asked. She had been silent all the way from town.

"It's probably best if we split up." Trent took charge.

"But don't go too far. We don't need someone else lost." Betty warned as she got out her cell phone. "Good, I've got a signal, I'll call the sheriff and report a possible lost hiker, at least alert them."

"Susan, you come with me. Betty you stay here, sound a blast on the horn every few minutes, if he shows up hit it several short blast and we'll know he's safe."

"Dave said there was a dry creek." Betty said as she dialed the cell phone. "If you find it, follow it, just don't go too far. I'll get some help." She looked disconcertingly at her cell phone. "Come on phone, work."

Trent took some bottles of water out of the back of the SUV and stuffed them in his buckskin bag, took a few steps south and bent down. "I think he went thru here." He said pointing and then held up a low branch for Susan.

Once past the obstacle she told Trent, "Go on ahead, I'll be right behind you." She was determined not to be a hindrance.

A short distance thru the heavy under brush, Trent stopped. "Hold up a second," he insisted as he reached down, placed his right palm flat on the ground and closed his eyes as if trying the hear something.

Susan was so fixed on the movement of his eyes behind his eyelids that she jumped with a start when he suddenly opened them with an intense stare into the distance. Susan didn't say a word as he started off in the direction of his gaze. Following, she struggled to keep up with his long strides; certain he knew where to find Dave. The sound of the horn encouraged her to keep pace with Trent as they worked their way through the under brush. When they came to the more open trail she could see fresh tracks. "It looks like Dave's boots."

Trent pointed. "There's the creek."

Another blast of the horn echoed through the trees. They followed the footprints in the sand as they climbed over the boulders up the dry creek bed. By now Susan was struggling to keep up with Trent. Suddenly she slipped and fell, the fine gravel cut into the palms of her hands as she caught herself, tired and hurt, she fought back her tears, but she wasn't about to stop. The sound of the horn urged her to her feet before Trent saw that she had fallen. She pushed herself to catch-up when at last he stopped ahead of her.

What has he found? She wondered and started to run. *Why has he stopped?* Within a couple of seconds she was beside him. She gasped. "Dave!" Dave's lifeless body lay on the rocks below them.

"Stay here." Trent shouted as he bounded down the bank like an elk.

His words didn't register with her as she hurried to Trent's side. Dave had a blank stare and she couldn't see him breathe.

"Is he?"

Trent stood and took her in his arms. "It's bad."

"Is there anything you can do?" She asked.

"I'll try."

As she stood in his arms she knew his work was before him, but had her desire for him blinded him? Had her temptation diverted him from his true reason for being there? Was it too late?

"Do it, if you can do anything, please, do it." She pleaded.

He knelt beside Dave and looked up at her. In his eyes she saw pain in his heart. She knew for him to help Dave she would have to let him go.

Another blast of the horn snapped her into action. "You must forget about me and do all that you can to save Dave."

For a long moment he stared up at her, his face frozen in agony, then suddenly he shouted, "Go to your mother and stay with her. Don't, whatever you do, don't let her come here. Understand?"

253

"I understand, I will keep her there."

"Wait by the vehicles until I come. No matter what you think or how long it takes. Don't let your mother come here. If she sees him like this, it's over, is that clear?"

"Okay! Yes, but what—"

"No time for questions now, go. Wipe what you've seen from your mind; what you see is an illusion, don't let it manifest itself. Now go to your mother. Hurry!"

With newfound strength Susan scurried up the bank, but when she got to the top she stopped to look back. Trent was knelt beside Dave and gently closed Dave's eyes with his fingers. He then put his hand over Dave's heart. There was silence, not a bird or insect whispered and the air didn't move. Trent turned his face to the sky. His dark eyes reflected like fire in the afternoon sun and it appeared as if he was looking into the very face of God.

There came another blast of the horn. She turned and ran to her mother.

CHAPTER 29

"Where are they?" Betty asked as she continued to pace.

"It takes time." Susan blasted the horn to keep up the charade.

"And where's Trent. Where the hell did he go off too?

"He's looking for Dave." Susan's ability to lie to her mother began to fade.

"Oh God, I can't stand this. I can't wait here anymore. I've got to go look.

"NO!" Susan put her arms around her mother to stop her and comfort her. "He'll—they'll be along soon, I'm sure of it. Where is your faith?"

"Oh honey your right. I'm acting so foolish. It's just that Dave showing up was an answered prayer. Now I feel he's being snatched away from me."

Susan reassured her mother a little longer, then returned to the pickup and sounded the horn.

"Can't we stop that? Every time is sounds, I can't help but feel it's useless."

"But Trent said to—yes, your right. We can space it out I guess. They are probably out of hearing range anyway."

Betty sat on a bolder. "Come sit by me."

Susan got two bottles of water out of the SUV and instead of sitting next to her mom, sat on the ground at her feet.

Betty ran her fingers through Susan's hair. "When your father died, I didn't want to go on, but you were only ten, so I did. As time went by and I watched you grow I began to dread the day you would leave. I had become so afraid of being alone. Now it's time for—"

"But Mom, I not going to leave you."

"You must and you will, you have a life of your own, that is the way life is meant to be. You're growing up, in time you will find someone to start a life of your own with."

"No it won't be like that. I'll always be near by."

"You could live next door, but it's not the same. It is still your life." Susan laid her head in her mother's lap. "You don't understand, your dad and I, we had a good life together, we even loved each other in our way, but . . . ."

"But?" Susan looked up, she had never heard her mother talk like this before.

"But, there was something missing. When you came along, I thought, now we are complete, but we weren't. Your dad knew it too. Oh, we never cheated on each other."

"Mom stop." Susan didn't want to hear her mother's words.

"You're a big girl now, you should know the truth. When your father and I started dating it was because of our friends, they thought we were right for each other, and in a way we were. We became friends. Our relationship was comfortable and convenient, but we were never really in love with each other."

"But Mom, everybody said you were the perfect couple."

"That's what everybody said and thought. We tried, but there was something missing. I didn't know what it was until I met Dave. True love transcends time and space. When they speak of a match made in heaven, it's true. I know virtually nothing about

Dave and yet in my heart I know I've known him throughout eternity."

"Oh Mom, you can't be serious."

"Your dad knew it. He knew we were to be together for only a short time. He prepared from the beginning for you. He knew he was going to leave us. It was in his chart, he'd say. He had prepared for everything, our home, the insurance, and your education. He took care of everything. A few days before it happen, he said he knew something was going to happen to him soon, that he was going to have to leave, his work was done and someday I'd understand. He asked me to forgive him. He said it was the way it had to be."

"Well, do you understand?"

"I didn't fully until last night. Dave was telling me about the dream he had. And suddenly I was getting glimpses of what your father was talking about. It was like Déjà vu, but more, I could see Dave and me in other lifetimes. Then, after all these years I sensed your father's presence in the room. In the moonlight, I saw him standing by the bed and he smiled. I knew, I knew at last my time has come."

"Oh Mom." Susan began to cry. How could she tell her what she saw? That Dave was dead.

"It's okay."

"Mom, you don't understand, when Trent sent me back to you . . . well, he had . . . ."

Betty stood and lifted Susan to her feet. "What, what is it?"

"We found Dave, and it wasn't good."

Betty collapsed to her knees crying. Susan knelt down beside her and held her in her arms. "Trent sent me back. He said not to say anything, to erase even the image of what I saw from my thoughts. Trent, he's—

"Oh God NOOO!"

"Sssssh . . . Mom, I'm sorry."

"What's he doing?"

"He's called for help. If there is anyone that—"

"That can work a miracle? No Honey, Trent's just a man. You can't expect him to work miracles, to change what's not meant, raise the dead, he is not God." Betty stood. "Take me to him."

"But— maybe love can make a miracle."

"Take me there now." She helped Susan to her feet. "Now!"

Suddenly there was the snap of a branch behind them. Susan swung around. The unmistakable form of Trent, backlit by the afternoon sun, walked toward them then stopped. From the distance and the light she couldn't see his face. "Mom, it's Trent, he's here."

Betty took a moment before she looked up. Susan found a tissue for her mother's tears. Betty's knees started to buckle and Susan steadied her.

"There's something . . . ." Trent spoke slowly. "Someone here looking for you. He's been looking for a long, long time, and now that he's found you he's not going to let you go." He held out his arm and pointed behind him.

There in the brilliant haze of the afternoon sun, Dave stood.

Betty looked perplexed as she glanced at Susan, then Trent and then back at Dave and wiped her eyes again and finally turned back to Trent with a questioning expression.

"Yes," Trent said with a smile. "He's real."

Betty ran to Dave's waiting arms.

Susan looked at Trent. "But how?"

Trent took her in his arms, touched a finger to her lips, shook his head no, and whispered. "He found his true love."

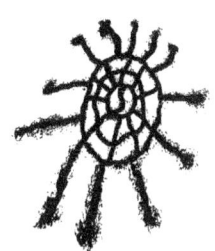

CHAPTER 30

"Shall I fix us some dinner?" Betty asked as they approach the front porch of her home.

"Trent and I will pass." Susan answered. "We are going for a walk."

"What about you?"

"Sure." Dave answered. "In a little bit."

"We'll see you later." Trent tossed Dave his pickup keys. "You ready?" Trent took Susan's hand and together they walked into the twilight.

"A handsome couple, those two," Dave said as he watched them leave.

"Yes, but I don't think Trent is the kind that will ever settle down." Betty paused a moment and then turned toward the door. "Would you like a glass of wine?"

"That sounds great. But can I use your bathroom a minute to wash-up a bit?"

"Of course. I'll make it red wine?"

*   *   *

Dave returned to the porch and waited for Betty. *I wonder if she is right? Will Trent ever settle down, or can he?*

Betty stepped out of the screen door with a tray. "Thought some cheese and crackers would go well with the wine."

"Perfect." Dave pulled the cork and poured the wine. "To us."

"To us." Their glasses clinked.

They sat in silence and sipped their wine in the warm summer's eve as the last vintages of the dazzling sunset disappeared and the crickets as numerous as the stars joyously celebrated life. Dave put his arm around Betty's shoulders.

"Aren't you going to say anything?"

"What? Say anything about what?"

"Today, about what happened out there, or is it none of my business."

"Oh, no, I want to tell you but I'm still trying to sort it out. I just don't have the words. I don't want you to think I'm crazy or something."

"You know I won't."

"Well everything was going fine, I had walked most of the property and had started back down the creek bed toward the pickup when I was startled by a rattlesnake. I jumped, lost my balance and fell backwards. I hurt myself but I wasn't bitten. The fall knocked me out, when I came to, I got up quickly because I didn't know where the snake was. I stood . . . ." Dave took a drink of his wine.

"Is that it?" Betty asked.

"I stood there and like I said I hurt all over, then I started back to the pickup. All of a sudden I got dizzy. I felt myself start to fall again, but there was no way to stop it. It was if everything was in slow motion. I hit the rocks, hard, but this time there was no pain. I remember laying there and looking up at the sky and then everything slowly went black. After that everything is a blur, vague impressions, a voice saying come to the light and a kind of courtroom or hearing. Then I heard the horn and you calling my name and Trent saying come back. I was confused. He said the council has decided, and not to forget, suddenly there was a mist around my feet and when I looked down, there you were just a few feet below me and you were crying and sounding the horn of your SUV. Then I knew. I knew." Tears filled Dave's eyes and rolled down his cheeks. "I knew you were more important to me than heaven itself."

They embraced on the porch swing.

*   *   *

There was enough moonlight filtering through the trees that Susan could see Trent's handsome face. She studied it knowing it would be the last time she would see it. She loved him wantonly, but knew she could not possess him. Her fingers ran across his chest as she lay in his arm on the sweet smelling grass.

"You promised to answer my questions, are you able to answer them now?"

"Go ahead, but I'll make no guarantee that you will like all the answers."

"When we got to Dave today, he looked . . . he looked like he was dead."

"If you define dead as one who's spirit has left it's body, yes he was dead."

"Did you bring him back, like, like Jesus raising Lazarus from the dead? Did you bring Dave back from the dead?"

"No. I reminded him that his work on Earth wasn't finished. He made the choice."

"You worked a miracle."

"No. Miracles come from the individual human spirit. A person chooses to be sick or well and how they are healed, they also choose if they are rich or poor, and how and when to leave this planet and most importantly of all, what they've come here to learn. I've explained that before."

"Are you an angel or a demon or are you a human?"

"You asked that before."

"But I didn't believe your answer.

"I'm human."

"Then could you stay here with me if you really wanted too?"

"Yes."

There was a long pause. She wanted to be angry but couldn't. She knew he had given her the choice. If she asked him to stay, he would. She wrestled with her emotions. She knew she could never ask him to stay. He held her in his arms and as he did she felt a energy flow from him into her.

"I will never forget you. I will never love another man." She whispered.

"You will." He assured her. "I saw a glimpse of the one you are destined to be with today."

"Will you remember me?"

"Always."

She felt her warm tears run down her cheeks. She lost track of time. When at last all her tears were gone, she wondered, had he worked some sort of magic on her to dull the pain? In the moonlight they walked long into the night silently and when they reach the creek they sat on the grass. Susan felt a strange intoxication.

Finally her heart began to lift. She looked at Trent and smiled.

Her thoughts went back to his words, *I saw a glimpse of the one you are destined to be with*. She pondered them for awhile then asked. "So when will I meet this someone, who will make me forget you."

"Your paths have already crossed, but the time wasn't right. He will come again in the spring."

"What's his name?"

"Oh I'm not going to make it that easy, but I will give you some clues."

"You're a rascal. So?"

"He's tall, with brown hair and pale blue eyes."

"That's no help. That describes a quarter of the guys in L.A.."

"He's educated and you have similar interest, he will arrive when you least expect it and he will complete your family. Oh, and he has a pet phrase. 'That's a corker'."

"How do you know all this? Humans don't know these things."

"Some do. I told you, I'm a Mystic Traveler, a Shaman. I've learned the techniques of journeying to the worlds of spirits, upper, middle and lower. You've studied shamanism, it's not just stories and myths, it is for real. I've committed my life to serve humankind. I go where the Great Spirit directs and serve those in need."

Susan tried to make sense of what he was telling her. Logic distorted with emotions simply made her more confused. Finally she decided to quit trying to understand and just except it, at least for now.

"Tell me what it's like there."

"There? Where?"

"There, heaven."

"What makes you think I know?"

"You know."

"Well the other side, what you call heaven, the upper world, is like Earth, just a different plain, actually it is near parallel, shifted just a few feet above the plain in which we live. Only it vibrates at a different frequency, that's why you don't see it. There is no decay, sickness, death or evil there. These things only exist on this level. It's incredibly beautiful there. We recognize each other even if we don't look like we did in our Earth life. Everyone is mature and looks about thirty, and yet we see our love ones as we remembered them here on Earth. People there are clothed in light, which can be opaque or transparent, and with or without color. Entities are either male of female, but there is no modesty there like on Earth."

"Do they have families?"

"No, there's no marriage or families, but loved ones do group together. On the other side there is no procreation, but people can merge, a higher form of shared pleasure than here on Earth, sexual intercourse is only a shadow of the true gift of love."

"Will I ever see you again?"

"Not in this lifetime, but we will be together again on the other side."

"When will you leave Mystique?"

"Early tomorrow morning."

"Then this is good-bye." Susan paused for a moment. "Hold me a little longer, then I will let you go."

They embraced on the grass.

*   *   *

Dave woke at the sound of the door. He had fallen asleep waiting for Trent. The clock on the nightstand glowed, 2:42 a.m..
"Are you leaving?"

"At first light."

"Can we talk?"

"I've been doing a lot of that tonight."

"You've got me really confused, you are not at all what I thought a holy man should be."

"Thanks. I'll take that as a compliment."

"I have some questions about what happened this afternoon."

"So what's on your mind?"

"Bits and peaces of what happen are coming back to me. Out there today I know I died and was in heaven and when I started to follow the guys, I heard your voice call me. I knew I didn't have to come back but I did, for Betty and I also know I have something yet to do. Silverhawk showed me it in a dream, what I was to do with the rest of my life, but now I can't remember what I saw."

"You are not meant to remember."

"How can I do the things I'm suppose to if I don't know what they are?"

"They are written on your heart. Live, if you get off track, Silverhawk will give you guidance. We are here to experience and learn from our mistakes. If we all saw clairvoyantly, what would we learn?'

Dave went to the refrigerator and opened it. "Would you like a soda or beer or something?"

"Soda would be fine."

"Are you clairvoyant, did you know what was going to happen today and what the outcome would be."

"No. Your providence is yours and yours alone. I knew you were to be tested but neither the nature of the test nor the out come."

Dave handed Trent a soda and opened a beer for himself. "I've made such a mess of my life in the past, I'm afraid I'm going to screw up again."

"Have you learned anything?"

"'Well yes, but that doesn't mean I'm not still a screw-up."

"You've made a one-eighty in the last few weeks and with your choice today, you have a new life before you. Oh there will be plenty of bumps in the road ahead, screwing up as you put it is part of life, but nothing you can't handle."

"Okay, one more question. I messed myself up pretty badly today. How come I'm not even sore? Yet after Carson City I hurt like a son-of-a-bitch for weeks." Pointing to his splint, "and I still have this."

"After Carson City you weren't ready for instant healing. This afternoon, your body, mind and spirit were ready. But don't push it, if you don't take care of yourself you will get sick and if you nail your thumb with a hammer, It's gonna hurt."

"Thanks for the warning."

Trent checked the bathroom, stowed his shaving kit and zipped his backpack close.

"So, am I ever going to see you again?"

"Not in this life, but that doesn't mean I won't be keeping tabs on you."

"You, and the old man, there's some connection, isn't there? He was there today and you weren't"

"There's something Shaman do, it's called journeying. We can project a part of ourselves to other dimensions and worlds including this one. Sometimes when we journey, we appear as a human form, a person to those around us, maybe even as our own grandfather."

Dave stood and hugged Trent. "I'm gonna miss you kid."

"It's been a pleasure. I'll miss you too."

The men retired, but talked no more and when Dave woke in the morning twilight, Trent was gone.

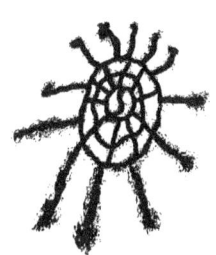

CHAPTER 31

"Well, tomorrow is the big day." Susan said as her mother stepped through the door to the backyard. Susan sat enjoying her morning coffee. "I brought the box I told you about. The one from the storeroom that was labeled wedding, I didn't know where you wanted it so I just put it on the table."

"Thank you dear." Betty looked at the box. "You are right, I don't know who's writing that is or where it came from. I'll look at it later." She fussed with a pot of flowers for a moment. "It's going to be perfect weather for the wedding. I was afraid that it was a little early in the season for a garden wedding, but I was wrong."

"Spring Break weather is always a little iffy. It has been a long cold winter for me, I'm glad spring has arrived." Susan looked at her watch. "What time is Dave going to be here?"

"Anytime now, Luke flew into Reno last night. They were going to get on the road first thing this morning."

"It's nice that he's reconciled with his sons."

"We had a wonderful visit with Luke the first of the year and he calls Dave weekly."

"What's he like?"

"A little nerdy, but I guess that's to be expected for an assistant professor at Berkley." Betty poured herself coffee and sat on a lounge. "But you can tell he's his father's son."

"And what about Ted?"

"Ted works for a publishing company in New York. Luke took Dave to New York to meet him in February." Betty paused. "Ted's gay. Luke wanted to be there when Dave found out. The three had a great time together."

"Why isn't Ted coming?"

"Prior commitments. However, he and Dave have been spending a lot of time on the phone."

The doorbell sounded followed by Lorelei's giggle. "I let myself in, I just had to check on the happy couple. Everything is ready at the teahouse for the first wedding of the year. I was holding my breath, but it looks like the weather will be perfect." She held out a handful of mail. "You've got mail. Where's Dave?"

"He's not back from Reno yet." Betty put the mail on a side table as she stood. "Would you like some coffee?"

"Heavens no, got to go, just stopped by on my way to the grocery store. There was something I wanted to tell you though. Now what was it, oh yes, Pastor James is sick, won't be able to do the ceremony, but I got a substitute, Reverend Santa something."

"Do I know him?" Betty asked concerned.

"Great, mom and Dave are gonna get married by Santa Claus, is he coming in by sleigh?"

"Lorelei shot Susan an irritated look then addressed Betty's concern. "I don't think so. He's from Termo, but you will love him. I've never met the man, but I'm told he's as cute as a bugs ear. Older gentleman, real sweet, Native American I think. Has Dave heard anything about his property proposal from the county?"

"Yes, yesterday, they approve the subdivision of the lower sixty acres, and his plans for us to build a home on the upper forty."

"Well I've got to run."

"Hey, where is everybody?" Dave's voice was heard coming from inside the house.

"Out back honey."

Dave stepped out the French doors to the backyard followed by his son. Betty greeted Dave with a kiss and then Luke. After a quick exchange she took Luke's hand and led him to Susan.

"Dear, I'd like you to meet Luke."

Luke nodded to Susan. She stood to greet him. *He was taller than his father*, she observe as she extended her hand. He pulled off his hat and extended his hand, but didn't remove his dark glasses. *He's got the same hair as his dad's, but without the gray, he's cute.* She extended her hand. "Hi," was all she could squeak out.

"Hello, I'm Lorelei." She said as she stepped up and extended a greeting.

"Pleased to meet you."

Susan stood and watched. *He looks familiar.*

"I think I'll have that cup of coffee after all." Lorelei took a cup from the tray and helped herself to the last of the coffee.

"I think I need to make another pot." Betty picked up the empty cravat and started for the house.

"I'll help." Dave followed.

"Betty says you're a Professor at the University." Lorelei grinned at Susan.

Old busybody. Susan smiled back.

"Assistant Professor, probably will have to wait until someone dies before I get a full Professorship, the way things are with the State these days."

"Do you have your doctorate already." Lorelei buzzed around like a pesky mosquito.

I wish the old biddy would just leave. Susan was annoyed.

"Yes."

"So then it's Doctor Hoffsted?" Lorelei batted her eyes at Luke.

Susan was so irritated she turned away. She fought back saying something she knew she would regret.

"No, I go by Starr, my stepfathers name, so it's Doctor Starr."

That's it. Susan turned back at the recognition. "Luke Starr." Susan finally found her voice. "I was on the dig with you last spring in New Mexico, doing field work. Remember. You called me Miss L.A.."

"Yeah." There was a momentary hesitation in his voice. "Last year's spring break, the anthropology group from U.C.L.A.. I remember."

Susan smiled and stepped toward him. He grinned and pulled off his dark glasses and she looked up into his pale blue eyes.

He looked down at her and smiled. "Isn't that a corker."

"Coffee will be ready shortly." Betty said as she returned. Dave will bring it as soon as it finishes brewing. "Susan, is there something wrong?"

"No!" At that moment Susan could care less about coffee or anything else, she took Luke's hand and she started to lead him to the side gate. "We are going for a walk." She announced.

"Isn't that something, Susan knows Dave's son from school, small world." Lorelei remarked. "Oh look at the time, I've got to pickup the rest of the order at the grocery store. Susan wait for me." She said as she ran after her.

*   *   *

"Coffee's ready?" Dave stopped and looked around. "Where is everybody?"

"Susan and Luke went for a walk. It seems Susan and Luke know each other from school, at least that's what Lorelei said before she followed them out the side gate saying something about getting to the grocery store." Betty turned toward Dave. "So it's just you and me."

"So Luke knows Susan, what a coincidence."

"I agree." Betty remarked as she poured them some coffee. As she put the cravat down she noticed the stack of mail, picked up the top letter and turned to Dave. "It's from Trent."

"Trent? Open it."

"It's a wedding card. He sends his regrets that he can't be here for the wedding. He's in Brazil."

"Is that it?"

"Best wishes, that's it."

"A man of few words. I didn't think we would ever hear from him. I sent a wedding announcement to him in care of his friends in Nevada." Betty looked over the card and envelope again.

Dave pointed to the box and asked, "what's this?"

"Susan found it in the store room and thought I had put it there. "Open it. It's not sealed.

"You are not going to believe this." Dave reached in the box and lifted up a buckskin bag.

"Isn't that Trent's bag?" Betty asked?

"Yes, I can't imagine him going off without it."

"He must have put it there, look inside."

"I started to once the day we met and almost got caught. I only got a glimpse inside and saw he had a gun, after that I left it alone."

"We can send it to him, but aren't you curious."

"Yes, and we can't send a gun."

Dave opened the bag and dumped the contents on the table. In the collection of odd bits of paper and envelopes the gun clattered on the table. Dave carefully picked it up. "I hope it isn't loaded." Then he realized, "It's a cap gun, a toy cap gun." Dave held up the toy. "It's exactly like the one I had as a kid and threw away. No, it is mine I carved my initials, right there."

"I wonder what this is." Betty picked up a plastic bag full of folded paper packets of herbs.

"I think it's some of his Chinese or Indian medicine, pretty powerful stuff, I know first hand how well it works."

Betty opened the bag and smelt the contents. "Chamomile, that's all it is, chamomile tea."

"That stinker."

"What?"

"Nothing, just thinking. Look at these things, baseball cards, a Vet Nam war metal, an Aids ribbon, a . . . ." A cold chill went up his back. "These are all my things from . . . ."

"What's this?" Betty picked up a small black velvet bag, opened it and she poured a gold ring into her hand. "Oh my god, it's the ring I made in jewelry class." Betty examined the ring.

"Had you lost it?"

"Yes. I designed and made it in a jewelry making class I took the year after Jake past away. I didn't know why I made a man's ring, so I was going to melt it down and recast it into something else, but when it came time, I couldn't find it."

"May I see it?" Dave asked.

"Sure, try it on."

"It fits." Dave admired the ring.

"It's Yours. Maybe now I know why I made it. It seems that Trent's bag was really a bag of our treasures. No wonder he left it."

"That kid, he never ceases to amaze me. Anything else?"

"A feather, it looks like a real eagles feather. I wonder what that represents?"

They both stood a moment in bewilderment and looked at the things before them, then put them back in the buckskin bag.

"Oh, I Almost forgot, I have something for you, a wedding gift from me to you." He handed her a small wrapped package.

"What is it?" Betty asked as she unwrapped the package. "A Book?"

"It's just been published. Ted's been helping me with it, I've been keeping it a secret. I wrote them for you."

"LOVE LETTERS FROM THE SOUL, by David Hoffsted." She kissed him. "It's perfect."

*   *   *

The afternoon sun streamed through the trees of Lorelei's garden. In the light Betty and Dave knelt before the minister as Susan, the Maid of Honor, and Luke, the Best Man stood beside them. Dave looked at the minister for the first time when he heard his voice.

"Dearly beloved, we are gathered together here in the sight of God . . . "

It's the old man from Kramer Junction. Dave trembled. Betty placed her hand on his visibly trembling hand.

" . . . and in the presence of this company, to join together this man and this woman in holy matrimony . . . "

A glimmer caught Dave's eye. Reverend Salvador wore his silver belt buckle with the gold S. *I didn't think you'd miss our wedding.*

" . . . which is an honorable estate, instituted of God, signifying unto us the mystical union that is . . . "

Dave looked up in the old mans eyes. *Thanks kid, thanks for everything.*

" . . . by the power invested in me, I now pronounce you husband and wife, and what God has joined together let not man put asunder." The old mans eye's sparkled as he winked at Dave.

"You may kiss your Bride."

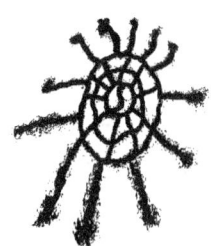

EPILOG

A dashing young man stepped out the golden doors of one of the elevators that lined the foyer of the great Hall of Records. Above, the vast marble dome was lit by a thousand rainbows from the refracted sun through the crystal windows. The colors blended as they cascaded down the layer upon layer of carved bas-relief, facades, balconies and colonnades until it spilled as pure white light onto golden oak reading stations that circled out from the central counter of the great reading room. He hastily crossed the floor of the rotunda to the central desk. The librarian scanned the tag on his lanyard and handed him an access card. He located a vacant desk, sat and inserted the card into a slot. The flat screen on the desk lit up. He scrolled through and read several documents.

When he was finally finished reading, he returned the access card. Just then a beautiful young woman in a leopard coat approached.

"Greetings." she said, "Visiting today?"

"Yes, preparing for another assignment?"

"Are you finished with the Brazil project?"

"Yes. I've got a new assignment, a young cowboy in California, is going to win a lot of money in the lottery."

"Are you going to help him spend it?"

"Hopefully save it."

"You are a glutton for punishment aren't you?"

"It's never a punishment." A pleasant smile appeared on the man's face. "So, how have you been?"

"Fine, but I miss you?"

"I've missed you too, but I still have a lot of work to do."

The elevator doors open behind the man.

"I know." The woman kissed him on the cheek and whispered, "but I still miss you."

The man stepped back toward the elevators. "You can come visit."

"I will."

"Is that a promise?" He grinned.

"You can count on it."

"I have to go," He said as he stepped into the car. "See you soon?"

"Soon." She said and as the elevator doors started to close she added. "May peace be with you, Trent."

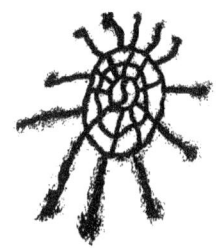

GENE STIRM
SHAMAN

There are two types of journeys in life, The Ordained and The Mundane. The mundane is easy to recognize, it's the path you choose. The Ordained journey is only recognizable when you look back on your life and see how far you've come and wonder, how you got on this path?

Over a trek of sixty plus years, Gene Stirm has realized his *Ordained Journey*. As he approaches the summit of the mountain that he didn't know he was climbing, he can now see the many forks and turns that have led him to where he is today.

No one chooses to be a Shaman. A Shaman is chosen by a higher power. And though they are directed to the path by a mentor or elder, they are instructed by the Spirit.

Gene made his first vision quest when he was twenty-two. Without a vision for his life, he quit school in his third year of college and went to the mountains. It was the Sixties, the Vietnam War was getting hot, hippies were cool and confusion rained supreme. The day after Christmas, 1967, he packed up his camping gear and drove to Yosemite. He pitched his tent in *Camp Four*, the warmest part of the valley, where the diehard climbers and campers stayed. He didn't have a formula or plan. He just intended to stay until he figured out what he wanted to do with his life. He stayed for almost a year.

As spring arrived, he spent more time on the trails and by summer he was soloing in the high country for weeks at a time. He spent time reading the Bible, the Life of Buddha, Kahlil Gibran's 'The Prophet', Lao Tzu's 'The Tao' and the poetry of To Fu, among others. Finally, at the first winter snows in late 1968, he moved to the town of Ahwahnee, California. He says the most important lessons he learned, "was to follow my heart, seek the high ground and that there is more to life than meets the eye." He finished art school and began a career in Graphic Arts. A career that spanned thirty years and include art director for Josten's Publishing, owner of both a printing business and menu design company, which brought him to live in Los Angeles.

His next vision quest was in the mid-seventies. This time he was more mature and with reasonability's, married with three children, he couldn't go off to the mountain for a year. So he fasted and meditated. His refreshed vision changed his and his family's life, and started him on the road to the ministry. Within five years, he had graduated from the seminary and was pastor of a church in Southern California.

A number of twists and turns took him to the healing ministry and the study of alternative medicine. He received a Holistic Practitioner Certification in 1996 and began a practice in Anaheim, California. More recently, He has received Certification in Hypnotism. He blends East, West and Native American philosophies with modern and ancient practices of healing and Shamanism. He has been given the name Paka by his granddaughter and called a Shaman.

In 2004, he and his wife moved to Tehachapi, California, where he continued his studies of Native American art and culture and Shamanism. It was at that time he began rewriting a number of his screenplays into novels. In 2008 he received a Doctor of Shamanism Degree from ULC Seminary. Gene has been connected with publishing, book design and editing most of his professional life. However, *Mystical Path To Mystique,* is his first published novel.

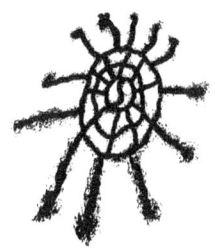

THE SHAMAN SYMBOL

The Shaman symbol that appears in this book is from a petroglyph found in Little Petroglyph Canyon, in the Coso Range, near Ridgecrest, California. Petroglyphs in this canyon are believed by some to date back as much as 16,000 year.

Find out more about Shaman Symbols, Shamanism and Petroglyphs, by visiting: www.shamanway.com.

View Gene Stirm's website at: www.genestirm.com and learn more about the Mystical Path To Mystique at: www.mysticalpathtomystique.com